D1474879

K. M. WRAY

Twilight's Curse
Book 1 in the Twilight Realm Series

First edition

This book was professionally typeset on Reedsy.
Find out more at reedsy.com

To my mom. Thank you for your support.

Contents

Acknowledgement

A huge thank-you to my editor Dana Hopkins. You were such a pleasure to work with brought the best out of my writing.

A huge thank-you to Lena Yang for her beautiful work on the cover art and design. Such a pleasure to work with you again.

A huge thank-you to Sue and Doreen for reading through the manuscript and giving valuable feedback.

A huge thank-you to the support of family and friends.

Chapter One

Nix

"Wake up, Prince Phoenix."

"What is it, Elek? It's the middle of the night," I said, letting a groan escape. I wasn't young enough to complain or moan about the inconvenience, so I tried to keep my voice neutral. Ignatius Elek, royal advisor to my father, the king, wouldn't wake me without reason. "It's too early for sword practice."

His subtle shaking of my shoulder had pulled me from my dreams. As I sat up in bed and wiped the sleep from my eyes, I caught a glimpse of the veil of night, full moon and stars dotting the sky through my bedroom window. I flopped back onto my bed.

Elek drew back my covers and held up a cloak. "You must get up and come with me. Hurry."

I shifted my weight to the edge of bed. "Where're my clothes?" I glanced around for my pants. Usually the brownies—servants to the royal family—had them ready in the armchair next to my bed. Prickles ran over my skin.

"There's no time. I'll explain once I've taken you to safety."

Cool dread coated me, turning my blood to jelly at his words. "Has the Twilight Realm been attacked?"

I pulled my boots on, adjusting the legs of my pajama bottoms overtop, and then swung the cloak over my shoulders. I tucked my pendant under my shirt. It was a symbol of the Royal Tree and a seal my sister and I always wore.

Elek's face fell. "It is worse."

I froze. "My parents?" And then I thought of my little sister, only six. "Zyanna?"

"Her nurse has her. Come, Prince. There really isn't time and I swore to your father I'd keep you safe."

I held back a grunt and fastened the cloak with a bit more force than was necessary. Was the Royal Tree under attack? No one could breach the Royal Tree. It certainly couldn't be the brownies; they would never betray us. It would go against their nature. And no other elf in the Twilight Realm had access. Even Elek needed permission to enter the Royal Tree.

The air sizzled and popped. Cocoa, the head brownie, suddenly appeared next to Elek. It was something I'd seen her do before, but it was still startling to have her unexpectedly pop into existence next to us. Like all brownies, she was tiny, only coming up to Elek's waist. She had long black hair, wide eyes, and a pointed face.

"Prince Phoenix, Royal Advisor Ignatius Elek. These are for you." Cocoa thrust a small black bag at Elek.

He took it, then his eyes slid in my direction and Cocoa nodded.

"Very well." Elek stuffed the bag into the folds of his robe.

2

"We must get the prince out of here."

"My family and I have kept the back stairs clear. They run straight to the kitchen's entrance. There is a door to the outside you can use."

"Thank you, Cocoa."

The brownie nodded, then as suddenly as she appeared, she was gone with a pop.

I shook my head. I knew the brownies had magic, but they were sweet, happy creatures who got pleasure from cleaning and cooking and remaining unnoticed. They seldom revealed themselves in the homes they inhabited and were able to pass through most, maybe all, magical barriers without issue.

If the Royal Tree really was under attack, shouldn't the brownies be leaving? The image of the childlike creatures trying to defend the tree was so comical I had to struggle to keep my laughter from busting out of me.

Guilt followed. My family and our home were in danger. I shouldn't find anything amusing, but the momentary distraction helped me focus and calmed my racing heart. I sobered back to the reality of my precarious situation.

I followed Elek into the darkened hallway, lit only by an eerie glow from the occasional window.

"This way." He motioned me forward to the kitchen.

I bit down on the questions and scenarios that surged through my mind, each unthinkable and impossible.

We tiptoed down the back stairs that led us directly to the brownies' quarters. I didn't see any of them, but brownies by nature kept themselves hidden, perhaps invisible. I didn't know the range of their magic since they were so secretive. Experience and knowledge about their race told me they were there keeping the path clear as Cocoa had promised.

My attention was stolen by the sound of muffled cries and scuffling in the distance. I tripped down the last two stairs.

"Careful, my prince."

My hands smarted from the fall, but I accepted Elek's help and bounced back onto my feet. I glanced down the corridor to the front foyer. The noises were coming from that direction. My heart froze in my chest. Were my parents okay? Had the Royal Tree really been breached? It was supposed to be impossible. The reality of this situation caught up with me and my fists clenched. Who was threatening my family? My home?

Cocoa's petite, childlike face popped through the kitchen door, pulling my attention from the foyer. She looked only a few years older than my sister, though it occurred to me that as the head brownie of the Royal Tree, she had to be least one hundred years old. No one knew for sure. The brownies rarely told elves personal information.

Cocoa waved us through into the kitchen. "We have kept the kitchen safe," she said, nearly running to keep up with Elek's long strides.

Again, the image of Cocoa and the other brownies fighting off invading forces entered my mind leaving me with a scowl. I didn't want any harm coming to these childlike creatures. What could they possibly do? Hit an attacker with a frying pan? Polish the floor to such a shine that whoever was attacking the tree would slip and fall? That might be kind of fun to watch, but I still couldn't imagine the innocent creatures ever fighting.

Elek turned in time to catch the twitch of my lips. "Do you have something to add?"

"I just wondered what a brownie could possibly do to fight

4

off an attacker."

Elek grunted. "More than you think."

Cocoa stopped in front of me and planted her hands on her hips. "Never underestimate the power of nurture."

I gave her a quick nod and then padded after Elek. I kept my expression neutral, but inwardly I continued to question their defensive or offensive abilities. The distraction helped keep me from worrying about my family.

A cluster of brownies peeked their heads above the kitchen counters and watched us as we passed, their eyes wide like amazed children but their lips set grimly. I didn't know how many brownies the Royal Tree housed, but seeing so many of them surprised me.

Elek paused at the door we'd just come through and peered back into the corridor.

Voices drifted toward us.

"Check every room." A deep, gruff voice carried into the kitchen. "Lord Leski wants the whole family."

"Yes, sir," a younger-sounding male voice replied.

"Elves! Loyal to Leski and Sirina Dion," Elek muttered. His words were coated in curtness, giving them an edge.

The royal advisor hurried away from the door, pulling me along with him. Cocoa scuttled ahead, leading us to the back exit out of kitchen and out of the Tree.

Footsteps from the hallway reached the kitchen. I glanced back as the door leading to the corridor opened a crack. The brownies were all focused on the sound as well, moving from behind the counters to form a line in front of the door. They really were going to fight for me and Elek. Did they even have a chance?

"Now, you must go." Cocoa forced us the last few steps

toward the back exit of the Royal Tree. "We'll protect you."

Elek and I stumbled outside just as a blinding flash of light from the kitchen lit up the darkened forest around the Royal Tree. Before I could look back, Elek grabbed my sleeve and yanked me to follow him through the underbrush.

I hoped the brownies were safe and hadn't lost their lives to whatever power was thrown at them.

Our feet padded noiselessly over the soft ground. The sound of the river gently trickling by as it ran past the Royal Tree felt oddly comforting, but I couldn't see it because of the thick fog. We moved with stealth through the dense foliage, the leaves and branches from closely growing trees pressing against us.

Elek nudged me away from the tree and I followed with reluctance. I still had no idea what had happened to my home and my family. Curiosity filled my thoughts. I couldn't leave my family, no matter what the advisor had said. My family came first. I paused and turned around. I had to go back to the Royal Tree and help my parents and sister.

A glow up ahead pushed through the fog, and it called to me. Elek was next to me a moment later and tried to lead me away from my home, to stop me from walking toward the Royal Tree, but I ripped free of his hold. But before I drew near, I stopped and crouched behind a bush, my eyes riveted on a small crowd forming in front of the Royal Tree's main entrance. Among them were Lord Leski Dion, his wife Lady Sirina Dion, a few soldiers—and my parents.

Hadn't Lord Leski come to the Royal Tree and sought audience with my father only a little while ago to request reinstatement to the Twilight Realm? He and his wife had just returned from their exile to the Night Realm. They had instigated resistance against the monarchy before I was born.

Now, seeing the soldiers holding my parents as if they were the criminals turned my stomach. Was this why they returned? To take the throne from my parents? To finish what they had started before they were banished? Impossible! The line would never be broken unless every last member of the royal family was murdered.

Elek settled in beside me, navigating with such stealth that the bush didn't even move.

"My prince, we must leave," he whispered, his warm breath tickling my ear. "I promised your father I would keep you safe."

"Elek, my parents." I pointed to the front of the Royal Tree. "Did you know they were taken? That the Royal Tree was breached? That this was happening?" I managed to keep my voice low but felt my anger rise with each question. It wasn't Elek's fault. But my parents were captives. Held by elves they should never have allowed back into the realm.

Elek looked at the ground and shook his head. "The Dions got in. I don't know how, but Cocoa came to me and brought me to the Royal Tree to rescue you. Please, my prince. It'll do you no good to stay."

Elek wrapped his hand around my arm, but I jerked it from him, disturbing the bush in the process. We both grew very still, and I checked to see if we'd been spotted. Leski and his crowd seemed oblivious to our presence.

Anger ignited in me. How could Elek think of walking away? I glared at him. "I'm staying. You might not care, but I do."

I couldn't leave my family. There had to be a way to save my parents.

The royal line had been established by the first rulers, Paz

Mier and his wife Nazira. They established their five children as rulers over each of the realms: Day, Night, Dawn, Light, and Twilight. My family line had ruled over all the elven races of the Twilight Realm since then. Our line was protected by the strongest magic in the realm which gave us favor with our subjects, though I was too young to fully understand how it worked.

The royal line would be protected. I felt confident of this. There was no need to rush away like Elek wanted. My parents' abilities would subdue Leski and his followers. I'd seen how the royal power worked to calm crowds when my father gave a speech. It would work here.

"Phoenix!" Leski Dion called out, his voice carrying clear into the forest. His long, blond hair was tied neatly at the base of his neck and snaked down his back. "Son of the king and queen, crown prince of the Twilight Realm, step forward if you wish to spare your parents' lives."

Leski stood with his arms outstretched, as if expecting me to run to him in an embrace. His loose-fitting shirt and pants hung on him in the motionless air.

My heart stuttered in my chest. I inhaled deeply to slow my breathing, then brushed my blond hair back over my pointed ears and shook it over my shoulders. I wiped the moisture from my forehead with my sleeve.

My parents were bound and kneeling—weak and helpless. Impossible! They shouldn't be forced to kneel. Not the monarchs. Not here. Not in the Twilight Realm.

Leski had once been a high servant of my father's, but due to his rebellious behavior he and Sirina had been expelled to the Night Realm a long time ago. They'd recently returned, however, asking for redemption—and the king and queen had given it to them.

My gut churned seeing my parents' state. It had only taken the traitor and his small squad of soldiers a matter of hours to somehow break into the Royal Tree. From the look of them, dark hair and creamy skin, the members of the squad were all from the Night Realm. Twilight Realm elves usually had lighter brown to blondish hair and a warmer golden skin tone.

I shook my head in confusion; it was impossible to enter another elf's home. Access to an elf's tree was tied to our magic. I'd place my hand on the marker and the magic within the tree would recognize mine, allowing the doorway to peel back giving me entrance. If I didn't have access, or if the tree's magic didn't read mine, then the tree would remain sealed. Had someone given Leski access to the Royal Tree? But who? And how? It wouldn't have been the brownies. They would never betray the family they served.

"Phoenix, we're waiting," Leski said. He then whispered to a soldier just behind him who grabbed my mother, Calla. She moaned.

"No, take me," my father, Alistair, cried out. "Calla!" He struggled against the elf holding him down.

The guard raised my mom to her feet, and she did not protest. I watched her vibrant blue eyes dart wildly as the elf's arm encircled her waist. His other hand raised a sharp blade and pressed it to the main artery in her throat. A cry escaped her mouth as a drop of blood, red and precious, trailed down her neck, reaching the collar of her nightdress. It pooled there and fanned out as the material absorbed it.

My throat tightened and my shoulders slumped. I had to help my parents. I had to do... something. But it would be more than a century before I was recognized as a mature adult elf. I had only just started my sword training.

"Phoenix, your parents' lives are in your hands," Leski said. "Come forward. Now!"

His words held a compulsion, strong and powerful, but I shook off its effects. This traitor had the ability to control those around him through either his voice or persuasion. A part of me wanted to jump out of my hiding place, wanted to move forward. Sweat trickled down the sides of my face in my effort to fight the pull of Leski's power.

I closed my eyes and calmed myself. A new resolve settled over me as my muscles relaxed and I filled my lungs with fresh oxygen. My fingers moved to the pendant I wore around my neck; it bore the symbol of my lineage: the Tree of Life, the Royal Tree, planted by the first royal family next to the river that ran only a few steps from me.

"Phoenix, I am a reasonable man, but you have pushed me beyond my patience." Leski turned sharply to the guard holding the queen. "Finish her!"

With a swift movement, the guard's blade sank smoothly into my mother's soft flesh.

No!

An internal roar rose from my depths. Then I heard another howl, this one aloud; in my peripheral vision, my father leaped forward against the elves who held him. My mother... she crumpled to the ground.

Raw terror engulfed me as her blood flowed like a fountain, saturating the earth. She struggled, gasping, her eyes roaming wildly, helplessly.

"Mother," I whispered.

Her eyes found me. I could read the pain in her expression and see her mouth move slowly: *"I love you. Live."*

Her body stilled and the spark of life left her eyes.

My heart pounded as I reflected on my mother's final wish. *Live?* How could I? I'd just failed to protect her.

My father's sobs filled the forest. The regular sounds of nature dimmed as if observing a moment of silence for their fallen queen. My tears fell and I turned from the sight.

Elek gripped my shoulder. "My prince, I wanted to spare you this."

I nodded. "I'm sorry."

"We should go."

"No, I can't… my father's still there."

Sobs threatened to rip from my chest, but I held them back. I'd save them for later. When my father, my sister, and I could mourn together. Hope—the expectation of a chance—hung in the air. Certainly now my father would exert his power.

I stilled my emotions and looked back at my mother's body, limp and lifeless. My father had crumpled at her side but was unable to hold her while Leski's soldiers restrained him.

My eyes settled on the gloating Leski, and this time I didn't sense fear but an ominous power creeping toward me. I drew on all my senses and dug my fingers into the dirt to keep myself stationary; if not, I might come out of hiding. I couldn't let that happen.

Leski grabbed a fistful of my father's hair and yanked his head back, exposing his throat. He brought his own knife to the king's neck.

"Last chance, Phoenix." His hand didn't flinch as his eyes scoured the foliage, searching for me.

"Phoenix!" my dad called, his chest heaving with effort. "My son, run. My life, your mother's life, we are nothing. Run." His breath came in quick gasps. "It's not… it's not your time."

My skin tingled and I felt frozen. My father then pushed forward, lurching as he stood up. With that movement, Leski's knife slid to the king's chest.

"No one takes my life," King Alistair declared. "I give it for the Twilight Realm. Let the elves know that their king was not slain, but sacrificed his life for them."

The king brought his bound hands up to the knife and thrust his chest upon it, falling forward. He tumbled, taking Leski down with him.

"Father…" I mouthed the word as tears flowed freely down the sides of my face. My parents, at the entrance to the Royal Tree, maybe twenty steps away, lay dead.

"Come." Elek placed his hand on my shoulder again and this time I did not resist him.

Slowly and with careful steps, we walked into the dark forest until I could no longer see the Royal Tree or hear the river that ran next to it. The emptiness of the dark night consumed me. My parents were gone.

I cried silently as we walked into an older part of the forest. The trees grew close here, but Elek navigated a path with ease.

We came to an old tree that had expanded to a greater circumference than the Royal Tree. Elek placed his hand over a carving in the wood, and in response a door peeled away, revealing an entrance. This was his home, and it was massive. Trees that elves inhabited were always larger on the inside. It had something so do with the way our magic connected with the earth and nature.

I followed Elek through a maze of corridors to a room containing towers of boxes and books. He walked through a small pathway between these towers to a desk, where he settled into a soft chair.

Elek pointed to a chair on the opposite side of the desk. "Have a seat."

Now that my tears had subsided, I noticed a small greenhouse bulging outward behind Elek. From the outside, it probably looked like a large root extending from the base of the tree.

Elek bent low. I heard the soft shush as wood ran against wood. I couldn't see from this side, but it sounded like Elek had opened a drawer. He lifted a box and set it on the desk. With a swift movement, he lifted the lid, but the box was empty. He dug into a pocket in his robe, and he pulled out the black pouch I had seen Cocoa give him. He set it beside the box. It was round like a small pillow, closed with a drawstring.

"You, as the crown prince, are now the king of the Twilight Realm," he said. The weight of his words dropped on me, and I slouched in my chair. "But you aren't ready. What Leski did tonight took planning, and I fear that crowning you king now would only put you in greater danger."

I cleared my throat, not fully trusting my voice. "Then what do you suggest?"

"I suggest you give yourself a chance to grow and become an adult."

"I'm only thirteen, Elek. Do you really think the Twilight Realm can wait eighty or so years until I reach maturity?"

He waved his hand. "At least wait until your child-adult years. We'll know the time when it comes. When you're ready to rule and govern the elves of the Twilight Realm."

I frowned, knowing that I'd never be ready. I should have had hundreds of years to train under my father's tutelage. I was pathetically unprepared.

Elek opened the black pouch and laid a series of royal

objects on the desk: my father's signet ring, his seal, and his crown, an unadorned circlet. I fingered each one, realizing they were now mine. When I slid the ring on my finger, it spun loose. Would it ever fit my hand?

"And in the meantime?" I asked, placing the ring back on the desk.

Elek slowly arranged each royal piece in the box and locked it. The black pouch lay flat beside it. "You can remain here. We'll change your name to Nix, and mine to Nate."

"Nate?" I raised an eyebrow.

"My first name is Ignatius."

I studied the older elf. He looked like he'd been alive for a few hundred years, unlike most other elves I knew. Had he served my grandfather? I pushed aside my curiosity for another day.

Elek cleared his throat. "You'll stay here and learn to be less regal, to blend with the populace. Once you've aged some, you'll be able to go out more, but for now, we must keep you safe and your identity a secret. In time, we'll decide on the next steps."

My lips curled at his statement. I didn't want to think about *next steps*. The raw pain of watching my parents being murdered was too fresh, and I didn't want to be king.

Elek studied me.

"And my sister?" I asked, thinking of little Zyanna.

"Wherever her nurse took her, we'll find her."

"Elek, my father. What did he mean when he said that he sacrificed himself for the Twilight Realm?"

Elek sat back in his chair and steepled his fingers. "These are mysteries best explained at a different time, but to give a brief understanding: When your father gave his life, he ensured the

Dions wouldn't gain any power. The royal magic is ancient. It is blood magic, meaning it is tied to the generational line of Paz Mier and Nazira. Its descendants—you."

A cool sensation like water being poured over me made me shiver. "If they had killed my father?"

Elek shrugged. "They wouldn't have gained access to the royal magic running through your blood. It might have weakened though. And the Royal Tree might have lost its magical seal. At present, it is tied only to you and your sister Zyanna, and the brownies who serve there have access. Cocoa will ensure the Royal Tree is well maintained. The tree will have sensed the passing of the ruling monarch and you will have to regain access one day."

One day. The Royal Tree could remain sealed as far as I was concerned. I never wanted to return.

Elek pushed back from the desk and rose. "Come, I'll show you to a room where you can get some rest."

I followed him through another maze of corridors until he left me in a room with a bed, soft carpet, and a well-padded chair in the corner. A small round window about the size of my head perched above the bed. The sky was still dark. I didn't know the time but since the black of night hadn't dulled to charcoal or deep gray, there were still a few hours before daylight. I buried my face in the pillow, wanting sleep to take me so I could wake up and find out this had all been a horrible nightmare. But I couldn't sleep.

As I lay in bed, I replayed the scene of my father giving his life for the kingdom. It seemed a useless gesture. Elek's explanation didn't satisfy me. Why hadn't my father done something, used his power? I closed my eyes, but the scene continued to play in my mind, mocking me.

My parents were dead. The truth of that settled on me. My father had died for me.

I shook my head as the emotions raced through me in a torrent.

He's dead... for me... for the Twilight Realm.

I made the decision to never again let someone else sacrifice themselves for me or this kingdom. I wouldn't be able to survive it.

Chapter Two

Zoe

Eight years later

"Chim, you need to find the way out," I whispered to the black dragon. Chim was about the size of a large cat. I stroked his head as he stretched his neck and preened from the affection. His skin was smooth and silky, like my own.

We were deep within the gray stone monstrosity of my parents' fortress, of course. I had never been outside the building save once when we moved in when I was four. The air outside had been free of the dank, musty smell that clung to these dim corridors. The vibrant green vegetation called to the magic in my elven veins. Even now I could sense the life beyond this sterile building reach out to me. It was faint but I could detect it.

I don't know why we moved or where we had come from. I couldn't remember much from before. I think we had lived underground, though, because it was like all of me came fully alive for a brief amount of time and then once inside the fortress, that part of me shrank, stifled from the lack of life. Though those memories were from so long ago and I was so young at the time, I clung to them. I wondered if it was more my imagination than reality.

Chim rubbed his head into my palm. His intelligent gaze rested on me. "We have to leave."

"Who're you talking to?" a male voice asked behind me.

Startled, I spun. I clutched my hand over my chest and breathed a sigh of relief to see that it was Maximon, and not my brother. Though with my brother's ability to mimic the appearance of others, I could never be too careful. The cool blue of Maximon's eyes bored into me with curiosity.

Chim slipped through a slit in the back of my blouse and settled on my skin. It felt like soft fabric sliding against my skin. He was one of my three dragon tattoos.

I'd been walking through the brick-and-stone hallways of my parents' fortress. It was cold, always cold, and a confusing maze to navigate. Creepy etchings on the walls sent shivers down my spine. They reminded me of my tattoos, only these were eyes and lines with arrows. I didn't know what the lines were for, but the eyes always left me feeling like I was being watched. My teeth chattered and I rubbed my arms to generate some heat. This fortress was my prison and sucked the life from me. I desperately wanted—needed—to escape.

I peered at Maximon out of the corner of my eye. Would he help me? I couldn't risk asking him, though leaving him behind didn't feel right either.

"What are you doing?" Maximon asked.

"Nothing," I replied.

Maximon was around my age and an orphaned elf child my parents had found to experiment on—experiment on like me. My parents liked finding abandoned children for their experiments. All elves had magic and some, like mine, my parents found useful. Though I suppose any child would do, since I was their daughter: their first and favorite lab rat. I considered Maximon a friend, though I trusted him very little, and there were some things, like my living tattoos, I didn't confess to anyone.

Maximon regularly trained with the guards who served my parents. I too received my own special tutor, a guard named Derek, for learning how to fight with weapons. He wasn't mean or cruel like some, but he wasn't kind either. None of the guards were.

Maximon was taller than me, though, and unlike the guards he hadn't shown signs of unnatural heavy muscle mass. Even the guards were a product of my parents' experiments. He sauntered closer. "Who were you talking to?"

"Myself," I said, wanting to get his attention off me. "What are you up to?"

Maximon shrugged. "I'm supposed to take you to the laboratory."

My fists clenched and the muscles across my shoulders tensed. I thought about Pat, the healing dragon who was tattooed on my left arm. She moved, and warm comfort floated through me. Pat knew I hated these visits with my mother.

I fell in step beside Maximon as we walked back down the corridor toward a large foyer and then on to the laboratory. "What does she want now?"

"The Lady Sirina wants to see you."

"No doubt to add another tattoo," I muttered to myself. My whole body, save my neck, face, and part of my chest, was covered in them.

"She's come up with something different," Maximon said.

I held back a scoff as my nails bit into the flesh of my palms. "Do you know what she's planning?" I asked, hoping that my voice didn't tremble.

A new tattoo would mean a fresh wave of pain as my mother drew another mark. She was fascinated by unusual types of magic, which I'd unfortunately been born with. For the most part, my magic helped things like plants grow or healed sick animals, but ever the scientist, my mother wanted to test its boundaries. She had been experimenting on me for as long as I could remember. And she particularly liked imbuing the tattoo ink with magic, a dark liquid foreign magic that burned like acid whenever I received a new mark.

She and my father, Lord Leski, were the ruling regents of the Twilight Realm and had dreams of turning me into the ultimate assassin. That was why most of my tattoos depicted weapons such as swords, knives, and daggers.

But the tattoos didn't work quite as my parents wanted them to. They couldn't control them, or me. And they didn't know that I had long ago discovered that the tattoos themselves had *life*, that they could separate from my skin.

As Maximon led me down a familiar hallway, the burning scent of flesh and copper filled my senses.

I stopped in my tracks. One of my parents' unnaturally burly guards emerged from my mother's laboratory with a small elf girl passed out in his arms. The girl had long blond hair and I guessed she was about seven years old. Her arm swung limply as the guard walked; on her palm was a fresh black tattoo. My stomach twisted.

As they passed, I also noticed the stain of tears on the girl's cheeks. I clenched my jaw. The young elf must have similar magic to mine, so my mother had found another lab rat. I closed my eyes. This had to stop. I had to stop my parents. And somehow. Someday. I would.

Maximon motioned me inside the lab. "We shouldn't keep Lady Sirina waiting."

"No, we shouldn't." As much as I wanted to run, experience warned me that I had no choice. I had tried running once, only for the guards to catch me. I'd spent a week in the hospital recovering, even after Pat had tried to heal me.

Maximon left me at the door and I entered the laboratory alone.

It was brighter in here, the lights almost blinding against the white floors. To my right sat four medical beds. The walls were lined with shelves, and the counters were filled with my mom's lab equipment—test tubes, beakers and jars filled with… stuff. I didn't really care. My mother's desk ran along the back wall directly across from me.

"Zoe!" my mother cried, enveloping me in a hug. She led me to a chair near her desk. "I'm so glad you've come."

I closed my eyes. In all my twelve years, I had yet to figure out how she could manage to act like a mother yet experiment on me like a lab rat. I had long ago stopped thinking of her as anything other than my biological mother.

I sat, stowing away all the emotions I was feeling.

Just get through it, I said to myself. *Whatever happens, Pat will heal you—in time.*

"What do you have planned for me today?" I asked.

My mother clapped her hands. "You'll love it. I think I've

finally cracked the code."

"And is that what you did on that child the guard carried out?"

Her face fell. "Zoe, darling, don't be a spoilsport. The girl is new and she and I are only just beginning our work together. It was her first day, you know."

Her eyes gleamed with excitement.

I'm sure her mind spun with possibilities for the little girl, but I knew I couldn't let this newcomer suffer like I had. I decided that after I was finished here, I would go find the girl and… befriend her? Maybe she and I could escape together.

The door behind me swung open and my brother stepped inside. Every muscle in me tightened.

"Ah, Dimas, glad you could come," my mother said, craning her neck to watch him enter.

I glanced at my brother and asked her, "What's he doing here?"

He grinned and raised his eyebrows. I remembered the last time Dimas had been in the laboratory with me. My mother had let him try his hand at inking me; a permanent scar on my back testified to his ineptitude.

"He's here to help." My mother waved him over and arranged the tools she'd need on a tray at her side.

Dimas held the back of my chair and loomed over me. "Come along, sister."

"Where to? Surely you're not allowed to try another tattoo after what happened the last time."

Dimas scowled.

My mother moved toward one of her medical beds and patted its cushioned surface. Unlike the other beds, this one had straps for my arms and legs. "No, darling. Dimas is here to help *me*. Up you get."

I glanced warily at my brother, then back at my mom. My stomach clenched. The bed's straps and the presence of my brother alerted me to the fact that this marking would be different from anything I'd experienced before.

I willed myself forward and lay down as my mother and Dimas strapped me in, Dimas pulling so tightly that the bindings bit into my skin. I refused to wince, since he was watching for a reaction. I bit my tongue and tasted blood.

"Not so tight, Dimas." My mother shooed him away and loosened the bindings a little. "Hold her down."

Dimas planted his hands on my shoulders and pressed me into the bed. His ice-cold eyes glinted with excitement.

"This tattoo's special," Dimas said.

I closed my eyes, not wanting to look at him. I called on all three of my dragons and they released waves of comfort into me.

Cold scissors touched my belly as my mother cut my shirt off, exposing the skin. Now I understood why she'd brought my brother instead of one of the guards, and modesty had nothing to do with it. She wanted to keep the nature of my numerous tattoos a secret.

A hot prick pierced the skin right above my heart. The ink, infused with my mother's concoction of elf magic, sank into my skin. As it burned, I felt my dragons shift, sensing their nervousness. The pain filled my body and white blinded me.

I released a scream. It tore out of me until everything went dark.

When I woke up again, I was back in my room. I didn't know how much time had passed, but my chest burned and my whole body trembled, like I had a fever. I couldn't stop the shaking.

Pat was pouring her healing powers into me, but something about the tattoo felt different this time; my chest no longer felt like it belonged entirely to me. My magic felt wrong too, like it was blocked or being held back. Or like a piece had broken off. Fractured. Yes, that word felt correct.

I shifted in bed and glanced around. No one else was in my room. I lifted my shirt to examine my latest marking, but I couldn't see it in the dark. I removed a cloth from a light stone on my bedside table and a soft glow filled the room.

I gasped and my hand came to my lips as I saw the tattoo—a beast, with a sinister toothy grin and horns protruding from its head. It glared at me, sharp fangs jutting out from its surly lips.

A demon. Its laugh, cool and malicious, echoed in my mind.

Chim's power had erected a barrier between me and the new tattoo. Pat and Tupac were also at work supporting him. The dragons had been at work while I'd been sleeping. And I was thankful I hadn't woken to battle whatever evil this new tattoo carried. I readjusted my shirt down, not wanting to look at the demon anymore. I pulled my covers over me and lay back, understanding the odd sensations I could feel in my chest; each of my dragons was working to imprison that beast, to isolate it and keep it from entering my mind.

A tear escaped from the corner of my eye. My parents had finally figured out how to create a tattoo that would control me. If it weren't for my dragons, the beast would have taken over. It wouldn't be long before they'd ink another one on me.

I searched for my innate magic, trying to pull it forward to empower my dragons, but it felt sluggish and unresponsive.

Broken. I felt my last glimmer of hope and strength break too. My parents had finally achieved what they wanted with me all along.

I had to escape the fortress. Despite how weak I felt, I climbed out of bed and pulled on a fresh blouse and pair of loose-fitting pants, lacing them up at the waist. I slipped on my boots and grabbed a satchel. I'd only need a few changes of clothes.

I surveyed my room, knowing I couldn't stay and allow my parents to fulfil their plans for me. This latest tattoo proved that I'd lose in the end.

The face of the young girl I'd seen earlier came to mind. I had to find her and take her with me.

I poked my head out into the hallway and peered in both directions. Silence greeted me. Though the eye marked into the wall outside my room made my stomach churn. Who was watching me?

I gulped in a lungful of air. I'd have to risk escaping and maybe, somehow, my dragons would help me.

Tupac, the dragon on my right thigh, perked up, and a picture of him filled my mind—he was scouting ahead. I agreed with this shared thought and a sensation of cloth being peeled form my thigh let me know he separated from me. Once he emerged from the folds of my pants, he fluttered down the dark hallway. I followed along, sensing his direction. None of my dragons had ever ventured so far away from me before. But tonight felt different, as though they needed to do everything they could to help me escape.

I padded down the corridor until I came to a set of stairs. Moonlight streamed in from a window on the landing, and I heard voices drifting up from the main floor.

Guards!

I ducked into the shadows just as two elves came into view. If they looked up to the top of the stairs, they'd see me. Chim sent a wave of power through me; it felt like warm water running over my skin.

One of the guards did glance up the stairs but didn't notice me. Was that Chim's doing? He'd never displayed this kind of magic before.

I sensed Tupac's excitement and knew his location. He'd found the girl.

Once the guards had passed, I stole down the stairs and headed in Tupac's direction. I sensed him hovering outside a door tucked behind a pillar off the main foyer. And from his back-and-forth aerial pacing, I knew he wanted to get inside.

Arriving at the door, I tried opening it—but it was locked. Of course.

I rested my index finger over the keyhole. The pin-shaped tattoo on my right finger moved and wiggled into the lock. This wasn't the first time the pin tattoo had come in handy. With a soft click, the door opened.

We crept into the small room, which contained a bed with a small figure huddled under the covers, along with a few other pieces of furniture. Tupac hovered near the door. *Keep watch. And scout ahead if you can,* I told him as I pulled down the covers and saw the young girl's sleeping face.

The girl stirred as I brushed a lock of hair from her forehead. She pulled away when she saw me, her eyes were wide with fear.

"Who are you?" she asked.

"I'm Zoe. What's your name?"

The girl's mouth clamped shut. I sighed and lifted my hand,

showing her my tattoos. When she saw them, the girl leaned forward. She touched the flower image on the palm of my hand, similar to the one she'd received earlier that day.

"I'm like you, and I want to leave," I said. "Do you want to come with me?"

"I'm Dasha."

I smiled, taking the offer of her name as assent. "Let's go."

Dasha grabbed my hand and scooted off the bed.

"Is there anything you want to take with you?" I asked, looking around her room.

She opened a small dresser next to her bed and handed me a backpack. I held it while she stuffed in her meager belongings. I guessed she must have been orphaned. I couldn't imagine someone giving up their child for my parents' experiments.

"Ready?" I asked once she stopped throwing in clothes. It wasn't even half full.

Dasha shifted the bag onto her shoulders and nodded.

We crept to the door, and when I saw the foyer was empty, I held my finger to my lips. "We have to be quiet."

I didn't see Tupac, but I sensed him down one of the nearby corridors. Warmth rushed over me again, just like it had at the top of the stairs. It was the power of Chim flowing through me and into Dasha. The girl jerked her hand away. Puzzled, I looked down. Magic burned if it was forced on someone. Though neither Chim nor I had been aggressive with magic, perhaps Dasha was extra sensitive because of what my mother had done to her.

"Did that hurt you?" I asked.

The girl shook her head.

I knelt to her eye level and reached out again. "It's okay. Magic doesn't hurt if you welcome it."

She looked at my hand then me and slowly raised a hand to touch mine. This time, when Chim's magic flowed to her, she didn't flinch.

"It kind of tickles like a soft fuzzy blanket," Dasha said.

"Good." I smoothed the girl's hair back then stood.

Tupac sent me a picture of an arial view of the corridors. It looked like a map, and I realized Tupac was showing me the best way out of the fortress. I didn't know how or when he'd discovered this, but I followed the images.

Guards loomed ahead and were coming in our direction. We ducked into the shadows of a doorway. I squeezed my eyes shut and held Dasha close. But they didn't see us. I slumped with relief. It was odd they hadn't noticed us, but the warm feeling from Chim still settled on me and I was certain his power had something to do with it. Once free of this place, I'd figure out my dragons' abilities. We passed a few more pairs of guards on duty, but they never saw us, even when they looked right at us.

Soon after, I noticed Tupac hidden in the shadows at a large metal door—once again, locked. With the help of my pin tattoo, though, it creaked open. I winced at the sound, but fortunately no guards were patrolling outside. Dasha and I slipped into the woods and Tupac flew behind us then melded to my thigh.

Instantly I was overwhelmed with a sense of life. The foliage called to me, and I took a step back as I breathed in the fresh air and welcoming presence the greenery offered. After a moment, the intensity of an encompassing hug blanketed me, and I wanted to lay down and fall into the deepest, most restful sleep. Not because I was tired but because of how good it felt.

I glanced around the surrounding forest. I didn't know

where to go, but we walked as quickly and quietly as we could manage until I was certain we had put enough distance between us and the fortress. We'd been walking for an hour, maybe two, when Dasha stumbled over a rock. I caught her, but the girl could barely keep her eyes open.

We walked for another half hour before I stopped, sitting on a log to catch my breath. Perhaps it would be a good idea to wait for daylight. Dasha settled next to me.

I sensed Tupac wanting to scout, so I released him. Dasha gasped when he fluttered out of my pants.

"What's that?" she asked. She reached out to pet him, and he nuzzled her hand.

"This is Tupac. He's one of the dragons Lady Sirina inked into my skin." I didn't feel that Dasha needed to know the elf was my mother.

Dasha's face fell. "I'm sorry."

"Hey, it's okay."

"But… they hurt you."

"I know." I held the girl's hand. "And they hurt you too, didn't they?"

The girl nodded. Her skin, angry and swollen, reminded me of the pain of being given a fresh tattoo—before Pat, it had been almost unbearable. I then thought about the new, rawest patch of skin on my chest and sent some mental appreciation to my dragons for keeping the demon caged.

"I have another dragon, and she can heal you," I explained. "Are you comfortable with her helping you?"

My dragons were technically androgenous beings, as far as I knew, but Pat felt female to me, while Tupac and Chim somehow felt male.

Dasha stared at Tupac, then me. "Okay."

I called to Pat, and the healing dragon on my arm slid from my skin and emerged from the folds of my blouse. Dasha squealed softly as Pat sniffed the girl's small hand, then settled on her lap.

"It feels warm," Dasha said as Pat poured healing energy into her forearm.

"Why don't you try to sleep?"

"But what if…" Dasha looked in the direction we'd come from.

I wrapped my arm around her shoulder. "We left and we're not ever going back."

Dasha peeked up at me. "Not ever?"

"No."

She leaned into me and a deep sigh left her. I ran my fingers through her long hair and hooked it around her ears.

"Where will we go?" Dasha asked.

"I don't know, but we'll figure it out."

The young elf fell asleep as Pat's healing ability worked on her skin. After a while, the dragon finished the job, stretched, and drifted into unconsciousness. Sleep pulled at me as well, but I couldn't succumb. I had to stay alert.

The sky softened to gray and the edges of the horizon glowed with the promise of a new day. Tupac had long since returned and roosted next to me on the log, as if acting as a sentry. His company, silent and steady, offered some measure of peace.

I shook Dasha. She yawned, rubbing at her eyes. Startled, Pat fluttered from her lap and melded back onto the skin of my arm.

"We should get going," I said.

"Okay." Dasha stumbled to her feet and reshouldered her

backpack.

We walked farther into the forest and eventually came to a small clearing with a large tree in the center. I stopped to gaze at it.

"It's huge," Dasha said.

I jumped at the volume of her voice and wanted to shush her but doubted any elf would have been close enough to hear.

"And old." I patted the trunk. "Ancient."

A portion of the bark quivered, then peeled back. Dasha shrieked and I jumped in front of her. The daggers drawn on my forearms slid into my hands. Brandishing the weapons, I nearly stumbled with shock. I'd never used them, as I'd kept the living abilities of my tattoos a secret from my parents. When I'd trained with Derek, it had been with real swords and daggers. I hadn't ever used the tattoos—they had been summoned by instinct—but Tupac bombarded me with strategies for how to maneuver them, thrusting and swiping. The dragon had never done this before. It almost felt like a nicer version of Derek had taken up residence in my mind.

From the newfound opening in the tree, an old elf with long white hair stepped out. "Oh my," he said with a gentle smile on his face. "Guests!"

"Excuse me?" I dropped my hands, still holding onto the daggers.

Dasha peeked out from behind me.

"I had a sense someone was near my tree. Would you like to come in?" He stepped aside and motioned for us to enter.

I narrowed my eyes at him and his... home? I'd never known such a thing, though I'd heard snatches of tales among the guards about elves who lived in the trees. They had always sounded like fanciful stories.

31

"Is this your home?" I asked.

The elf nodded his head. "My tree, you could say. Are you hungry?"

My stomach betrayed me with a gurgle, and Dasha looked up at me with pleading eyes. We were both hungry and had nowhere to go. And nothing to eat.

Sensing no immediate danger, I willed the daggers to meld back into my arms. I doubted this grandfather elf would be a concern. It wouldn't hurt to have some breakfast, and the old elf seemed innocent enough. Not every elf was like my parents.

"All right," I said.

"Wonderful. Right this way."

We passed through the entrance and walked first into a sitting room. It was massive, and my jaw dropped.

He chuckled and tilted his head to the side. "Never been inside an elven home?"

"Uh, not like this." I gripped Dasha's hand. The magic of the place reached out to me with tentacles that rubbed up against my magic. It was searching for something and though my magic still felt fractured from whatever my mother had done to me, I could feel it surge, wanting to connect with the magic in this tree... house... whatever.

I studied the old elf and got the sense he was studying me too, though it felt a bit more intense.

My eyes narrowed. "Can you read my mind?"

"No. I haven't the ability. My magic is one of knowledge and wisdom." He shrugged. "I sense things, guess things and sometimes I'm even right. The magic is useful sometimes."

"And what is your magic telling you?" I shifted my weight uncomfortable with what his magic might reveal about me.

"That you need a good breakfast and a place to sleep. Beyond that, time will tell. I don't like making quick judgments. Did that when I was young and found it unhelpful." He cleared his throat. "Elven homes are always bigger on the inside. It's the magic we infuse in them when they're created." He tapped his lips with his index finger. "I'm Nate, by the way," he said. "And you are?"

"I'm Zoe, and this is Dasha."

Nate nodded and took in our backpacks. I quickly ran my fingers through my hair, and then Dasha's, trying to work out the knotted mess.

"Over breakfast you can tell me a bit about yourselves." Nate paused glancing back at us as he started down the hallway. "And you're welcome to stay as long as you need."

Twilight's Curse

❀

Chapter Three

Nix

Six years later

My heart pounded, my breath came in shallow bursts. My unconscious mind informed me that it was the dream I had almost nightly. The lush foliage surrounding the Royal Tree pressed against me. I knew I had to look, but the thought of seeing my parents' dead bodies once again sent needle-sharp tingles through me. Seeing their prone forms would finish the recreation.

I slowly moved my head and took in their still bodies. I stumbled up to them and released a yell.

"Mother! Father!" I caressed my mother's cheek. Cold. Lifeless. Her glassy, staring eyes would never look upon me with affection again. And then there was my father, no longer strong and unbeatable, but still my hero. "I can't... I can't be the king. I'm too young. I'm not ready."

The trees around me moved and a gentle breeze lifted my disheveled hair. My parents' lips offered no comfort, no answer.

"My king," a soft female voice said.

I shifted and spun to face a woman. She was new to my dream. She wore loose pants, and her fitted top hugged her slim waist. My eyes traveled up to her face. Her hair was wrapped tightly beneath a scarf and she held a loose portion of the material over the lower part of her face. All I could see were her vibrant green eyes and dark brows. She stood at the borders of the forest.

"Who are you?" I asked, my noble training taking control of my emotions.

The woman gently pulled the scarf away and revealed her face. A long lock fell down the front of her garment; near the roots her hair was a creamy blond that gently darkened to black at the ends, which fell over her shoulders. Her eyes, as green as emeralds, stood out against the canvas of her skin, which was golden. She looked like a paler version of the Twilight Realm elves. Though not as light as elves from the Night Realm.

"We will meet again, and I will assist you," she said. She crossed her arms and gave a slight bow.

"Wait! When will we meet? Where? Why? And how are you going to assist me?"

A smirk played at her lips. She strode toward me and touched my hand. Warm magic pulsed with my own. It was inviting and I didn't fight it. It raced across my skin and beneath, merging with my magic.

"I will fight with you as Nazira did with Paz Mier."

"My ancestors," I whispered.

She nodded. "It is time to free your people."

"But I'm not ready."

"Your readiness matters not. You have all you need. Do not doubt yourself. The peace of Paz Mier's Vaim Na'quab is with you to guide you. Your time has come."

Vaim Na'quab, which imbued the royal lines with magic. The words rolled in my mind and I pictured the painting of the soaring bird—the symbol of peace—that hung in Nate's office. Legend said the bird resided with Paz Mier as he defeated the ancient darkness that once held all of elvendom—an evil spirit also part of our origin legends. Once Paz Mier, Nazira, and their army defeated the evil—the ancient stories never gave details on this part and only highlighted the first king's success—Paz Mier married Nazira and established his rule over all of elvendom. And when their five children were each given a portion of the kingdom to rule, the peace of Vaim Na'quab was to guide them.

I shook myself from the enchantment of this elven female's mysterious words.

"How will I find you? You said you'd help me."

She smiled and her eyes softened. "We will meet." Her gaze lingered on my face. "Until then, my king."

She replaced the scarf and then slowly faded from my sight like a mist dispersing in the night.

I reached for her arm only to swipe through empty air. "No, come back." Had she really been here? I glanced down. There weren't even footprints where she had stood.

I wandered back toward the Royal Tree, standing tall and white behind my parents' bodies. In my dream, it was completely untouched by time and remained as I saw it the day my parents had been killed. The leaves had scattered over the earth as they always did when a monarch died. The Royal Tree had taken on the deadened appearance of a deciduous tree in winter.

I approached the trunk and stretched my arms toward it. It felt lifeless beneath my touch and I willed my magic to enter it.

"I am your king," I said to the tree. Startled, I jerked my hand away. I'd never spoken those words in any previous dream. They were forbidden by my own vow, which I'd made the night I'd witnessed my parents' murders.

Stepping back, I took in the massive feat of nature. The tree trembled. I felt my magic connect to the tree and sensed its own ancient magic awaken from deep within, stirring it from its deep hibernation. The trunk started to gleam white as fresh buds of leaves tinged with gold started to sprout.

* * *

I gasped for breath and sat up in bed, my sheets soaked with sweat on this humid night. It had been a dream, a familiar and constant one I'd had ever since that night fourteen years ago. The dream always ended with the tree dying, going completely black.

This time, at my words—I shuddered remembering that I'd told the tree I was its king—life was restored. *Was it really my time to take up the throne?* Nate said I'd know.

I climbed out of bed and ran my fingers through my thick blond hair on my way to the bathroom. I splashed cool water on my face from a freshwater fountain, which sprouted from a branch jutting from the wall. The cold water cleared away some of my grogginess and the eerie dread that had filled me since I'd woken.

I wandered back to my room, changed into clean clothes, and arranged my bedding. Today was Zyanna's twentieth birthday. I hoped that she was still alive—and if she was, that she was celebrating what this day meant. I wished for her to be happy and safe, wherever she was.

The night that had taken my parents had also taken her. She'd only been a child of six when she and her nurse had disappeared. Nate and I had searched for her throughout the Twilight Realm, but we'd never been able to find her, not even with Nate's tracking skills. It wasn't his magical ability, but as the royal advisor, he did have skills and connections I knew nothing about. I wondered if he was still in touch with the non-elven citizens who'd been around in my childhood—the centaurs, dwarves, fawns, and such. They'd all disappeared once the Dions came to power, and I wasn't sure if they had been massacred or were in hiding like me.

The dream played again in my mind. I mentally scanned through the details and shook my head to return to reality.

Those green eyes flashed in my imagination as I thought about the mysterious woman. She too was different from my previous dreams. I'd never seen her before. Just as I'd never before spoken to the tree and told it I was the king.

No! I thought. *I'm no king. The son of a king, but not the king. And I never will be.*

I went down to the first floor of my home and sifted through the notes on my desk. I'd stopped living with Nate five years after my parents died. I riffled through a pile of paper and ran my finger over a page on the bottom. The papers were nothing more than notes from my study of the books Nate had given me. He was diligent about my education as the future monarch and ensured I had knowledge of our history, rules, laws, and everything else he deemed I should know. Everything I'd be learning from my parents if they were still alive. Despite Nate's efforts, there were still gaps. Things only my father and mother could have passed down.

I was a mere child-adult. If my parents were still alive, my father would only expect me to observe and mostly shadow him in his duties. It'd be boring, but we'd be together. Wistfulness squeezed my heart. But I remembered that Nate wanted me to meet him in Haven, a small city near the Dion fortress, and it pulled me from my dismal thoughts. I needed to talk to the advisor anyway, about my dream and that woman's enchanting green eyes.

I left home about an hour later, stepping through the entrance of my simple tree. Like all elven trees the doorway was magical and prevented anyone but me from entering unless I allowed it. So far, Nate was the only other elf who had access.

I strode through the forest until I came to the bustling city of Haven. Most elves lived in trees and traditionally would never consider felling a tree or using brick and mortar to build anything. But under Leski and Sirina's rule, Haven had, as its rulers described it, "modernized." The buildings surrounding me were elf-made and the ground beneath my feet was cobblestone. It was unnatural.

A young elf woman with a daughter and two sons hurried past, nearly bumping into me. My foot almost tangled with the daughter's.

"Excuse me," she said without giving me a second glance.

Like the rest of the populace, she was making her way toward the center of the busy marketplace.

Carts creaked by, pulled by horses and donkeys. I patted the golden side of a nearby mare and she flicked her tail at me as she sauntered past, bearing the weight of the elf family she pulled in a wagon. I cringed inwardly. Horses were meant to be ridden. And trees were meant to grow, not be cut down and manipulated into boxes that carried elves.

Already I missed the richness of the forest and the magic that permeated the foliage. Though all elves had innate magic, the city of Haven had very little. With the rise of the Dions, most elven magic had fallen into disuse due to fear. There were rumors that any elf who showed strong magical potential would be taken by the Dions. These were only rumors, which I believed to be true, since elves had disappeared without a trace for years. And the public working of elven magic had become a bit taboo.

I passed a vendor selling cloth.

"They say the tree's changing," a customer said, holding a child while his wife perused the material.

The vendor leaned forward. "You mean the Royal Tree?"

My heart drummed a little faster and I pretended to be interested in a blue swatch as I listened.

"Yeah," the elf said. "My cousin passed it the other day and said he saw leaves starting to bud."

"You don't say." The vendor folded a piece of fabric the customer's wife had discarded in favor of another bolt. He rested his hand on top of the material and the fabric wiggled under his hand then flattened with not a hint of a wrinkle.

I smiled at the vendor's subtle use of magic. Elves found a way to discreetly use their abilities.

The elf holding his child shifted his weight as the child reached up and stuck her fingers in the father's mouth. The patient father merely smiled and tucked his lips around his teeth then plucked the child's fingers from his mouth. He turned back to the vendor.

"I hear there's to be an announcement today," the customer said. "My wife's thinking it'll be a marriage announcement."

"Do you think a royal has finally come forward?" the vendor asked. "When the king and queen died, the children disappeared, some say they're dead as well. His royal highness the crown prince should, by rights, be king."

I dropped the fabric in surprise. I quickly picked it up and brushed off some dust, moving closer to the two elves.

"He'd just be a child-adult. It's good the Dions stepped up as regents when they did." The vendor spun to face me. "Can I help you?"

Startled, I glanced up, catching the vendor's fierce eyes. "Uh, no, just looking. This blue's quite nice." I patted the bolt of material.

"Are you planning on buying?"

"I'm just looking."

The vendor grunted. "Try not to touch what you don't plan to buy," he grunted and hitched up his pants.

"Of course. I'm sorry, sir." I could feel the warmth of embarrassment reach my cheeks. The brownies who lived with Nate still made my clothes, cooked my meals, and even came over to clean my home. I didn't know a thing about fabric.

The customer and vendor moved away and there seemed no sense in following them or they'd grow suspicious, if they weren't already.

I wandered back out into the street, troubled by their words. I stuffed my hands in my pockets and kicked a loose stone off the cobbled street.

"Ouch!"

I turned and saw the stone had struck a woman, who rubbed her ankle, and I darted into a cluster of elves before she caught me staring. I hadn't intentionally aimed the stone at her!

"Nix, there you are," Nate said.

My mentor's familiar voice carried above the din of the market. He wove his way through the crowd and slapped me on the shoulder when he reached me.

"Morning, Nate. What's up?" I grinned, feeling relieved to see him.

"There's to be an announcement from the fortress," Nate said. "Lord Leski and Lady Sirina have news of an upcoming wedding."

I felt the warmth leave my face as my blood drained away. Idle gossip between a vendor and customer was one thing, but this was Nate. He knew these types of things. I shook my head, trying to relieve the cool dread I felt. This announcement didn't mean anything. The regents responsible for killing my parents hadn't been able to claim the crown since the Royal Tree had gone inert. As far as I knew, the brownies alone enter the tree. But no elf could enter it—save me and possibly my sister. She was of the royal family but I was the crown prince. I wasn't sure if the tree would only open for me or both of us. And one day, when I was ready, I'd have to unseal it. I shivered despite the hot, humid air as my dream pricked at my mind. *Is it time?*

"You look whiter than a howlite stone," Nate remarked. "Relax. They'll never claim the throne."

The world seemed to stand still in my little bubble as the elves of the city raced by in a blur of color, all heading off to hear the announcement.

"Do you think they've found her?" I dropped my voice and leaned in close to Nate. "After all this time?"

Nate nudged me along. "I don't know and don't want to give you false hope."

I knew Nate couldn't say more. Our real identities had been hidden that fateful night and it wouldn't be wise to reveal even a hint of who we were in public. No one could find out about me—or my sister. But I feared she'd been taken by the usurpers.

We arrived at the center of the market where a permanent stage sat. The city speaker motioned to the crowd, silencing all the buzzing voices.

"Our realm has been without a proper ruler for almost fifteen years." The speaker's voice, aided by a touch of magic, projected to all corners of the open square. "We suffered a great loss when the king and queen died and the crown prince abandoned the kingdom."

While surveying the crowd, the fluttering of dark fabric in the shadows of an alleyway caught my attention. As if sensing me, a woman's head popped up and my heart tripped in my chest. A loose scarf covering her head slipped down, revealing blond gently merging to black tones of her hair. It was her! I'd recognize that hair anywhere.

I pushed against the unyielding crowd, but the woman secured the scarf tightly over her head and ducked back into the shadows.

"Nix, where are you going?" Nate asked, tugging the back of my shirt.

I pulled away from him and weaved through the dense crowd, growling internally. I'd lose her at this rate. I wanted to yell at all the elves enraptured by the speaker to get out of my way, so I pushed a little harder than I should have, jostling a woman holding a baby. She nearly fell over, but her husband caught her and glared at me.

"Sorry." I stopped to help steady the woman. "Are you all right?"

The woman nodded and held her baby closer.

"Mind yourself, son," her husband said in a deep, warning voice.

As I turned away from the family, I heard Nate whisper-shouting at me, "Nix, get back here!"

The speaker droned on and I half-listened.

"The Lord and Lady Dion graciously took the place of the royals, but without rulers of royal blood the Twilight Realm has been without proper leadership. Thankfully, we have not suffered." The speaker's dull voice tickled my ears, but it was just background noise. In every speech, he offered a long preamble giving glory to the Lord and Lady, as if their actions were heroic.

Using greater caution, I slipped between the elves who were riveted by the speaker. I'd only seen a glimmer of the woman's green eyes, and now that I looked around, I saw any number of women with the same eye color.

I needed to find this woman. She hadn't been focused on the speaker like the other elves. She'd hung back on the fringes of the crowd instead of pushing forward. Perhaps she wanted to hear the latest news but maintain a quick retreat.

Thankfully, I soon located her in the shadows. She hadn't moved and I was able to come up beside her.

"Hi, green eyes." I felt stupid the moment the words left my mouth.

She gasped as she glanced sharply at me. Without answering, she turned and headed down the alley.

I ran to catch up to her. "Hey, wait!"

"Leave me alone," she called, but suddenly she rounded on me and pointed a black dagger at my chest. I held up my hands.

"Hey, it's not like that," I said.

"Yeah, then what's it like?"

"I just…" Now that I could see her face, I was certain she was the woman from my dream—although in my dream she hadn't held a knife to my chest and had seemed much more pleasant. I couldn't just tell her I had dreamed about her. That would sound crazy!

The door to a nearby restaurant banged open and two regent guards spilled out into the alley. They loomed over me and I shuddered. I didn't know what it was about regent guards, but they were unnaturally tall and muscled.

The woman stiffened and darted into the shadows of a side street. I called after her, but she was gone.

"What's that?" one of the guards hollered at me.

"Sorry, I was… I thought I saw someone I knew," I said.

"Move along, boy. You should be in the city center with the rest."

I nodded curtly and made a dash back the way I'd come. The woman lingered in my thoughts. It *had* been the woman from my dreams. I needed to find her again.

Reaching the edge of the city center, I saw Nate listening to the speaker, who had finished with his preamble: "It is with great joy that we announce the upcoming nuptials between Dimas Dion…"

I stopped in my tracks, my heartbeat ringing in my ears. I

closed my eyes. *Please no...*

"...and Zyanna of the royal house and lineage."

A thunderous cheer drowned out the rest of the speaker's words. The elves around me emanated joy at hearing the news that one of the royals had survived.

I sank to my knees. I no longer desired to find the green-eyed woman—my sister was alive! After all this time, hearing her name had both winded me and sent energy coursing through me. I was no longer alone.

But my heart sank again when the reality of the news hit me: my sister would be married to Dimas. Was it her choice? Was she being forced to do it against her will? I clenched my fists.

The crowd around me opened up and dispersed in all directions. On shaky legs, I righted myself and looked around. The elves were moving in a steady stream.

A guard was nailing a parchment to the message board by the stage. I'd missed the details of the regent speaker's final words and decided to read the official announcement.

Pushing against the tide, I reached the board and scanned the notice for any mention of the wedding date.

"Nix, there you are," Nate said when he came up beside me. "We'd best get out of here."

"One week, Nate. We have one week."

Nate nodded and in that moment I decided: As soon as I got out of the market, I'd go to the fortress of Leski and Sirina. I'd find a way in. And find a way to rescue Zyanna.

Chapter Four

Zoe

My skin itched as sweat trickled down the sides of my face. It was only late afternoon, but after leaving Haven because some random elf decided to flirt with me, I had decided to come here. Should I be flattered by his attention? Some elven females might be, but I didn't care about such things. I liked my simple life with Dasha, Nate, and the brownies. Plus, I didn't want to encourage him. Pulling my dagger on him surely spoke of my lack of interest.

Moving with stealth required me to wipe away the moisture on my forehead with practiced grace. The beginnings of a spectacular headache grew from my tense shoulders, and I rolled them, willing my muscles to relax. I called on Pat and her healing abilities.

I hated being here—near the fortress where I'd grown up and my parents still resided. I didn't come often and always watched from a distance, though I'd slowly creeped closer over the years.

I often thought of the children my parents experimented on, the young male elves they turned into their bulky guards. Had they found another with magic like mine or Dasha's? And Maximon. He had been a friend, sort of, since we'd explored the maze of corridors together. He knew my parents experimented on me, but not the details, and I'd never trusted him enough to tell him about my magic or how it had given life to my tattoos.

The fog-drenched air around me added to my need to remain alert. The foreboding structure before me rose to an impossible height. My parents had forgone the traditional tree dwellings of elfkind, preferring structures of wood, brick, and mortar.

I needed to find the way in—not that I wanted to return.

I felt a familiar rub along my upper left arm and ran my hand over the skin there.

Be still, Pat, I thought. In response, my dragon tattoo swirled around my arm. When she settled, I felt her calm.

Chim rested on my back. His hyper-alert senses helped me discover there was no one nearby. If I were attacked, he would throw up a protective shield.

Tupac functioned as a warrior. He rested on my right thigh, like a sword.

Each dragon had a purpose, and although they had started out as nothing more than androgynous drawings on my skin, I now felt a bond with them. In fact, I felt a bond with all my tattoos—save one—and I'd assigned the dragons names and genders to fit their personalities.

My dragons were the most animated of my tattoos. They could leave my skin when I permitted, and often communicated to me through images of flying free or constant squirming on my skin that they wanted to be released for a while. They never went too far, as it taxed me, and they returned to my skin when they wanted to. I never commanded them to return unless it was important. And if I needed them, they willingly and readily helped.

I considered calling forth my dragons as I sized up the fortress.

Was I really crazy enough to re-enter this place? It had been six years. When I thought of all the orphaned children inside being subjected to my mother's experiments, I knew what I had to do.

I shook my head, a sardonic smile creeping to my lips. Had they really expected me to be grateful? Little did my parents know that while they had been *enhancing* me with their manipulations, they'd forged me into their enemy.

Chim? I asked, aligning my senses to the guardian on my back. We still felt nothing from the surrounding forest, aside from the movement of animals.

I drew my scarf tight around my head to hide my hair. If the guards ever caught a glimpse of it, they'd haul me back to my parents without a thought. I crept through the trees, barely making any noise as I got closer to the building. I kept my breathing slow and even as I made my way to the back door, hidden behind a coating of ivy.

Tupac, I thought, summoning the warrior. I felt him lift from my skin like the peeling back of fabric. He flew away from me. Chim then separated from me and joined Tupac. I sensed their alertness as they flew around me. Pat could fight and defend me if she needed to, but she would serve me best by staying close and providing healing energy. With her help, I seldom tired in a sword fight, unless the dragons had separated from me for extended periods of time.

Stray voices traveled toward me, and I froze. Tupac and Chim fluttered to my side, perching on my shoulders. Their dark coloring provided them with a sort of camouflage in the forest.

When the voices drew close, I ducked down and the dragons settled on the tree branches above me.

"Hurry!" commanded a feminine voice. My mother.

My muscles tensed. I hadn't heard her voice in six years.

The dagger tattoos on my forearms slipped free into my waiting hands. Fighting the guards wouldn't be easy. I couldn't see how many there were, but Nate had mentored me both in magic and weapons.

From my position, I could make out the dull brown of the guards' uniforms as they snaked through the trees. What were they doing out here at this time of night?

I willed my daggers to return to my skin, then crouched down and waddled forward to get a better view. I settled behind a bush and pressed the palm of my hand over the leaves. I called my magic forward; the flower tattoo on my palm encouraged growth among the foliage to keep me hidden while giving me a sight line to the passing entourage. Even after all these years, my magic had never really healed from whatever my mother had done the night she tattooed the demon on my chest. The magic was fractured, and it didn't feel like it fully belonged to me.

I counted five of the large guards with my mother. I stilled.

Suddenly, a thick arm wrapped around me and a hand pressed itself over my mouth, muzzling me. I wouldn't scream and expose myself, but instinctually I held still and waited as the procession passed. Then I'd fight whoever had snuck up on me. Through my connection with Chim and Tupac, I sensed that the unfortunate fool was a male. I doubted he was a guard, or I'd have been taken straight to the fortress for trespassing. But how had he managed to get past Chim?

My daggers fell into my hands and I slowly began to twist the blades so I could stab him at just the right moment.

With my hand lowered from its previous position on the bush, my hiding place was exposed, but Chim extended his cloaking shield over me—just in time before my mother passed and glance in my direction. For a moment I forgot to breathe, certain she'd call for her guards.

As I watched, a smirk lifted the corners of the woman's mouth. Soon after, the group had passed.

I felt the elf behind me sigh with relief. "You're safe," he whispered.

I chomped on the elf's hand and he flinched. Taking advantage of the opportunity, I burst out of his grasp.

"No thanks to you, fool!" I whispered, mentally signaling my dragons to settle behind the elf.

Having struck the first blow, I gripped my daggers and planted my feet firmly in a fighting stance.

The man held up his hands. "Woah! Easy there. I'm not looking for a fight."

"Then why start one?"

"I was just trying to protect you."

I stepped closer. "I don't need protection."

He rested his hands on his hips. "Clearly I was mistaken."

"Next time don't butt in where you're not needed." My voice sounded stronger than I felt, but this elf was a nuisance. He'd spoiled my plan and now I'd have to return another night.

"Can I ask what you're doing so near to the fortress?" he asked. "It's forbidden territory."

I sheathed my daggers. His eyes bugged out a bit when he saw them slide up from my hands.

"How'd you do that?"

"Your questions are irrelevant. Now, why don't we go our separate ways?"

The elf cocked his head, suddenly looking like he'd recognized me. Impossible!

My eyes narrowed. Was this the same elf who'd followed me in the market? My back tensed and Chim, in his heightened state, threw out a protective shield, knocking the elf to the ground.

Chim!

At my chastisement, the dragon pulled in the shield, allowing the elf to crawl onto all fours, shaking his head.

To my surprise, he chuckled. I squinted, studying him. I should have run, but now I was curious. He didn't look like anyone I'd known from my previous life, yet I was certain he recognized me.

And he'd been following me.

"Do I know you?" I asked.

The elf stood up. "No, but I believe we can help each other." He extended his right hand. "I'm Nix."

I stared at him.

Nix shrugged. "Usually this is where you shake my hand and tell me your name."

"How can you help me?"

"So that's a no to your name then."

"None of your business." I folded my arms. I didn't like him and doubted he knew what he was talking about.

Chim, Tupac, knock him out, I ordered. *It's time to get out of here.* The dragons responded immediately and a moment later Nix was lying facedown in the dirt.

I knelt by his side as Chim and Tupac melded back onto my body like soft fabric running against my skin. I then felt for a pulse and allowed a small sliver of healing flow from Pat into Nix, enough to make sure he hadn't been hurt too seriously but not enough to wake him.

I disappeared into the shadows of the forest but couldn't resist glancing back.

Chim, do you sense anything?

The dragon used his power to check, but nothing registered. I shook the creepy feeling that had come over me that someone out in the forest was watching me, then sighed and turned toward home.

A smile blossomed on my lips when I came into view of Nate's tree. I laid a hand on the tree's entrance marker and a moment later the door peeled back, allowing me to step through. The entranceway was large. Curving stairways wound up the sides of the tree with landings on each floor. The interior was lit with glow stones placed on small shelves that resembled pouting lips. Hallways extended in all directions.

I decided to check on Nate and made my way to his private wing.

Along the way, I passed the part of the home dedicated to housing orphans—children I'd rescued from the streets—as well as the brownies who cared for them.

Brownies wore only brown garments and were about waist-high in stature, with dark black hair, rich brown eyes, and light skin. They were such cheerful creatures. They lived to serve, but they only offered their services willingly and freely. It was believed among the elves that if a brownie chose a home, the home became a safe place and the elves who lived there would have the highest reputation. The creatures also preferred secrecy and only revealed their presence to a homeowner after they'd already lived and served in the home a long time. No one knew how long they'd been in a home by the time they revealed themselves.

A small brownie appeared to my left. "Greetings, Mistress Zoe."

I turned and smiled at her. "How are the children today, Cocoa?"

"Well." She tilted her head, trying to look around me. "And have you brought more for us?"

"I'm sorry, not today. My mission was… interrupted."

"I'm glad you're all right." Cocoa's voice was light and soft.

"Thank you, but it wasn't a fight."

"Oh?"

"It's nothing. Just someone…" Words failed me.

Cocoa traced a pattern on the carpet with her toe, her hands clasped behind her back. "Was it a male elf?"

"Yes."

Nix's blue eyes and warm smile floated through my mind. He was handsome, and meeting him had been kind of entertaining… but he was a nuisance and had spoiled my plan.

Cocoa giggled and clapped her delicate hands.

"Don't get any ideas." I waved my finger at her. "He *was* a nuisance."

"A nuisance can be a good thing."

"Not for me."

"Why? You are beautiful."

56

I stared at the brownie. No one had ever complimented me that way before, and so I didn't know how to respond. Finding a mate seemed so complicated and I was content with my life in Nate's home. I had the freedom to come and go, I had a roof over my head, and I helped with the children, which was important. Besides, I'd only just entered my child-adult years and wasn't even twenty years old. While some elves married as child-adults, many waited until they had become full adults and passed their first one hundred years.

"Are you going to see Nate?" Cocoa asked, her soft voice interrupting my musings.

"Yes, but first... how's Anansi settling in?" I thought of the newest addition I'd found on the streets of Haven city a week ago. I inwardly winced at his name. It meant *trickster* and was an unusual name for an elf. His arrival rounded our number of children to fifteen.

Cocoa shrugged.

"What's wrong?" I asked.

"He's settled in fine, but I don't know," she said uncertainly, patting her chest. "Something doesn't feel right about him."

I knew what she meant. The boy had given me odd vibes as well, but most street kids did when they first arrived.

"I'm sure he just needs time to settle."

"Perhaps."

"How's Dasha?"

The elf child I'd escaped the fortress with six years ago had turned out to have a gifting similar to mine, though she wasn't a life-giver. When someone was in Dasha's presence, they felt full of life. Peaceful. Energized.

"Dasha is worried for you," Cocoa said. "She wouldn't see Nate until you returned."

I fell in step beside the brownie, who took us down a spacious corridor with doors on either side, each housing one of the children. The hallway was well lit with the glow stones.

"Is she feeling better?" I asked.

"She's not as congested as she was, and her energy has returned. She was playing with the other children today. Her house mother, Coffee, felt she was well enough to join with the other children."

"That's good to hear. Then what's wrong?"

Cocoa's forehead crinkled. "It's hard to say. She won't tell us… just that she needs to speak with you."

I picked up my pace, and in three steps I had reached Dasha's door. I knocked gently.

"Dasha? Can I come in?"

When she didn't respond, I opened the door a crack and peered inside. The warmth of the young girl's magic filled the room and radiated against my face. It was like wrapping myself in a warm blanket on a cold day.

"Zoe! You're back." Dasha scooted off her bed and tossed aside the book she'd been reading.

I thanked Cocoa, and the brownie bowed.

"I'll let Nate know you're here," Cocoa said, then disappeared back into the hall.

Dasha took my hand, and I felt her magic flow into me, removing the irritation I'd felt toward Nix.

"I hear you're feeling better," I said.

Dasha settled back on the center of her bed as I perched on the edge. The small flower tattoo on Dasha's palm moved up to her forearm. I watched, puzzled and curious.

Dasha coughed. "I am, but I had an odd dream last night."

"You did? Is this what you wanted to talk about?" I stroked the girl's hair, tucking it behind one of her ears. I marveled at how much the girl had grown and thrived during the past six years. She was the same age now as I had been when we first arrived at Nate's home, yet there was an innocence about her I had lacked.

"Yes."

"Then tell me about it."

Dasha's eyes darted to the left and right, then settled on me. "Please don't think I'm crazy."

"Of course not. I'm thrilled you want to talk, since you're obviously bothered by something."

Dasha inhaled, as if filling her lungs with air gave her courage. "It was a dream about… the king and queen. They… well, I saw them die."

I tried to keep my face neutral but was troubled by the revelation. "That does sound scary. Are you okay?"

"Yes."

"And how do you know it was the king and queen?"

"That's what *he* called them."

I couldn't help the sharp intake of breath that caused me to pull back. Dasha was referring to my father; she rarely said their names.

"Continue," I prompted, "and leave nothing out."

"Well, *he* was calling for the crown prince, demanding him to come forward. But the prince didn't. I couldn't see him, but I sensed him in the dream, as though he were watching the same scene play out. Then the king and queen were murdered. It was…"

Dasha turned and buried her warm face in my shoulder.

I kissed the girl's head and hugged her. Wanting to help, I

summoned Pat, who fluttered through the sides of my sleeve and landed next to the girl. Dasha ran her fingers over the dragon's inky black snout. Pat then climbed into the girl's lap and curled up like a cat, thrumming with contentment. I felt the dragon's healing flow into Dasha.

"What happened next?" I asked.

"*He* and his guards left the bodies of the king and queen on the ground. For a long time, no one came. The bodies just lay there... and then a boy, maybe my age, stepped out from under a bush and knelt by the king and queen. He was the prince. I don't know how, but I just knew it. And then..." Dasha stopped petting the dragon and looked up at me. "You showed up and spoke to him. You said you'd help him one day."

My blood ran cold. I knew the child wasn't lying; she often had dreams that carried premonitions and prophecies.

"Have you told anyone else about this?" I asked. Dasha shook her head. "I need to go and see Nate. I believe you, but..."

I didn't know how to put my thoughts into words. A dream. About me. Helping the crown prince... the king...

Impossible!

* * *

I made my way through the maze of towering shelves and pillars of boxes that filled Nate's office; he used a small corner at the back of the room, his cluttered desk in front of a small greenhouse that let in some natural light.

On the wall hung a painting of a dove, Vaim Na'quab, with golden accents on its wings. It was a symbol of peace for all elves, and whenever I looked at it, I longed for peace amidst the turmoil that churned within me. The bird was so calm as it soared! Today, I chose to avoid looking at it.

The rest of the office was filled with shelves bursting with books, scrolls, beakers, and boxes filled with items Nate had perhaps forgotten he owned. Without the help of the brownies, I was certain the place would be coated in dust, perhaps even a breathing hazard.

I cleared my throat.

Nate lifted his head from the parchment he was writing on. "Ah, Zoe. I'm glad you're back."

I settled in a chair across from him and launched into Dasha's dream. When I was done, he leaned back in his chair, his eyes closed. He was thinking. Needing to move, I entered his greenhouse and looked over his struggling plants.

Ten minutes later, Nate still hadn't said anything. As I paced in front of Nate's desk, my dragons zoomed around the room, chasing each other and exploring the maze his office provided them. I worked to hold my impatience at bay while waiting for my mentor to offer some insight into Dasha's dream. Certainly he'd see it was a dream and nothing more.

"So?" I prompted.

Nate's eyes were closed and I wondered if he was even thinking about what I'd told him just a few minutes ago.

Nate adjusted himself, as though he'd been startled. He had been drifting off. "It's hard to say."

"Do you think it's true?"

My mentor leaned back, one elbow resting on the arm of his chair and his left hand cupping his chin. "Yes."

I stopped my pacing and stared at him. "Excuse me?"

Nate glanced up at me. "I said yes. I do think the dream is

true, and I do think you will be helping the crown prince."

"But that's… that's impossible."

"Your tattoo?"

I folded my arms across my chest, sensing the demon tattooed there move beneath the dragons' shielding. I shuddered. How could I help the crown prince with that demon inside of me? What if it got out? What if it turned me into some monster and I killed someone, killed the prince, in an attempt to help him? What if I became the thing my parents had wanted all along? I dropped my head. Nate knew how I felt about the tattoo. We'd discussed it at length many times and our opinions always differed.

I turned away. The familiar conversation was about to start. "How could I help a prince with…" I waved my hands in an attempt to find the right word but couldn't. "…this!" I pointed at my chest.

"You think it defines you? Keeps you from doing good? Or perhaps you think it's greater than you?"

I squeezed the bridge of my nose. "No… It's just…" Nate didn't understand how the demon tattoo made me feel. It had been years since I'd received it, but I still felt like that part of my body didn't fully belong to me, and it left me with a dark emptiness in my chest. And while the demon was kept contained by my dragons, I worried that it would one day take over and I'd lose the control I had. I shook my head. I couldn't help a prince with something so vile living in me.

"There is only one way to free yourself of that particular tattoo. You have to forgive and let your magic merge with it," Nate said.

"No!" Anger rose in me. That was the conclusion Nate always came too. He just didn't understand. He made it sound so simple. But it wasn't. I felt the demon rioting inside its cage. It always grew stronger when my emotions turned antagonistic.

Chim, I called. There was a rustle as the small dragon flew out from beneath a stack of paper to my right and landed on my shoulder. Had the dragons been playing a game of hide-and-seek? He climbed down the back of my shirt and moved between the folds of cloth before melding back onto my skin.

The raging demon settled down, and so did my emotions. Next, Tupac flew to me and settled on my leg.

"Zoe, your tattoos aren't all bad."

I tapped my chest. "I know, but this one is."

Aside from my family, Nate was only elf who knew the extent of my tattoos and what they could do, what I was capable of. I kept the tattoos covered so no one would see them.

Nate stood and shuffled into the greenhouse where a few plants struggled to survive. He claimed he liked plants but was easily distracted with his reading and studying to really tend properly to them. I followed, reaching out to touch each of the plants. Every time I did, new life blossomed. I enjoyed this aspect of my magic. It brought a smile to my lips and quieted my emotions.

Nate watched me and winked. "You're a life-giver. I do my best to help them grow, but they don't thrive under my care like they do under yours."

"Meaning?" I leaned against a table holding some depressed roses.

Nate touched the leaves, then picked at a thorn with his nail. "Meaning, here's a lovely rosebush. But there are thorns and weeds—"

"So pull out the weeds."

"True, I could do that." Nate pulled at some of the small shoots, then tossed them into a nearby garbage bin. "But what of the thorns? I can't get rid of those. They'll just grow back."

I studied the rosebush, my brow furrowing as I waited for Nate to offer some insight. He tended to teach metaphorically, than literally. "Okay, there's a lesson in here somewhere."

He offered a smile instead and settled back into his desk chair. "You always were my favorite student. You learn fast."

My mouth dropped. "But I haven't learned anything."

"I beg to disagree. You have. You just haven't worked it out yet."

I ran my finger over the sharp edge of one of the thorns. What was Nate trying to teach me?

"Take a plant home with you if you need to think about it more," he said. "The plant will do better with you than me."

I grunted but picked up the most unfortunate rosebush from the greenhouse and balanced it against my hip. I'd at least give the plant a better life. Perhaps the mysteries of Nate's words *would* unveil themselves.

Chapter Five

Nix

I rested my hand on Nate's old cedar tree and waited for the doorway to peel back, allowing me to access the foyer.

After waking up in the forest outside the fortress, groggy but with no bumps or bruises, I stumbled back to my tree to quickly freshen up before making my way to Nate's. I needed to speak with my advisor.

"Nate?" I called as I walked into the living room with its neat, lived-in feel. A book lay open on a side table next to Nate's recliner and a throw blanket had been tossed over the arm rest. Otherwise, the room appeared relatively untouched.

I smiled. Being here felt like coming home.

I made my way through the familiar hallway. If Nate wasn't in the living room, he'd be in his office.

In all my years of living here, I'd never fully explored the place and had stuck close to Nate's living quarters. The external structure was quite large, so I guessed there was more to the tree. Perhaps one day I'd take time to admire its internal structure. It wasn't that I wasn't curious, but since only Nate, the brownies, and I had shared the tree during the years I'd lived here, exploring had never appealed to me. It was also common for elves to block off parts of their home they didn't want anyone to enter. An outsider would see a wall instead of a hallway, but to the elves who set the boundaries, they'd see their home as usual.

"Nate?" I called again as I rounded a corner into the office, pausing when voices reached my ears. That was odd; he seldom had visitors.

"Now tell me, how did visiting the fortress go?" Nate was asking someone.

A woman's voice replied softly, "Not as planned."

I dared to peek around the doorway and considered walking through the maze of towering clutter to find out who Nate was talking to. I wasn't one for spying, but my curiosity got the better of me.

A flutter of black wings greeted me in the doorway. The animal, with its wide black eyes and protruding snout, dove at me and I raised my arm for protection. It was a dragon, I realized. A very small dragon. It stopped in midair right in front of me and stared into my eyes.

I held my hand out to the creature. "Hey there, buddy."

"Pat!" the woman who'd spoken earlier shouted. "Oh no you don't!"

"What is it?" Nate replied, sounding concerned.

The sound of stomping alerted me to someone's rapid approach. It wasn't Nate's soft shuffle, so it had to be his guest. The woman rounded into view, balancing a pot with a dead plant on her hip.

"You!" she said, her light cream-blond hair hanging straight along the sides of her face, darkening to black at the tips. I found her hair fascinating—but my gaze was drawn once again to her mesmerizing green eyes.

I plastered what I hoped was a friendly smile onto my face and held out my hand. "I'm Nix. We met earlier."

She called for the dragon to return, and it fluttered back to her arm, disappearing beneath the folds of her loose-flowing blouse.

"Neat trick," I said.

The woman rolled her eyes. "I'm going," she called to Nate over her shoulder. She then rounded on me. "And you, next time stay out of my way."

She brushed past me out of the office.

Next time, I thought, feeling hope for our future encounters. I watched as she sauntered down the hallway and left the tree.

"Well, I see you've met Zoe," Nate said as he approached me.

"Zoe?"

"She didn't tell you her name?"

"No, we didn't get that far."

"So you disrupted her plans earlier?"

"I thought I was helping."

"Not according to her."

"I noticed," I said, following Nate through his towering piles of possessions. I had no clue what all these boxes and shelves held. Had Nate ever thrown anything away? "How long have you known her?"

Nate laughed. "A while."

"Why do I get the sense you're not going to tell me?"

"Zoe likes to keep to herself. You're lucky you were able to interrupt her as you did. Not many are able to do that."

"Can you introduce us?"

Nate rearranged some stacks of paper on his desk, then opened a book called *The Royal Line: A Comprehensive History.* He left it open to a particular page for me to read. I glanced down and saw my family's seal on the page—an engraving of the Royal Tree. There was also an image of the royal crest, the same image featured on my father's signet ring.

I looked away, not needing to read further. Since the night my father had died, I'd never worn the royal symbols—and as far as I knew, they remained in the box where Nate had hidden them.

Nate dropped another book on the desk in front of me, this one called *Royal Magic*, and found a page for me. He pointed to a paragraph, which I scanned. It described how to access the Royal Tree—specifically, revealing that only someone of the royal line could gain entrance.

"Is there a reason you're showing me this?" I asked. Through the years, Nate had tutored me often on my royal station and duties for when I'd become king. I grimaced at the thought.

Nate had gotten onto a ladder and was perusing the bookshelves. "There's a purpose in everything. You want to meet Zoe, you say. Why?"

Instead of answering, I asked, "Why haven't you introduced us before?"

But he didn't answer. I sighed and lowered myself onto one of the chairs in front of his desk. He wouldn't answer my question and was waiting for me to answer his.

"I had another dream last night. Same dream as always, but there were some additions," I said.

I told him of the Royal Tree, how it had responded when I told it I was its king. Then I described the woman who had spoken to me and that I was convinced she was Zoe. Some elves did have the gift of prophetic dreams—I wasn't usually one of them, but it wasn't unheard of for elves to sometimes have a dream that guided them or was a message left to interpretation through the unfolding of life events. By the time I finished, Nate had returned to his desk chair.

He pushed a third book toward me, entitled *The Royal Family*. I ignored it for the time being.

"This woman had green eyes, you say?" Nate asked with a pleasant smile on his face. "And as you stated, you assume it is Zoe."

I shifted in my seat. I thought back to first seeing her at the market and then outside the Dion fortress.

"When I'm around her, she seems to inspire hope in me. I don't know. It sounds kind of stupid."

Nate leaned forward and steepled his fingers, his elbows resting on the desk. "Listen, Nix, Zoe is independent and hard to get to know. She keeps to herself and won't help you without reason. To get close, you'll have to get her to trust you."

"How do I manage that? She'll barely stay in the same place as me for more than a minute."

"That does present a challenge. But I suggest that first, you show her respect. That's important."

"Okay," I mumbled. Despite trying to help, I could see how accidentally interfering with her plans could have been construed as disrespect. This was going to be harder than I thought. "And second?"

Nate chuckled. "Be yourself."

"I am."

He tapped the third book he'd opened on the table. "Your

real self."

A cold dread washed over me. I knew what Nate was telling me: I had to step up as king. But how could I? I knew nothing. I had no power and no army with which to fight Leski. And I'd never ask the other elves for help—to do that, I'd have to reveal myself to them and put others in danger. I'd promised myself on the night my father died that I would never let another elf die for me.

But then there was Zyanna. I had one week to rescue her...

Nate stood and handed over a fourth book. "Here, read this."

I glanced at the word *Ascension* pressed into the smooth worn leather surface. There were other sophisticated patterns etched along the edges. He'd shown me the book many times but never opened it. He said he'd give it to me when I was ready to be king. *I wasn't!* I stared at the book, not wanting to touch it.

"Thanks," I muttered as I took the book and attempted to lift the front cover. It wouldn't open; I held the book by the spine and shook it, expecting the pages to fall open. It remained sealed. "Hey, is this a trick?"

"That book will only open for one of royal birth. Your father would have given it to you when he passed on his crown. Since time is of the essence, I need you to take it now."

I fiddled with the book. There was no way I was becoming king anytime soon. Though it did occur to me that he was referring to rescuing Zyanna before she was wed to Dimas. "So how do I open it?"

Nate shrugged. "Don't know. Royal secret."

"Great." I sighed. "Anything else?"

Nate studied me and I winced. It was such an intensely

focused stare.

"I'm not your father, but let me offer a bit of advice that I think your father would want you to hear," he said. "It's not the magic that makes you a ruler, or even your family line. Rather, it's a choice. Your father knew this, and it's all you need to be a good king."

I laughed sardonically. "That's all I need, huh? Somehow I think my dad would have a lot more to say."

As I held the book and studied the intricate pattern on the cover, I felt remorse. I shouldn't have snapped. I was angry at not having my dad here to guide me. "Sorry, Nate."

"It's been a tough day and you're facing it alone. But greatness is often born of adversity."

"Meaning?"

"If you keep your heart right, you'll make out all right."

"I didn't ask for any of this."

Nate's sharp, penetrating eyes left me feeling he knew more, understood more than he ever let on. He nodded and spoke softly. "No one ever asks for the path they're dealt in life."

Twilight's Curse

Chapter Six

Zoe

I rested my chin on my knuckles while picking at a rose thorn. It pricked me, and I brought my finger to my mouth to stem the flow of blood.

After my meeting with Nate, I'd returned to my small apartment in his tree, which had its own external and internal entrances. A living room, kitchen, and little office, which I used as a reading nook, comprised the main level. A pillar rose through the middle, supporting a stairway that circled up to the bedroom loft.

As I examined the plant Nate had given me, Pat settled on my shoulder. She released a healing pulse, repairing my finger within moments. I thanked her and she flew back to join Chim and Tupac on the bookshelf for their evening nap.

I let a burst of my own energy flow into the plant, causing five new buds to form. As much as I loved watching my life-giving magic take effect, I pulled it back. Unnatural growth created weak plants.

A soft knock sounded at my door.

"Come in," I called.

Cocoa entered, balancing a tray in one hand while managing the door with the other. I hurried over to help her with my evening meal.

"Sorry," I said. It was dinnertime and I should have known it'd be the brownie.

"It's okay. I'm used to it."

I took the tray from her and the rich scent of onions filled my nostrils. Lifting the lid revealed the tray was ladened with soup, bread, and a garden salad with a tangy dressing. On the side was a bowl of peeled oranges.

"Do you want to join me?" I asked her. "I think there's enough for both of us."

I put the tray on a small dining table and pulled out an extra bowl and plate from my kitchen.

"Sure." Cocoa went to my cutlery drawer and grabbed what she needed.

I eyed the brownie with suspicion—had she intentionally set it up for us to eat dinner together, or had Nate arranged it? He always seemed to know when I needed someone to talk to.

After dividing the meal into two portions, we dug in. The first touch of bread melted in my mouth and I held back a moan of appreciation. The brownies were amazing chefs.

"This is so good."

"I will let Chocolate know."

I considered the brownies living here. I had the most contact with Cocoa, though she was evasive most of the time. I rarely saw the others unless they were tending to the children.

"Do all brownies have names that resemble things that are brown?" I glanced at Cocoa and watched her expression. She wasn't always forthcoming when it came to details about her race, and I wasn't confident she'd answer now.

Cocoa giggled. "No, but everyone here comes from the same family. Our mother named us."

I nearly spit my soup back in the bowl when I thought of the… at least twenty brownies who lived here. "*All* of you?"

Cocoa nodded. "Brownie families are quite large."

"No kidding." I filled my mouth with a forkful of salad.

"So… is there anything on your mind?" Cocoa rubbed her spoon against a serviette.

Yes, she was here to talk. "Did Nate send you?"

Cocoa wobbled her head back and forth in a yes-no-maybe gesture. "He suggested you might like to have dinner together. And I assumed that meant the two of you had discussed something you'd want to talk about."

"You know us well."

"It's the brownie way."

"Right." I thought of Nate's lesson on weeds and thorns, though I still didn't understand it as I stumbled my way through telling her about it.

Cocoa gulped down the rest of her soup before answering. "Do you ever wonder why such horrible things happened to you?"

My spoon paused midway to my mouth. I hadn't expected that question. "No." That wasn't true. "Sort of. I mean, bad things happen all the time, so obviously everyone is bound to experience bad things at some point. Why am I any different?"

"This is wise. What lies at the core of your dilemma?"

I leaned back from the table. The demon inside squirmed,

and instinctively my hand moved to my chest.

"Ah, I understand. You wonder why you weren't spared from that particular tattoo."

"Not exactly." I sighed. "Are you familiar with the deity of the Night Realm? My parents believe in Nosh Dem. And a few months ago Nate gave me books to read about the history of elves and our magic. He tells me that if I accept what's happened to me and let it go, *forgive* is the word he uses, then my magic will be able to deal with the demon tattoo."

Cocoa nodded. "This is true."

But what of my other tattoos? I wanted to ask, thinking of my beloved dragons. Would it be worth getting rid of one tattoo if I risked losing them all?

"I don't know, Cocoa. It sounds so simple, letting go of what my parents did to me..."

"I understand your fear."

"You do?" I asked, surprised.

"You're looking at all this through your fear. And you interpret something as being good or bad through the lens of your experiences. But you're forgetting the abilities within you."

"You mean my magic?"

"Yes, it is very powerful and special. You are favored."

I snorted. I was many things but not favored. "My parents saw my abilities and wanted to control them. Control me."

"True, but you control what's inside you and how you react to what happens to you. Once you really understand this, it'll change your perspective."

I had no response to that, so I distracted myself with the remaining crumbs on my plate.

Cocoa placed a warm hand on my forearm. "What happened

to you, it was a nightmare no child should experience, especially not at the hands of their parents."

I ran my fingers over the smooth surface of the table. "You and Nate make it sound so simple."

"It sounds like you have things to work out. Weeds and thorns." Cocoa nodded, as though she understood the so-called metaphor perfectly. "It's a good lesson. And when you figure it out, well… you'll know what to do."

I smiled, thankful the brownie didn't push the issue further.

"I need to help put the children to bed," she added. "But come find me later if you want to talk."

"I will."

I gathered up the dishes and washed them in my small sink. The brownies didn't like it when I got near their large kitchen. After six years, I had yet to see the inside of it. I was certain the small creatures were guarding some secret.

After putting everything away, I paced through my apartment, my mind churning over recent events. When I heard the clock ring half past nine, I realized it was too late to help the brownies herd the children to bed. Feeling restless, I decided to go out.

Twilight's Curse

Chapter Seven

❦

Nix

When I returned home, I placed my hand on the entry marker and the door peeled back. I tossed the *Ascension* book on my desk and sank into the chair. I closed my eyes and let my body relax.

A moment later, a tap like a branch striking my door disturbed me. I groaned and scrubbed my face. No one ever visited me, as I knew very few elves. Perhaps it was mail.

I opened the door and glanced around at the twilit forest. The greenery paused in an eerie stillness. Seeing no visitor, I stepped back inside.

As the doorway began to reseal, though, my eyes landed on a scrap of paper on the ground. I stepped forward again and the door peeled back.

I picked up the small white slip, no bigger than my palm.

"Someone must have come after all," I mused, waving my hand over it to detect the use of magic. There was no trickery here, no spell, just a blank piece of paper without any writing on it. Why would someone leave this? Was it a prank?

I stroked the paper's flat edges, then held it up to the light when I returned inside. Two mysteries in as many hours.

Sitting down, I flipped the piece of paper between my fingers, thinking back to the few memories I had of my family. I thought of something Zyanna and I used to do, a game we'd played when our parents hosted boring dinners. Since we had been meant to sit quietly all evening, and I knew how hard that was for my little sister, I entertained her by sending her notes with pictures drawn on them. It was a silly game, and sometimes she'd laugh and the guests would give her a questioning glance, but it had helped the evenings to pass more quickly. The game helped her to behave.

Before such an evening, we'd take small slips of paper and each run our royal pendant over them. Our markers would infuse the paper with bits of our magic, so only we could see the messages we sent each other.

The excitement of realization struck me, making me feel freshly alert. I raced to my room to find my pendant, which was hanging around my bedpost. Not well hidden, but I'd always been told that the best way to hide something was often to put it in plain sight. I snatched it off the post and raced back to the desk.

Impatiently, I rubbed the pendant on the front of the card. Nothing happened. Then I rubbed it on the back and waited. Still nothing.

In frustration, I tossed the pendant down on the book Nate had given me. To my surprise, it suddenly gave off a soft glow.

Gingerly I tried to lift the cover, but it still wouldn't budge. I ran the pendant over the book again, with the same result.

The book recognized my seal, but it wasn't the right symbol. It was the symbol of the prince, not the king.

My heart sinking, I searched my memory for another clue to the paper scrap. Did I have anything of Zyanna's? It didn't seem possible that she still had paper from all those years ago... but maybe...

I walked outside and dropped to all fours, crawling through the grass as I looked for something I may have missed before. Maybe the deliverer of the note had left a pendant behind.

I must look like a fool, I thought to myself.

Finding nothing, I returned inside.

I had felt so close to something from my sister, the first contact in so long. Feeling deflated, I returned to my bedroom to rehang the pendant on my bedpost. Then I picked up the clothes I'd discarded before heading to Nate's. I tossed the shirt in the laundry bin, then grabbed the pants by the bottom hem—

Something fell out, landing hard on my toe. I hissed, hopping on one foot until the sharp pain wore off.

Kneeling, I studied the flat, rounded stone that had assaulted my foot. There was nothing unique or special about it other than I'd never seen it before. My mind raced with possibilities. While in the market, I'd bumped into a few different elves...

Was it possible? Had someone put it in my pocket on Zyanna's behalf? Hope lurched in me as I sprinted back to the living room, fumbling to pick up the piece of paper again. My pulse was so fast that it left me breathless. My fingers trembled as I placed the flat stone against the paper—and waited.

Nothing.

But then, just as hope extinguished, a dark line appeared

on the paper. And then another. My heart sped up as they formed a series of numbers. It was a time—written in elegant and flowing handwriting: *Ten Forty-Five.*

I glanced at the clock on the wall and saw that it was half past ten right now. Was something going to happen today at quarter to eleven? I drummed my fingers on the underside of the paper, wishing for more writing to appear.

It felt like it took forever, but in reality it was only a few seconds before the next line of writing was revealed: *The Misty Inn.* That was a tavern in the city.

I stuffed the flat stone and paper into my pocket and dashed out of the house.

I darted through the light sprinkling of rain, my footing sure on the slippery stone path. I could sense the foliage around me and it energized me.

As I turned a corner and reached the entrance to Haven, I slowed, trailing my fingers over the leaves of a dripping tree. Was this the wisest thing to do? I brushed aside the niggling question. Nate would no doubt have wanted me to exercise a great deal more caution, but this was my sister.

I entered the city, walking past the closed shops until I got to a building with a hanging sign out front that read *The Misty Inn*; it dangled from the branch of a centuries-old cedar that glowed softly in the moonlight. As I recalled, the tree had once been the estate of the Mist family.

I squared my shoulders and marched forward. The note hadn't said anything about there being a meeting today. I pushed the front door open, shrugging off my doubt.

"Sit anywhere you like," the proprietor, Nyla Mist, said. She was tall and thin like most elves, but her sun-kissed complexion radiated as if a soft light shone on it. "Yoli will be out in a minute to serve you."

I nodded. Yoli and Toli were Nyla's daughters—twins, which was rare. Twins were known to share an uncommon gifting of magic which strengthened when they were together and went dormant when they attempted to use it alone. I had no idea what the Mist twins could do, and with the threat of what the Dions did to elves with exceptional magic, I doubted I ever would see their magic at work.

Rain puddled behind me as I walked to the back corner of the tavern, finding a table where I could sit with my back against the wall and observe the room. It was a bit darker here, but I didn't mind. I'd be less noticed. I scanned the other patrons looking for someone, anyone, who might be waiting for me.

I sighed in disappointment, finding no one likely, but decided to wait a little longer. In all the years since my parents had died, this was the first time I'd had any hope of finding my sister alive. I'd wait all night if I needed to.

"What'll you have?" Yoli asked, smiling.

I glanced up at the tall elf. Her long blond hair fell halfway down her back, and she swept it over her shoulder.

"Hey, Yoli. I'm waiting for someone. Has anyone mentioned me?"

"I'm Toli, actually. My sister's on her break." She handed me a menu, a small piece of glass that listed the evening specials.

"Sorry. Never can tell the two of you apart."

"No one can. Except Mom." She paused. "But to answer your question, no. No one's asked for you."

"Oh." I glanced at the menu, not reading the words. Had I gotten it wrong? No. I was certain that I'd read the message correctly.

"Do you need a minute to decide?"

I tapped the menu against the table. I wasn't hungry and the sticky humidity did little to encourage my appetite. "Coffee."

Toli raised an eyebrow. "That's all?"

"All for now, or do I need to order more?"

She glanced over her shoulder and I followed her line of sight to her mother. Clearly her mom wanted customers to order food.

Toli turned back to me. "Well, we're not busy. It shouldn't be a problem. I'll let her know you're waiting for someone."

"Thanks, appreciate it."

I watched her walk over to her mom, admiring how beautiful the Mist twins were. Maybe the twins had a magical ability to grow their hair long. I chuckled, doubting that was their ability.

I watched the exchange, then caught Nyla nod in my direction; she wouldn't require me to purchase a meal.

Leaning back in my seat, I allowed my gaze to roam over the room again. There was a table of four older elves in the center of the tavern. They weren't as old as Nate though. I'd never seen another elf that old. It looked like they were playing *doh'l*, a game made from painted stones. Most gambled while they played. Usually the stakes were low, and no elf had ever lost their livelihood over a pot. The type of coins on the table had no real value and weren't even in circulation among the populace anymore.

A young couple sat in one of the booths, and a lone elf was finishing his meal at the bar. It was too late in the evening for families.

Toli returned and placed a steaming mug of coffee before me.

"Thanks," I said, reaching for the sugar.

"No problem."

Just then, four guards burst through the doorway. Two were large and had enhanced muscles. They were probably older guards. And the younger two were leaner but still larger in height and muscle mass than average elves.

Their voices filled the room. Their brown uniforms announced that they were from the fortress. They sauntered to the table beside the elves playing *doh'l*. Chairs scraped against the floor as the new arrivals settled down.

The largest elf hollered at Toli, "You, girl! Come and serve us instead of chatting with him."

Everything in me wanted to get up and say something to Bulky, but that would risk exposure. I tamped it down.

Toli was standing in the shadows near me. She looked warily at me and blushed. Her body tensed and she faded sightly as if the shadow was embracing her. I blinked and a moment later she was back to normal. Or maybe my eyes had been playing tricks on me. The corner was poorly lit.

"Hello, good sirs," Nyla said, walking closer to the newcomers. "What an honor it is for the regents' guards to visit my establishment. I'll be serving you this evening."

I chuckled inwardly and felt relived at the proprietor's interference. Nyla was no fool. She knew what the guards were like. Everyone did.

"You deny us a pretty barmaid?" Bulky asked.

Nyla kept her voice light. "That barmaid is my daughter and I'll deny any elf with wrong intentions. Now, what'll you be having?"

Twilight's Curse

Chapter Eight

Zoe

I'd made my way through the warm drizzle to the Haven. I pulled my scarf up, ensuring it hung loosely around my head to keep me dry and hide my distinct hair. If anyone from the fortress saw me, my parents would stop at nothing to drag me back and continue their experiments.

Not having a direction in mind, I walked through Haven, pulling my cloak tighter as the misty rain continued to fall. The humidity kept the air warm, but I didn't want to get sick. Even though Pat would heal me if I did.

As I thought of the dragons, I felt them moving just under my skin.

Settle down, you three. You're distracting me.

I needed to be alert while walking through the city. I never knew when my parents would have their guards out looking for me.

Chim, I need your senses. Immediately my eyesight sharpened.

From experience, I knew all my senses were heightened even if I didn't need them at this moment.

A scuffle from a side street drew me off the main thoroughfare. I kept to the shadows and Chim helped me move closer, undetected. On my right thigh, I felt Tupac tense; the dragon was ready to fight if I needed him.

We're not fighting, I reminded them. *It might just be street kids.*

Nothing gave me greater pleasure than bringing in a new kid off the street. I thought of Anansi, the latest addition to our household. He was always lurking around Nate's tree, and unnerved Cocoa. I needed to spend more time with him, get to know him.

Coming to a darkened corner, an overpowering scent of sweat assaulted my senses. I padded forward, hearing the soft murmur of voices.

"It'll bring him out," a deep voice said. "That's what Lord Leski wants."

My ears burned and I leaned closer, not daring to round the corner. I guessed these elves were my parents' guards.

"How's it work then?" someone asked. This voice was lighter; perhaps he was young.

"That's not for you to know. We don't need to understand Lord Leski's ways. Now, are you going to obey or am I going to have to report on your behavior?"

My stomach clenched as I remembered when the guards had made the same threat to me as a child. They weren't empty threats. I'd often ended up in the medical ward when I didn't comply. Thanks to Pat, I had healed quickly, though my mother had only seen that as an opportunity to draw a new tattoo.

Chapter Eight

The voices lowered and I chanced moving closer.

"I'm obeying, sir," Young Voice said. "Just wanting to know what to look for."

"We're looking for anyone sitting alone. He was sent a message to head to the Misty Inn at ten forty-five. He'll be there. And we get a free meal just for spotting him," Deep Voice responded.

"Sir, if we know where he lives, why don't we just go pick him up?"

"You idiot. You know nothing of living in trees. There ain't no address. It's the magic that carries a letter to the tree. The best way is to lure him out into public when it's quiet." Deep Voice spat.

"Whatever you say, sir."

Chim, I want you to get closer, I nodded toward the guards.

The dragon stirred and the sensation of smooth fabric running down my back told me when Chim lifted from my skin. I watched through his eyes as he kept to the darkest corners. The elves, both wearing the brown of guard uniforms, were physically enhanced. And they were headed this way.

Moving quickly, I shifted my cloak and darted my eyes around the alleyway. There was a doorway nearby, and I ran toward it and hid in its shadow. I felt warmth flow down me, as though I were standing under a shower, and realized that Chim had cloaked me with invisibility.

As the two guards passed, I saw Deep Voice—a large elf built like a tree trunk. He had a barrel chest and muscles bulged from his arms. Young Voice was leaner and well-toned but still formidable. Both strode by my hiding place with an air of indifference.

Once they'd gone, Chim returned to me. I followed the

guards, maintaining the dragon's stealth, and watched as they paused outside the Misty Inn. Two more guards—another pairing of large and lean—joined the first set and all four entered. Before going inside, I waited to give the guards a chance to settle down. I considered sending in one of my dragons, but they'd be too obvious.

I stole inside, listening as the guards gave an order to the innkeeper.

No one seemed to notice as I slid along the wall toward a booth… but then my eyes landed on someone who had *seen* me—that idiot, Nix. I rolled my eyes.

With a quick glance around the establishment, I noticed he was the only elf sitting alone. I broke my cover, lowered my scarf and hood, but left the dark ends of my hair tucked underneath my collar. I strode across the room toward Nix. I smirked at the surprised expression on his face.

I plopped down in a chair next to him.

"Glad you came. I hope you haven't been waiting long," I said, loud enough for the guards to hear. Then I leaned in close to whisper. "Get the confused expression off your face and pretend you're happy to see me."

Nix changed his expression to a broad smile. "Good to see you. No, I've only been waiting a short time. Just got here."

"Good. What are we having?"

I gave my order to Nyla when she came around, then picked at the table with a fingernail while I waited for my tea to arrive. Nix still looked confused, but he'd have to be patient. Maybe I'd tell him later that the guards were looking for him. It was the least I could do, but the idea grated on me. My gut still churned with irritation about his interference earlier.

Who was I kidding? I'd tried to enter the fortress at various times over the past six years since I'd run from it and each time I'd got no farther than I had today.

"Here you go," Yoli said, placing a steaming mug of tea before me.

"Thanks." I gave a weak smile and sighed.

I glanced up at Nix, my irritation dissolving. He'd had a mission to get into the fortress, too, and perhaps he really was trying to help me like he'd said. How long had it been since anyone had cared enough about me to help? Besides the brownies and Nate.

My mind flashed to Maximon and I wondered if he was still alive. Had he even cared about me? My mother often sent him to bring me to her laboratory for my *procedures*. My gut churned. I had never fully trusted him. He'd never given me reason to. No one in the fortress had. Maybe I had slightly trusted Derek, my weapons trainer, to not land a killing strike during practice. And he'd never threatened me when I struggled with my training or harmed me on an off day. He actually offered the odd word of encouragement. Even so, his loyalties would always rest first with my parents.

"So, why the pleasure of your company?" Nix asked.

I leaned in close, like we were a couple, and rested my hand on his forearm. Nix raised an eyebrow.

"Any reason why those guards are interested in you?" I whispered.

Nix didn't flinch and he didn't look at the guards. I had to give him credit.

"Hey now, don't be like that," Deep Voice said.

In unison, Nix and I turned to look at them now. The largest of the guards was gripping Toli's arm in his meaty hand.

"I'm just serving drinks. That's all," Toli said firmly as she

91

tried to pull away. Deep Voice laughed and pulled her closer. Toli twisted and seemed to fade slightly. I shook my head but the opaqueness had left. Or perhaps it was a trick of the lighting. The guard twisted her to himself.

"We've got to help her," Nix whispered.

I nodded and commanded my dragons to prepare for a fight. It would risk exposing me; if the guards had been in the fortress all those years ago, they might recognize me. My grip tightened on Nix's arm.

"Hey, loosen up," Nix said.

I glanced down at my white knuckles and the fingernails biting into his flesh. "Right, sorry. What do you have in mind?"

Toli continued to struggle as Nyla came out of the kitchen. Her face was blazing with brightness.

"I told you lot I'll be your server tonight and you're to leave my daughters alone," the innkeeper said. "They aren't here to serve you more than drink and food."

Nyla strode into the midst of the room and laid a hand on Deep Voice's arm. He laughed at her and pulled Toli onto his lap.

"We're from the regent and you won't be speaking to us in this way." Deep Voice laughed and the other elves around the tabled joined him.

One of them, Large from pairing number two, scraped his chair against the floor as he stood and wrapped his arms around Nyla. A look of terror passed between the mother and daughter and my muscles tightened, ready to respond.

I called my dragons forth, and a moment later they fluttered next to me.

"Where'd they come from?" Nix asked as Pat perched on his shoulder, purring in contentment.

92

I ignored his question. I was risking enough just letting my dragons be seen. I asked Chim and Tupac for strategies, and they responded by sending me pictures of potential plans. Tupac showed me that I could take the guards one at a time. Pat would keep my energy up and Tupac would help me with my strikes and blows by guiding my limbs as I fought. Chim would protect me if one of the guards managed to land a blow. And all the dragons would spit their inky, magic-infused saliva, which would burn the skin of the guards. They'd distract the other guards, keeping them from rushing me if needed. It seemed a reasonable plan.

Toli and Nyla continued to struggle as Deep Voice and Large forced them to stay on their laps. The remaining patrons were sneaking out the front door, and pretty soon Nix and I were the only ones left. I felt better about these odds and pulled my hood up to cover my face again.

"You help Nyla and her daughters," I whispered to Nix. My daggers dropped into my hands. "I'll take on the guards."

"No way. I can't let you."

"Look, with my dragons it's four against four. You're just one elf and you don't look like much of a fighter. I can do this."

Nix looked taken aback. Maybe he could fight, but I doubted he had proper training.

Not giving him a chance to respond, I made my way to the guards' table.

"Come to join the party then?" Younger Voice asked me as I approached. A ripple of disgust passed through me.

"Let them go." My words were low and controlled.

Young Voice stood and crossed his arms. "And what are you going to do to make us?"

His friends jeered, and I readied my stance then lifted my black blades.

"We can fight, if that's what it'll take," I said as I felt Chim's shielding wash over me, followed by a surge of strength from Tupac.

"Go on," Deep Voice said, egging on the younger one. "You'll like a feisty elf maid like this. Teach her a lesson."

"You're next," I said to him as Young Voice lurched toward me.

His movements were sloppy. Either he wasn't a good fighter, or he'd already had too much of Nyla's beer. I smirked as he unsheathed a sword; it was a stupid weapon for such a confined space. He swung, landing a blow against a chair that sliced it in two. I deftly moved to the left, swinging my dagger up and landing its hilt on the back of his head. The blow, guided by Tupac's battle strategies and Pat's knowledge of elven physiology, knocked Young Voice out.

Lean, from pairing number two, grabbed me from behind, but Tupac and Chim clawed at his head and spat black ink into his eyes. The guard shrieked; the ink stung like acid.

"Dragons," Deep Voice said gruffly. "Black dragons."

Unable to see Nix, I stuffed my elbow into Lean's midsection and he screamed. But he didn't let go. I twirled my blades in my hands and thrust them into his thighs. He let out a cry of pain and released me as he crumpled to the floor.

I glanced down and saw the red pool around his pants. I hadn't hit anything major. But I didn't need a surprise attack from him later, so I swiped the back of his head and knocked him out.

The two remaining elves tossed Nyla and Toli aside. Nyla stumbled into a table and Toli into a barstool. Then they ran.

Good.

Large and Deep Voice stood. My energy was waning, but with the help of my dragons, I hoped I could take these two.

Feeling Pat replenish my strength, I flexed my fingers around the hilts of my daggers. The guards circled me.

Finally, Large struck. I ducked his punch and swiped back, nicking his arm.

He flinched. "We'll teach you a lesson, brat," he snarled. "Just like we did when you were at the fortress."

My spine tingled as I realized Large and Deep Voice had recognized me.

"First blood goes to me," I replied with mock courage, my heart pounding in my chest.

"Your parents will be glad to have you back."

Large lunged at my midsection and my feet lifted from the ground as he plowed into me. He swung me over his shoulder, then barrelled me into a wall, knocking the air from my lungs. My head cracked against the wall. I sputtered, my lungs grasping for oxygen.

But as he spun, my dragons attacked, clawing at his face and spitting ink.

The elf holding me let go and dropped to the floor. I gasped as I landed awkwardly on my ankle and pain shot up my leg. I needed a moment to stop my head from spinning—but I dared not pause, not even for a second. I jabbed one dagger into my attacker's arm and he backed off. I crashed to the floor and tried to shake off the dizziness.

Suddenly, something heavy and fast came at the side of my face—and my neck snapped. My vision dimmed and blackened.

Twilight's Curse

Chapter Nine

Nix

I winced as the younger guard lunged at Zoe, but she ducked out of his reach, moving with precision and grace. I was captivated by her martial pirouette. As she advanced on one guard, then another, she never uttered a single command to her dragons. Nonetheless, they fought with her in synchronized movements. I watched her take down the second guard with ease.

Who was she? My mind whirled with possibilities.

I shook my head, remembering that I was supposed to help Nyla and her daughters. The guards had flung them aside so I padded across the empty tavern to reach them. I waved for Toli and Nyla to follow me into the safety of the kitchen, where they were reunited with Yoli.

Nyla embraced both her daughters as they shook and sobbed. We couldn't waste any time, though, and I didn't want to leave Zoe to finish the fight alone. She had dragons and was probably as good with a blade as I was. It had irked me that she assumed I couldn't fight. Nate had trained me and he was an expert in fighting, though no one would know the bookish advisor had such skills. Perhaps the same could be said about me.

I thought of Zoe taking on the two larger guards. She couldn't last much longer. Those guards clearly had the advantage of height and strength.

"Do you have somewhere to go?" I asked Nyla.

"We could stay with my brother." Nyla looked wistfully at the door to the dining area. Her radiant glow lessened in the kitchens. It seemed darker in here. "But my tavern, I can't just leave it."

"You'll have to for tonight. If you give me the keys, I'll lock up for you. Promise."

"You seem like an honest enough elf."

"Is your brother far?"

"No, he's two shops down. He's the butcher."

"Good."

There was a brief lull in conversation as Nyla nodded and dug through a deep pocket in her apron. No further sounds of a scuffle from the dining area reached my ears. Had Zoe beaten the guards? Or had they gotten her? My stomach soured. I couldn't let that happen.

"Here." Nyla handed over a large steel key then turned to her daughters. "Come on, girls."

"But Mama, what about our things?" Yoli asked.

"No sense bothering with them tonight. This young elf will lock up. Come now." Nyla grabbed a shawl from the hook near the back exit and wrapped it around Toli's shoulders. The girl flinched under her mother's touch. "There, there, dear. We'll be with Uncle Drew soon."

I peeked through the back door and stared into the empty street. "Do you want me to come with you?"

"That's nice of you to offer, but you should keep watch from here." Nyla glanced at her daughters. Her lips were pursed.

I nodded and turned to Yoli and Toli.

"Don't," Nyla hissed as her daughters shifted their stance.

The two elves disappeared as if sliding into the shadows near the back door. I blinked and looked then looked again. The twins were gone.

"What? How?" I couldn't move my eyes from the darkened empty space.

"We have light magic." Nyla's voice trembled. "My daughters, they can polarize light. They're still there, but when they moved, it looked like they disappeared. Come back, girls."

Yoli and Toli came back into view. They hadn't moved other than to turn their positions.

"I'd always heard about twin magic," I said, thinking back to how Toli had faded slightly when the regent's guard had called on her in the dining room. "They need each other to do this, don't they?"

Yoli and Toli clutched each other and looked away from me.

"Yes," Nyla answered. "Please, tell no one."

I tore my eyes from the twins to their mother. "Of course not. Thank you for trusting me with this though."

Nyla sighed and her body slouched with relief. A soft glow grew on her cheeks and I guessed it was her magic at work. She touched her forehead as if massaging a headache. "Things were different under King Alistair and Queen Calla. We didn't have to hide our abilities."

I stifled a wince at hearing the names of my parents. She

didn't know who I was. By all rights, I should be on the throne and governing the elves.

"They cared for our race," she said. "This was a safe and happy place. The royal children need to be found. Rumor says they're dead or they'd have come forward by now. For the Twilight Realm's sake, I hope they're alive. Though only a child-adult, the crown prince would make a far better king than the regents."

On the night my parents were killed, Nate said I needed to learn how to blend in with the citizens and be less regal; perhaps I had adapted and aged too much for anyone to recognize me. The thought churned my core. The truth was, I was the rightful king. My core liked that thought less.

"You best go now," I said, my voice was soft and thick.

Nyla's words weighed my shoulders down. She believed I'd be a good king, and her confidence strengthened me. I was still too young, but when I was ready, maybe I could be the king that the elves of the Twilight Realm needed.

Nyla patted my arm. "You take care of your elven maiden and yourself. You're our heroes tonight."

"Thank you."

The elven females were through the back door a moment later. The twins, holding hands, shifted and once again blended into the shadows. I watched Nyla scuttle down the back alley. Then, a few doors down, she pounded on a door and the twins returned to view. The door cracked open. Soon a large bald elf with a goatee ushered them in. I inhaled deeply, knowing they'd be safe, at least for the night.

As I pivoted back to the tavern, I found it eerily quiet. I cracked open the door and saw Zoe sprawled on the floor. Muscles, the guard, rolled her over and lifted her shirt to expose her midsection. What were they going to do to her?

My gut clenched. It was no longer an option to hide for my safety—not right now, and not anymore. I had to do something to help Zoe.

I slipped through the door and hid behind the counter.

"Is it her?" Bulky asked.

"Look for yourself," Muscles said.

I closed my eyes and breathed deeply, calmly. I had to be strategic. I'd never willingly entered a fight, though Nate and I had sparred regularly over the years. I knew skills and strategies.

The other two guards were still passed out; Zoe must have hit them pretty hard.

I noticed a rolling pin next to me and grabbed it.

Where were Zoe's dragons? I looked around, but they were nowhere to be seen. Odd. I brushed the thought aside and moved silently across the wooden floor, thankful that no creaks gave away my presence.

Muscles lifted one of Zoe's arms and shoved up her sleeve.

"Here it is. And I'll be, there's a tattoo just like it on the other arm."

"The Lord Leski and Lady Sirina will be glad to get her back."

"No doubt. Lady Sirina's not been the same without her daughter to experiment on."

Daughter? I stopped in my tracks, having made it to the edge of the bar in a crouch, three steps from Bulky. This was the daughter of the regents?

I'd ask questions later. Nate trusted her and she obviously had a story.

I sprang up and swung the rolling pin, but Bulky, despite his size, spun and caught it in midair. He twisted it, wrenching my wrist. My grip loosened, but I held on then twirled, ducking under Bulky's arm and reversing the twist in the process. The rolling pin slid free from the guard's grasp and I quickly swung it again. The pin met the side of his head with a loud *thwak*. He toppled, landing on Zoe.

Muscles looked up from his crouch, surprise registering on his face. My makeshift bat hit the side of his skull before he had time to make a move. His eyes rolled and he flopped down.

I pushed Bulky off Zoe and patted her cheek.

"Come on, wake up," I said. Relief washed over me when I saw her chest rise and fall. She was alive.

Moving quickly, I scoured the back of the bar for a tablecloth and laid it out on the floor next to Muscles. With a grunt and a shove, I managed to roll him onto the material then dragged him out onto the street. Sweat sprouted across my forehead and I wiped it with the now free tablecloth then returned for the three remaining guards. I checked on Zoe but she hadn't changed, so I set about straightening up the dining room a bit.

Zoe was still out cold. I felt around her head and discovered a large bump the size of a goose egg forming at the back of her skull. But she didn't appear to have any further injuries, no bleeding or even bruising.

I sighed and lifted her over my shoulder. She wasn't heavy. I locked the back door on my way out.

Nyla and I hadn't made a specific arrangement for the key, so I wondered if I should just slide it under the door of the tavern. But what if she didn't have a spare key with her?

I glanced up and down the street. Since the light at the

butcher's was still on, I made my way there and placed Zoe on a barrel in a seated position before knocking on the door. The tall elf I'd seen earlier opened it, a slight scent of coffee wafting out.

"Is Nyla here?" I asked.

The butcher crossed his muscled arms and narrowed his beady eyes. "Who wants to know?"

"Drew, is that the young elf I told you about?" Nyla's voice called from inside. She peeked over her brother's shoulder. "This is him. He helped me and the girls. You, get out of the way."

She smiled widely and gave a gentle swat to her brother's arm. Drew disappeared inside.

"I came to return your key," I said, handing it over.

"Thank you. You both okay?" She glanced down at Zoe.

"She's resting." I didn't want Nyla to offer to take care of Zoe. It was best that we return to my tree, which was much more secure than any elf-made structure in the city. "We'll be going."

I stepped back and pulled Zoe's hands up as though I were helping her to stand. Nyla waved and closed the door.

Slinging Zoe's arm over my shoulder and holding her limp body close to mine, I kept to the shadows as I hustled out of the city, then once I was confident no one was around, I lifted her over my shoulder.

I made my way back into the forest and waved my hand over the entrance of my home. Once inside, I lowered Zoe onto the couch and covered her with a blanket.

A dark pattern on her arm caught my eye as I adjusted the blanket, and I remembered that the guards had said something about a tattoo—and about Zoe being the daughter of Leski and Sirina. Curiosity got the better of me, and I moved her sleeve up. There, inked on her skin, was an intricate tattoo of a dagger. It looked very much like the ones she had fought with.

Tattoos weren't common among elfkind. In fact, they were a bit taboo. Was this connected to the experiments her mother had apparently done to her? It didn't seem so bad. Definitely odd, though. Perhaps there was more to it.

Or maybe Zoe just liked body art. Who was this enigma?

I sighed as I sat across from her and watched her sleep. I wouldn't get any answers tonight.

Eventually my eyes grew heavy, but I fought to stay awake.

Remembering the book Nate had given me earlier, I grabbed it from my desk. It still didn't open, but I admired the faint glow it gave off when I placed my royal seal over it. Nate had said my father would have passed the book down to me one day—and with it, I would have received the king's royal symbols: the signet ring, crown, and seal. Perhaps they had the power to unlock the book.

Zoe stirred, reaching above her head in a stretch. When she hit the arm of the couch, she bolted upright, and her head swiveled as she took in my home.

"Where am I?" she demanded when her eyes landed on me.

I cringed at her angry tone. "Relax. You fought off the guards brilliantly, but one of them knocked you out. Nyla and her daughters got away and I finished off the guards."

Zoe glanced around the room like an animal in unfamiliar surroundings. She looked wild and tense.

When her steely gaze settled back on me, gone was the sweet innocence I'd witnessed while she slept. "And where is here?"

I sighed. If I hadn't overheard her kindness with Nate, I

might have been offended. Her distrust made sense, though, given what the guards had said about her. We both had stories we would rather keep secret.

As I rose and came closer, she cringed. I held up my hands in a non-threatening gesture, my heart softening.

"Relax, you're in my home. I brought you here because I don't know where you live and you were in no condition to tell me. I just want to check the bump on the back of your head. It was pretty nasty."

Her hand shot up under her unusually colored hair. Cream-blond to black tips.

She ruffled through her hair feeling for the bump, then her hand dropped in relief.

"You won't find anything," she said.

I moved behind her, suspicious. "I'm just going to make sure your head's all right. Do you feel lightheaded or sick?"

I started at the top of her head and gently moved my hands down to her neck. There was nothing there. I ran my hands over her scalp again. Incredible! The lump had been huge.

She turned to face me. "I told you you wouldn't find anything." She watched as I crossed the room back to my seat. "And no, I'm not dizzy or sick or anything."

"How?"

She tensed and her eyes wandered around the room again. I wasn't sure if it was a diversion from my question or if she was just interested in her surroundings. I settled back in my chair and studied her. She wasn't about to divulge any secrets.

My eyes flicked to her sleeve, my thoughts returning her tattoos. She saw my gaze shift and pulled her sleeve lower to cover her hands—but not before I saw a line on one of her fingers and a black flower etched on her palm.

"The guards," she said. "They wanted something from you. Before they entered the inn, I overhead them say they were looking for an elf sitting alone. It was a setup. When I came inside and saw you sitting by yourself, I decided to join you."

A cold shiver pattered over my skin and it took considerable focus to keep from shuddering. Had they or the regents sent the note, as a way of drawing me out? Why would they do that? "Thank you."

My estimation of Zoe soared. I knew she didn't like me very much, and after watching her fight, I understood that she clearly didn't need my help. But the fortress still held something for her. It was her former home, and now my sister was there. Or was that another ruse? It didn't matter. If there was a chance my sister was in the fortress, I had to rescue her.

My feelings toward Zoe were muddled by this new information. Nate clearly trusted her, and now she had risked her own life to keep me and the Mist family safe. Trust was built, given, and earned. And I was willing to start.

"I think we both have secrets to share," I said. She flinched at my words. "I'll go first and then, if you feel comfortable, you can share your story. The guards, after they knocked you out, were looking at your tattoos."

Zoe adjusted her shirt again and looked down.

I leaned forward. "You don't have to tell me your story, but Nate is a mutual friend. I've known him all my life, and he told me that you respect honesty."

Her eyebrow arched. "Doubtful."

"Excuse me?"

"I doubt you've known him your whole life."

"I have, and he can verify my story." I licked my lips and

106

hesitated before sharing with her the truth of my identity. The words felt heavy and my voice hollow. Was this the right moment?

Deciding to forge ahead, I cleared my throat.

The air suddenly sizzled and Cocoa popped into my living room.

"Cocoa! What are you doing here?" Zoe said. Her voice softened.

The brownie's gaze darted between the two of us, then rested on Zoe. "It's Nate… his home's been attacked and the children—"

Zoe rose. I stood, too.

"Are the children safe?" Zoe asked.

Cocoa shook her head, her long black hair tumbling around her shoulders. "The regents' guards took them."

Zoe fled from my house without another word. The brownie glanced up at me then popped out of view. I guessed that she had returned to Nate's.

I grabbed my sword and daggers, then looked back at the book lying on my desk. It seemed like an odd thing to bring, but I didn't feel right about leaving it. I stuffed it in my satchel and ran out the door.

Twilight's Curse

Chapter Ten

Zoe

I raced through the forest to Nate's house, taking advantage of the enhanced speed my dragons gave me. And I was so thankful Pat's healing had worked during my nap. My conscience twinged. I should be thankful for Nix, too, for helping with the guards. I'd tell him later. Right now, Nate and the children needed me. Chim helped me see better in these darkest hours of the night as I hurdled over felled logs and darted around trees. I had to get to the tree and the children. Nate could take care of himself, but the children were another matter.

I couldn't let Dasha be taken back to the fortress. Ever. She had amazing abilities, and I knew my mother wouldn't hesitate to continue her experiments on her. She had learned so much through her experiments on me.

I skidded to a stop about three trees away from Nate's, hearing the scuffle of the regents' guards. Despite being elfkind, they didn't move with the stealth we innately had. Perhaps it had been bred out of them with their training, and whatever my mother had done to them.

I caught my breath and moved to a neighboring tree, then crouched behind it and allowed Chim's camouflage to coat me. I'd be nearly undetectable unless someone walked into me or was a few steps away and looked directly at me; even then the elf might think I was a trick of the eye.

The metallic scent of blood wafted toward me and my stomach rolled. Scanning the guards milling around Nate's tree, I didn't understand what was going on. Why would such heavily armed guards be here?

Moving silently to the cover of bushes, I crouched to get a closer look. My heart nearly lurched from my chest when I saw the children gathered in a tight circle with three guards posted around them. I couldn't tell if all fifteen were there, but the cluster hinted at it. Why didn't the children run or scatter? The guards would have no chance of catching them all if they fled in every direction. The guards must have bound them somehow. I shivered, remembering the restraints I'd seen while I'd lived in the fortress; the *zing* they gave off whenever someone touched them would leave the arm numb for hours.

I carefully inspected the children's faces, looking for Dasha. I couldn't see her from this distance, but that didn't mean she wasn't there.

Under the cover of darkness, my dragons would easily remain hidden. I called them forth and felt the familiar peeling sensation as they left their roosts in my skin.

Go and look for Dasha, and anything else that might be useful, I instructed.

I watched Pat move to the children while Chim darted high

110

and Tupac flew around the perimeter of Nate's tree.

One of the guards—leaner than burly—turned suddenly, startled, and I prayed he hadn't seen the dragons. I crouched lower and watched the guard move toward me. Even with Chim's enhanced eyesight, I couldn't make out his face. He was mostly in the dark, but I caught a glimpse of his profile. There was something familiar in his movements; he was probably one of the kids I'd grown up with in the fortress.

My thoughts wavered toward Maximon, the friend I'd left behind. He'd been one of those kids, training to fight, so it was only natural that he'd have become a guard by now. He'd always been fast and strong.

I watched this guard as he moved. He said something to another guard, then disappeared into a cluster of trees.

I glanced back at the front of Nate's tree, worried that I couldn't see my mentor. I also wondered how the guards had managed to breach the tree, since it was heavily warded with magic. Someone must have let the guards in, but who? Certainly not the brownies or the children.

I thought of Anansi. Had he been planted in Nate's tree to betray us? I shook my head. Nate was a kind old elf who took kids in—or at least, he'd taken me in and let me take in other kids. He stayed near the tree and wasn't anyone important.

Chim sent a flutter of images into my mind of the forest around me and the guard I'd found familiar. Each picture spilled over the others. The onslaught masked the warning, and I was too late to do anything as a hand clamped over my mouth, pulling me from my hiding place. The dragons instantly responded to my distress and shot in my direction, intending to fight off my captor.

"Don't say anything," a light tenor hissed in my ear. "And

call off your dragons."

With all the guards around, I knew it was futile to scream, but I struggled against his hold. He only wrapped his arm around my waist tighter. If my arms had been free, I would have elbowed him or struck at him with my daggers, but they were trapped in his vicelike grip.

Even as I called to my dragons, he was leading me away from Nate's tree. How had he been able to sneak up on me? It was the second time in as many days someone had breached Chim's cloak of stealth.

The guard brought me to a stop a few trees away.

"I'm going to remove my hand from your mouth," he said. "I just want to talk, Zoe. Don't run, okay?"

Something in his voice sounded familiar, especially the way he'd said my name. Could it be...?

The hand slid from my mouth.

"Who are you?" I asked.

He spun me to face him. "Don't you recognize me?"

I examined his features. He had the face of a grown elf, but when I looked into the cool blue of his eyes, the color reflecting the sky of a perfect sunny day, and the line of his nose, my heart leaped in confirmation.

"Maximon?" I reached forward, my fingers trailing along the side of his face.

He nodded. "Yes. When I saw the dragon, I guessed that you'd be close. Don't worry. I doubt anyone else noticed them."

A cool set of prickles danced over my skin. I'd never told Maximon about my dragons. How did he know now? I wanted to ask but I couldn't trust him, not as long as he was bound in service to my parents. Instead I asked, "But how did you sneak up on me?"

Maximon rested his hand on his hips and glanced around the small clearing. "We don't have long. I can't answer your questions because I have to get back."

"They turned you into one of their guards," I said.

Maximon grimaced and I wondered what else my parents had done to him.

"They've been making plans for a while now," he said. "They've devised a way to control the entire population of the Twilight Realm."

"But that's impossible," I whispered.

"No. They've found a way."

"When?"

"Soon. By the end of the week."

Another wave of cold shivers ran through me as I thought of what that meant. If what Maximon said was true, every elf and creature that lived in this realm would become a slave to my parents. I shook my head, determined to ask Nate about it later. Nate! My heart jumped, I had to get back to the tree and try to rescue the children.

"We've got to stop them. Maximon, you must desert, now. Come with me and help me take down my parents."

Maximon shook his head, then looked into my eyes. "I can't. After you left, everyone had a tracker placed on them. Wherever I go, they'll be able to find me."

"Oh." I looked down and scuffed the ground with the toe of my boot. What else had my parents done? "But we have to do something to stop them."

"We can, and we will. Can you come to the fortress?" He paused. "But not alone. We're going to need help. Do you have friends?"

I thought of Nix. He was a friend, sort of. And there was Nate, assuming he had managed to hide from the guards. And what about the brownies? Would they help? Their sweet, nurturing nature did not incline them toward fighting.

Well, there was no sense in telling him any of this.

"Come with your friends to the fortress in two days," Maximon said.

"Why then? Why me?"

Maximon hissed. "Look, I've got to return. I've been gone too long already. Just come in two days. Or tomorrow if it works better. It doesn't matter. Just come and I'll know when you arrive."

My eyes narrowed. Why was he so cavalier? And how would he know when we arrived?

"Wait, how will you know." I grabbed his arm to stop him. His eyes flared with anger. I snatched my hand as if from fire and took a step back.

"Just come. Your gifting is the only kind of magic that can stop their plan."

I hesitated, needing more information. But he wouldn't or couldn't answer. I didn't think Maximon would set a trap for me, but it was hard to tell. It'd been six years since I'd last seen him. And there was even less reason for me to trust him now. He'd mentioned my dragon. I'd never told anyone in the fortress about what my tattoos did. How did he know?

Instead of arguing, I nodded. "Tomorrow or the day after. You'll know when I arrive. Got it."

As he dashed away, I wasn't sure if I'd actually go through with it. I needed to think about this more and discuss it with the so-called friends I'd implied I had.

Maximon's plan sounded weak, but then my parents always

knew my movements when I was at the fortress, except for the night I'd escaped. It had been quiet that night. Had Maximon somehow tapped into my parents' abilities? And was that how he'd know when I would arrive? The thought sent a shudder through me.

I creeped slowly back to Nate's tree, keeping under the cover of Chim's stealth and the shadows of night.

It looked like the guards had thinned out. I crouched in the underbrush with my dragons close around me. The last thing I needed was another surprise visit from a guard.

The children were huddled inside a covered wagon, which was hitched to two horses. Windows secured by bars running along the side gave me a view inside. I searched their faces, hoping to spot Dasha. As I watched, the horses began to pull the wagon away from the tree. Maximon was walking at the rear but quickened his steps alongside the slow-moving wagon until he'd reached the front. He swung himself up next to the driver. He was close in age to me. Rank among the regent guards was achieved through years served, so he'd only be a low-level guard. Why would he be riding up front?

A blond head popped up among the children, her vibrant blue eyes shining out in the dark. Dasha! My stomach plummeted. They'd gotten her.

Plan or not, friends or not, Maximon or not, there was no way I would let my mother experiment with this girl. Not again.

I climbed up the tree next to me to get a better view of the departing wagon, thankful that the foliage was thicker here. I crawled out on the limb as the wagon jostled over the uneven forest floor. Aside from Maximon and the driver, there were no other guards around that I could see.

I stood up, preparing to jump on the roof of the cart as it passed underneath, but as it got closer, I questioned my plan. I focused on Dasha and my plan to rescue the other children.

Turning in my crouched position, I saw two guards riding behind the cart on horseback. I doubted they'd see anything with the distance and the cover of night. Not to mention Chim's cloaking abilities. The guards were large and with my mom's enhancements they'd be hard to take down. I wanted to avoid that.

I called on Chim's magic, and its effects washed over me, allowing me to jump from my perch and land smoothly, silently, and with complete invisibility on the roof of the wagon.

Now to get in, I thought. *Any ideas, guys?*

The dragons responded with images and strategies. I thought through my arsenal of tattoos, searching for something that might help me get in and out again without the guards noticing. If I got inside, I thought Chim's magic could shield the children. He'd been able to shield me and Dasha the night I escaped the fortress, so I assumed he could do it again. I could then potentially take the children out through the roof and deposit them in the trees, since the limbs hung low in this part of the forest. That felt like my best option, but I still needed a way into the wagon.

I glanced through the cracks of the roof and saw the kids huddled in clusters, with Dasha alone in the corner. I didn't see Anansi, though. My gut churned. Had the concerns of the brownies been valid? Had he betrayed us? I didn't like thinking the worst of a child I barely knew. Perhaps he'd escaped or was hiding back at Nate's tree. I pushed aside my uncertainty.

I released one of my daggers and used it to saw at the wood. I cringed at the noise, but with the clop of horses, jangle of tack, and creak of the wheels, I was certain no one could hear.

Some of the children started to murmur when sawdust trickled down on them. They scooted back and glanced up at the ceiling.

From up front, Maximon banged on the wall of the carriage behind him. "Quiet back there."

I shivered hearing his voice; it was void of my friend's usual warmth and reminded me a little too much of my brother. Had my parents changed Maximon? It was entirely possible, but the thought saddened me. Maybe I could save him too.

Someone grabbed the back of my shirt and yanked me. My dagger slipped out of my hand and securely reattached itself to my forearm.

"What's this?" a large guard asked as he flipped me over and stared down at me. I recognized him as the driver of the wagon. How had he seen through Chim's cloak of invisibility? I made a quick glance at the driver's seat and saw Maximon leading the horses.

I scrambled up to a fighting stance, which was hard to do with the carriage still trundling along and so many trees overhead.

Maximon peered back at me, scowling. "I'll deal with her."

"Are you sure, sir?" the driver asked him.

Sir?!

The wagon slowed to a crawl, then stopped. I could leap off and flee into the forest, but the two guards on horseback would come after me. I was probably faster than them, and Chim's stealth abilities would keep me hidden—but I couldn't leave the kids.

"Come on down, Zoe," Maximon called to me.

I leaped to the ground.

"Sir?" I asked, raising an eyebrow.

Maximon squared his shoulders. "This doesn't concern you. Leave." The words were directed at me but he spoke loudly, probably so the guards would hear.

I leaned in close and whispered, "What's the deal? These are kids, and you're willingly taking them to my parents? To my mother?"

Maximon clamped his hand around my arm and led me into the forest out of earshot. I stumbled as he flung me to the ground, and I nearly landed on my backside. I trembled at his cold eyes.

"This is your final warning, Zoe."

"I can't let you take those kids." I flexed my fingers, sensing my dragons ready to fight. I realized I should have run when I had the chance and later doubled back to get the kids.

The demon tattoo on my chest shook his cage and roared. If I asked my dragons to drop their shielding and release him, I'd easily be able to take out Maximon and the guards, but I feared that would turn me into exactly what my parents had wanted me to become.

"You don't have a choice here," Maximon said. "If you want a fight, you'll lose."

"Maximon, they're kids. Innocent."

He placed his hands on his hips and shook his head. "You don't get it."

"Then explain it to me."

"Your parents are raising up an army."

"What for?"

Maximon shrugged. "To rule, what else?"

I narrowed my eyes. I knew that wasn't the truth. My parents had been rulers ever since they'd taken out the king and queen of the Twilight Realm. Maybe they themselves were still just regents, but no one in the Twilight Realm had ever attempted to defy them.

"Who's their enemy?" I asked.

Maximon shook his head. "I don't want to fight you, Zoe. Stop asking questions and come to the fortress. Tomorrow."

I folded my arms across my chest, not appreciating his forceful manner. He was keeping something from me.

"I can't come that quickly," I said. "I'll come in two days, that's better." I wasn't sure if two days would give me time to figure out what he was hiding and maybe come up with a different plan, but one day wasn't enough.

Maximon's jaw clenched. "Fine. No, tomorrow. Come—and don't come alone. Remember, I'll know when you arrive."

How? The question burned in me, but he turned and headed back through the trees. I was tempted to follow at a distance and try again to rescue the kids, but that would be hard now that they were alerted to my presence. Plus they'd managed to see through Chim's cloak. That unsettled me. First Nix, then Maximon, and now the driver.

As the wagon holding Dasha and the other children disappeared into the forest, I made a vow to myself: I would finally storm the fortress and face my fears.

Pat, Chim, Tupac... let's go. I thought of Nate and hoped he was safe in his home. *Nix is probably at Nate's tree and might need our help with the remaining guards.*

I turned and headed back to Nate's. Talking to Maximon and hearing that my parents were raising up an army stirred up memories of what they'd been trying to do with me and my magic. *What are my parents up to? And is this why they're enhancing all their guards?*

The dragons left their roosts on my skin. Pat settled on my shoulder, sending waves of calm through my body. I reached up and stroked her. Her skin felt like my own, smooth and soft. All my tattoos had been intricately inked, as was the demon on my chest.

Early on when my parents discovered the life-giving abilities of my magic, they had hoped to create a deadly assassin out of me. They thought the tattoos would come to life, and the inked creations did, though I never let my parents know the effect my magic had on the tattoos. It'd been my carefully guarded secret. My parents had never counted on me disagreeing with them or their plans and hadn't considered the bond I had with my tattoos.

I wondered if my parents had inflicted the same sort of demonic tattoo on Maximon and the other guards. Without living magic like mine, I couldn't guess what effects this might have had on them. Would any elf be able to resist?

My heart was heavy as I tromped back through the forest and thought more about Maximon's confession that my parents had a plan to take over the Twilight Realm. It didn't make sense me. There had to be more, or something else. They already had control. Sort of. They weren't considered monarchs. And if memory served me right from Nate's lessons, the royal line had a special magic that helped them lead their citizens. Maybe this was what my parents wanted.

My breath caught in my throat. What if my mother's experiments on my magic were to create some kind of influence like the royal magic?

I sighed. It didn't make sense. I was too young when I had run away to really know what my parents were doing and I hadn't cared at the time.

I thought of Maximon's order to come to the fortress tomorrow and to bring *friends.* I had no idea why he suddenly changed the timeline and that unsettled me. Was Maximon really going to help me with rescuing the kids? Or was this all a trap? I shuddered as uncertainty twisted my stomach.

Nix didn't really qualify as a friend, but he'd been skulking around the fortress earlier this evening… or was it yesterday? I rubbed my face. I had no idea how late it was.

I'd arrived back at Nate's tree and crept forward. I needed to make sure Nate was okay and then I'd help Nix get into the fortress. And maybe Nix would help me save Dasha.

Twilight's Curse

Chapter Eleven

Nix

I reached the trees bordering the edge of open space surrounding Nate's tree. I couldn't spot Cocoa or Zoe. I cursed my ineptitude for arriving too late. Ducking into hiding behind a bush, I saw a cart loaded with children being led away.

With no one else visible around the tree, I darted across the ground covering foliage for Nate's door, placed my hand on the marker, and entered before anyone noticed me.

I leaned against the interior wall as the door sealed behind me. I wasn't winded, but my adrenaline was pumping—and if I didn't take a moment to settle down, I might do something careless, especially if there were any guards still inside the house.

I quickly made my way to Nate's study and pulled out *Ascension* from my satchel, placing it on Nate's desk. I searched for *The Royal Family,* one of the other books Nate had shown me earlier—a record of my family line and ancestral history, including a few prophecies given by gifted elfkind. I didn't want the guards or Leski and his wife to get their hands on this book.

I found *The Royal Family* and placed it on Nate's desk.

I turned my attention to the next items I needed: my father's signet ring, seal, and crown. I circled the messy office, looking under files and stacks of boxes, but I couldn't find the box Nate had put them in on the night he'd brought me here.

I moved to Nate's desk and flopped down in his chair. When my father had breathed his last, the royal symbols automatically belonged to me, but both Nate and I had decided to keep the items hidden so I could be raised in obscurity. For a few years after my parents had died, I'd ventured out very little, which had led to the rumors that I was dead, captured, or in exile. After I'd learned to act in what Nate called "a less regal manner" to disguise my true identity, I had started going out again, intent on living a simple life. I liked my life this way. It was uncomplicated and no one got hurt.

But now my sister's life was in the balance.

As I yanked open a drawer and riffled through some of Nate's papers, voices drifted into the office. I froze, listening as steps grew closer. My best guess was that they belonged to guards, and there were at least two of them.

I slid the books off the desk and into my satchel, then glanced around the piles of stuff filling the room. I clenched my jaw. Here I was, rightful king of the Twilight Realm, looking for a place to hide. I felt disgusted with myself.

I headed into the greenhouse, where the floor was damp but the foliage offered shelter. I folded myself under a table that held potted plants with draping vines.

The scuffling of footsteps announced the two guards as they

entered the room.

"What's in here?" A loud baritone filled the room. "Tam, check the corners."

I adjusted the leafy vines so I could see the guards while remaining obscured from view.

"Looks like a library to me, Sarge," Tam said.

"We'll have to go through everything. Maybe we'll find a clue as to where she is."

Tam opened his mouth like he wanted to say something, but then clamped it shut. His eyes bulged as he looked at all the clutter.

I clutched the books in my bag closer to my chest, glad that I'd grabbed them.

"Heard she bested four guards at the Misty Inn earlier this evening," Tam said.

"Lady Sirina will be pleased to get her back." Sarge pushed around the papers on Nate's desk.

"Don't know what we'll find in here." Tam leaned an arm on a stack of bookshelves.

"Don't care what you think. Now get looking."

Tam turned back to the shelves and made a show of pulling books out and replacing them, but his movements were too quick for him to actually be looking at anything.

"What does any of this have to do with the girl?" Tam asked.

"Lady Sirina and Lord Leski told us to search for their daughter, and we will. But that old elf is hiding other secrets. The regents seem to think he has some ties to the child-king. Might know where to find him."

"The child-king? But—"

Tam never finished his sentence. He suddenly crumpled to the ground. Sarge reached for a dagger at his side. I couldn't see much of what was happening, so I shifted my position—and accidentally kicked one of the legs of the table.

Hearing me, Sarge spun around. I watched as he crossed the threshold into the greenhouse. Looking around, I tried to find something I could use as a weapon.

"Come out now," he said. "No sense hiding."

But before I could move, Sarge stiffened, then his eyes fluttered as his knees buckled and he crumpled to the ground.

Looming behind him was Zoe, and she was peering down at the fallen guard with her black daggers clutched in each hand. A dragon floated up behind her, then another slipped out of the folds of material at her thigh, and a third from the loose sleeves of her blouse.

How many dragons did she have?

I shook my head and wondered whether Zoe practiced dark magic.

But Nate knew and trusted her. He also told me that I needed to partner with her. Then I remembered my dream and her vibrant green eyes, as well as everything her parents had done to her. Maybe all those tattoos hadn't been her idea.

Zoe examined the guards. As if given orders, two of the dragons shot off toward the door while the third fluttered down to the younger guard and landed on his chest, staring intently at him.

I noticed Zoe was no longer holding her daggers. I hadn't seen her sheath them. Perhaps she had more hidden pockets under her clothing.

Despite my hesitation, I decided that I had to trust her and give her the chance to tell her story. If I ever did become king, I didn't want to be one who condemned subjects based on the accusations and opinions of others. I certainly wasn't that kind of elf.

I parted the vines and crawled out of my hiding place. Startled, Zoe's eyes shot in my direction. Her daggers flew back into her hands.

When she realized who it was, she sighed. "Nix."

I think that was the first time she'd said my name without her voice having an edge behind it. Were we making progress? I crawled out from under the table and dusted off my pants as I regained my footing and let my satchel fall to my side. The books thumped against my thigh.

"What are you doing here?" I asked in a cool voice. "You took off pretty quick."

"I saw you enter and wanted to make sure you were safe. Or help you, if needed."

I narrowed my eyes. "Is that the only reason?"

"Of course."

But she seemed confused about it. She cleared her throat and composed herself.

I glanced at her hands and saw that the daggers had disappeared. Again.

"Why are you here?" Zoe asked. There was no accusation in her tone. She sounded curious.

As Zoe studied me, it took a tremendous amount of control to remain neutral. "I have my reasons."

"Okaaaaay," she said. "Earlier, I saw the guards round up the children and cart them off to the fortress. I'll need help rescuing them."

I squinted. The request seemed odd.

"How do you know about the kids? And where do they come from?"

"They live here. They're orphans, or abandoned children. I

find them and bring them here."

"To Nate's tree? He lets you?" In all my years, I'd never known Nate to care for children. While he'd raised me for a few years after my parents died, he wasn't the paternal type. There were the brownies though I had a hard time believing they raised the children. They were too secretive about their race and seldom interacted with others unless they were cleaning and cooking. I twitched my lips at my poor summation of their character. I clearly didn't know very much about the brownie race. "Do you take care of the kids?"

Zoe nodded. "Yes, with the brownies. So will you help me rescue them?"

She was clearly a part of Nate's life that I knew nothing about.

I crossed my arms and leaned against the table I had crawled out from. "Why?"

"Why what?"

"Why do you want my help? Why me?" The sudden change in her was catching me off guard. Though she had sat with me at the Misty Inn, her sudden desire for my help seemed… unlike her. Earlier she'd told me to stay out of her way. There was something behind this request.

"Because any decent elf would help. They're children and they're—" Her voice trailed off and she shook her head. "It doesn't matter."

She stared up at me and my heart stuttered at the vulnerability I saw in her expression. The armor she'd been wearing since we'd first met was gone.

I relaxed my stance and moved toward Nate's desk.

"The guards," I said, nodding at their unconscious bodies. "Maybe we should go somewhere safer."

Zoe shrugged and pointed to the small dragon curled up on the guard's chest. "Pat's keeping them asleep and Chim and Tupac are ensuring the entrances are secure. If anyone else tries to get into the tree, they'll let me know."

"Your dragons?"

Zoe nodded. "Yes."

"Where do they come from?"

Zoe sighed and sat in one of Nate's chairs. "Me."

As if called, Pat flew to Zoe and perched on the arm of her chair. Zoe raised her sleeve, and as she did my eyes nearly popped out of my head to see the number of tattoos littering her skin. She shifted the underside of her arm and there was one of the daggers, perfectly inked. And then, when she nodded toward Pat, the dragon leaned against her arm and *melted* into her skin.

I sucked in a sharp breath.

The dragon re-emerged and fluttered back to the guards.

"She'll keep the guards sedated as long as she's with them."

"The dragons... they're tattoos? And your daggers as well. Why? How?"

"I didn't ask for them. I was born with an unusual magic." Her voice was soft but in it was a touch of anger. "My parents, they experimented on me." She held up her index finger, showing me a single line drawn down its length. It looked like a pin. "My first tattoo. For the longest time it seemed useless... until I learned how to use it to open doors. That's how I escaped the fortress. I was twelve, and by then my parents had covered my body in tattoos."

I was shocked. Leski and Sirina had killed my parents, but to have done this to their own daughter, a child... what kind of heartless beings were they?

Zoe rose fluidly and walked into the greenhouse. She touched one of the plants; it had looked beyond help a moment ago, but suddenly it began to flourish. Zoe smiled, a genuine, unguarded smile.

I nearly tumbled off Nate's desk.

"My unusual magic gives things life," she explained. "My parents attempted to manipulate my magic with another magic. I don't understand my mother's science, but she thought she could train my magic to respond to hers or whatever magic she used and then control my tattoos. It's kind of like how grafting works. You take a branch from one kind of apple tree and join it with a different kind of apple tree and you'll have two different kinds of apples growing from the same tree. Their hope was to turn me into an assassin. Somehow, they were able to control other elves by similar methods. And it worked, in a way... just not quite how they expected."

"Your parents are Lord Leski and Lady Sirina." I wanted to hear it from her.

"Yes."

It was a loaded word for her and I could see a range of emotions vying for prominence across her features.

I settled into Nate's chair, relaxing my posture and softening my voice. "Did the tattoos hurt?"

"They burned like acid."

I swallowed, the picture of a child screaming flashing through my mind. "Do they still hurt?"

"Pat's a healing dragon, so no. Not anymore. Tupac is a fighter and Chim provides shields and stealth." She faced me squarely, her gaze penetrating me. "I don't tell anyone my story. Only Nate knows it. After I escaped, I found his

130

home... or at least Tupac did. Nate invited me in for breakfast and ended up raising me. Together, we've been protecting children. There's one child, Dasha, who's like me, only more unique. When I fled from the fortress, I took her with me. My parents had only just started experimenting on her, but if they..."

She shook her head as tears welled in her eyes.

"They'll do to her what they did to you," I said, finishing her thought.

Zoe nodded. She trembled from the effort of fighting to hold in her emotions. But she was strong and had survived worse than me.

Now I understood why Nate had told me to trust her, and I knew we'd have to work together to save the elves we cared about. I also understood why she was asking for help. Her love for Dasha and the children was greater than her resistance to working with others. She was choosing to trust me, and I'd take any sliver of an open door she offered.

"The guards took Dasha, didn't they?" I asked.

"Yes, and now we have to rescue them all. Tomorrow." She glanced at a clock on Nate's desk. "I guess it *is* tomorrow already, so later today. One of the guards who took the kids, he's someone I knew from the fortress. He told me to come with help, that my parents are building an army to take over the Twilight Realm. I don't trust him. He claimed he'd know when we arrived, and that makes me trust him less. But this isn't about him. It's about rescuing Dasha and the other kids."

She turned to face me fully. Her composure had returned. "Will you help me?" she asked.

"Yes."

Twilight's Curse

Chapter Twelve

Zoe

Nix's willingness to help left me feeling empty and vulnerable. I wasn't used to friendship or relationships of any kind past those who lived in Nate's tree. I wanted to pull my dragons close for their company.

I'd told Nix more about myself than I'd told anyone else except Nate—and now he would help me. I studied his profile and found he wasn't impressive, though I could see an appeal to him. There was an innocent grace that lent him a bit of charm; it both mystified and drew me to him. Mostly, he made me feel safe. Perhaps it had something to do with his gifting.

"Zoe, there's something—"

But Nix's voice was cut off as Cocoa came hurtling into the room.

"Zoe," Cocoa said, panting as she clutched her tiny hand over her chest. "Come, Nate needs you."

My muscles tensed and Pat's head perked up from her perch over the sleeping guards.

You stay, I instructed her. *Keep the guards asleep. I'll make sure Chim or Tupac will stay with you.*

As Pat curled up on the younger guard's chest, I felt her power flowing between the two elves, keeping them sedated.

"Nate is hurt?" Nix asked. His expression had grown grim.

Cocoa jumped, startled at Nix's voice. "Forgive me, ah—"

Nix shook his head. I tapped my lower lip and wondered if these two knew each other.

Cocoa curtsied to him. "Right. Follow me."

With that, the brownie spun, her long hair flying out in a twirl around her. I began to follow but then turned back.

I crossed my arms, giving Nix my full attention. "Is there something I should know?"

"We need to hurry," Cocoa insisted. Her large round eyes had so much pleading and desperation in them that there was no doubting her sincerity.

"I have some secrets of my own to tell you," Nix said. "But right now, I think Nate is of greater importance."

He had spoken with enough grace that it almost seemed… regal. I tilted my head, studying his features more carefully. There was something familiar about him.

Cocoa grabbed my hand and tugged, and I let the brownie lead me out of the office. I would ask Nix about his secrets later.

"Wait, what about the guards?" Nix asked.

"Pat'll keep them sedated." Just as I was about to pass through the doorway, however, another thought occurred to me.

Cocoa scowled. "We need to go!"

"I know," I said. "But safety first. Is the tree secure?"

"Those are the only guards who remain inside," she said.

"And how did they get in?"

Cocoa looked down, fidgeting with the hem of her shirt.

"It was Anansi, wasn't it?" I asked. *Trickster! His name!* Inwardly, I fumed. I should have figured it out.

"Yes, he was a spy for your parents. He knew right where the children were."

My heart hammered against the prison in my chest, fighting for freedom. Anger sparked in me and I felt the demon tattoo rattle the bars of his cage. Fortunately, I also felt Pat's peaceful presence reach out to me. I thanked her, then took a deep breath and let it out slowly.

Chim, you need to reset the protections of this tree, I thought as Cocoa led me out of the office. *Make it so that no one can get in. We'll deal with reimprinting ourselves later.*

Chim, who'd been checking the various external entrances in the tree with Tupac, flew up next to me then darted off down the hall toward Nate's private entrance.

"Where's he off to?" Nix asked, stumbling out of the room behind me.

"He's going to reset the protections around this place."

"Right. So your dragons have magical abilities?"

"Sort of, I guess. I don't really know. They were part of my parents' experiments on me. Sometimes I wonder if the magic comes from the tattoos, or if it's mine."

I quickened my steps as Cocoa led us toward the part of the tree where the children lived.

"I should have known about Anansi," Cocoa said, stopping and squeezing my hand. "We brownies can usually sense these things, when an elf is being deceptive."

135

I wanted to reach out to her and tell her it was okay, only it wasn't okay. The kids had been taken and Nate... well, I didn't know what had happened to Nate. I hurried my steps along.

"Cocoa, you did suspect him," I said. "I just..."

Didn't listen, I finished internally, swallowing the lump in my throat. Was this my fault?

Cocoa shook her head. "But not enough. Brownies have the innate ability to sense good and evil in sentient beings. Nate trusted us and we let this happen."

I ran my hand over Cocoa's hair, hoping the small gesture would comfort her and relieve my guilt.

"Nate is the forgiving type," I reminded her. "He was deceived, too. We all were. And I should have sensed my parents' craftiness."

But what if the break-in, Anansi, and kidnappings of all the children weren't my parents? Icy tentacles crept across my skin as I thought of my brother's magical ability to mimic others so perfectly.

When Cocoa gazed up at me, her small face registered an acceptance of my words.

"It happened," I said. "We can't do anything about it but save the kids."

I hoped the words carried the assurances I didn't feel... and hid the suspicions still eating at my gut.

"We'll help," Cocoa said. "After we see to Nate."

The brownie's response was so sincere and passionate, I nearly laughed out loud. What could a brownie do to my parents? They were maternal creatures, nurturing, able to clean and cook. As far as I knew, they didn't even have any defensive training or strong magical skill.

Cocoa led us through the large playroom that doubled as a classroom.

"Nate's tree is huge. I've never been in this part," Nix said, his mouth gaping at all the open space.

"It's an addition," Cocoa stated and the two shared a quick glance that reminded me Nix had claimed he'd known Nate his whole life.

I yawned. It was late, and I felt drained; I wasn't used to being this far from my dragons for so long.

Cocoa rounded into the massive library, and I followed her in.

I gasped. All the shelves had been toppled over and books and paper were littered over every surface. Tentatively, I followed Cocoa, stepping over books and around broken shelves. I'd read many stories to the children here, and now the place was utterly destroyed. My heart plummeted, and frustration at Anansi and anger toward my parents' actions rose up in me.

"They're horrible," I muttered to myself. "They have to be stopped. All they do is destroy."

Pain seemed to shroud Nix's features at the mention of my parents. What had they done to him?

A moan rose from the middle of the room, and I recognized it as coming from Nate. As we drew closer, we entered my favorite part of the room, where we did the storytelling. Cushions were usually scattered about for children to sit on while they were read to. Low tables, now overturned, were places for them to study. We'd also practiced our magical giftings here.

But today all I saw was devastation—and at the very bottom of the debris, beneath a bookshelf, Nate lay prone.

"Nate," I cried as I knelt next to him. "We're here. We'll help you."

Nate smiled up at me and my heart melted at the affection I saw in his eyes. He was the only good adult I'd ever known. He'd become a father to me.

The older elf reached out and wiped a tear from my cheek with a trembling hand. His gaze shifted to Nix.

"You've found each other," he said, obviously in pain. "Good."

"Oh, Nate, we've got to get you out of here." I pushed some books away and reached for a cushion. Gingerly I raised Nate's head and slid the pillow beneath it. He grimaced.

Nix leaned over and shifted some wooden shelves from the mountain of books atop Nate. "Is it possible to move some of this?"

Cocoa helped Nix with the longer pieces. Because of her small size, she easily scaled the mound and handed down bits of debris.

"It's not as bad as it seems," Nate said. "I think I broke a leg, but thankfully it's nothing worse."

I shook my head, my daggers itching to be released. The surge of vengeance thumped in my chest and my demon roared. I suddenly wanted to hurt the regent guards who'd done this to Nate.

I'd never taken a life. I didn't want to... but for Nate, for Dasha, and for the children? It was all I wanted to do. I knew these thoughts were coming from the demon tattoo, and I was having trouble holding him back. A trickle of sweat ran down the side of my face. I needed Chim to help me contain the beast within or I'd do something I'd really regret.

Nate wouldn't release my hand. "Zoe, don't let it take over.

You're good. Rely on the strength of your magic. You're a lot stronger than you think."

"Okay, I'll think about it." I kissed his forehead. I knew he was talk about the demon tattoo and letting my magic merge with it. I told Nate I'd think about it more to appease him in his wounded state rather than start another argument about his theories. I looked toward Nix. "Are you coming? We'll have to deal with the guards so Pat can heal Nate."

Nix nodded.

"I'll stay here," Cocoa said as Nix helped her down from the mound. She took up my post next to Nate.

"We'll be back soon," I called over my shoulder. Soon Nix and I were back in the corridor.

"What'd Nate mean back there when he was talking about not letting *it* take over?" Nix asked.

I scowled. He'd picked up on that, had he?

"Nothing."

I quickened my pace and in no time we were back at Nate's study. Tupac and Pat were inside, keeping the guards sedated.

Tupac, help Chim finish setting the protections around the tree, I commanded.

The warrior dragon hesitated and then directed a wave of power into me. I felt that power flow around the demon's cage.

We don't have time for this, I growled at Tupac.

Tupac shot from the room, and I instantly felt bad for snapping at him. He was only trying to help me. Ever since my mother had imprinted me with the demon tattoo, the dragons had faithfully shielded me from its effects.

Pat looked up at me with tired eyes. She smacked her lips as I crouched to stroke her raised head.

You've done well, little friend, I told her.

"What are we going to do about the guards?" Nix asked.

The thought of killing them floated through my mind again. Pat gave a little squawk and tried to calm me. I felt her energy search for the demon tattoo and reinforce the prison around it.

Suddenly, my intense anger dissipated, along with my desire to kill.

"We could throw them out of the tree once Chim is done setting his protections," I suggested. "They won't be able to get back in."

"Won't they just return to the fortress and bring reinforcements?" Nix asked, crouching beside me and reaching out his fingers to Pat. The healing dragon sniffed his hand, then rubbed her head against it.

I smiled at the affectionate dragon.

"They'll already know we're here," I said.

I glanced at Nate's clock. It was two in the morning and sleep was pulling at me. I knew the added weariness came from the fact that the dragons had been working so long. Because they were part of me, their energy was connected to mine. I needed sleep...

But there was no time to rest. Not now, not yet.

Nix shifted his weight, waiting for further explanation. My focus was distracted as I sensed Chim and Tupac soaring through the tree back to me. A moment later, they landed on the floor on either side of me.

"We could tie up the guards," Nix suggested.

"I think our best bet is getting them out of Nate's home."

Nix sighed and rubbed his eyes. "I hate letting them get away."

I leaned against Nate's desk, clutching its edges as the demon roared in my chest. Noticing the state I was in, Chim fluttered up next to me and clamped down on the demon by reinforcing the shielding around the demon's cage. I closed my eyes.

"We need to take care of these guards, then go back to help Nate. His life is too important."

"You're right." Nix picked up Pat. "Hey, wake up, buddy."

"What are you doing?"

Nix looked at me confused. "You said we should move the guards. I was getting her out of the way. I thought—"

The healing dragon stretched her wings, and at the same time the two guards shook their heads and sat up.

"Sarge, we found her," the younger guard said, leering at me and making my skin crawl.

"You take her, Tam. I'll take the child-adult." Sarge shifted his weight under him and rose to a menacing height.

"You idiot!" I said to Nix as my daggers slid into my waiting hands. I felt the demon tattoo beat against his cage. "Pat was keeping them sedated."

"I thought she could keep them sedated while we moved them. I didn't want—"

Sarge lunged at Nix, cutting off his response.

Tam leaped to his feet and swung at Tupac with his fist, sending the warrior dragon spiraling through the air. He landed with a thump and one of Nate's carefully constructed pillars toppled to the floor, burying Tupac beneath. At least I could sense the dragon was still okay.

Tam sneered at me and rolled his shoulders; behind him, I saw that Nix and Sarge were already locked in a wrestle hold. Pat was hovering around Nix's head, pouring energy into him. I was impressed; Nix was holding his own against an elf at least twice his size.

Tam sneered then thrust a short sword at me, and I dodged even though there wasn't much room to maneuver. Chim flew in and attacked the elf with his claws, but the guard grabbed the dragon and pitched him into the greenhouse. The little creature landed hard on his backside and slid into a table leg.

I rolled my daggers in my grip. I wasn't used to fighting without my dragons, but I would if I had to.

But as I stared down the guard before me, something inside me broke. The demon roared with newfound freedom and I lunged with my daggers. Everything went red.

Chapter Thirteen

Zoe

"Zoe?"

Nix's voice filtered into my subconsciousness. Everything around me was dead quiet and I felt the nervous energy of my dragons.

"What happened?" I asked.

My eyes open and all four faces—dragons and elf—peered down at me with concern.

The demon.

I sat up, not realizing that Pat had settled on my chest; she toppled to the floor and I had to scoop her up. I apologized and she nuzzled her cheek against my palm.

I searched my chest for the spot where the demon tattoo was contained, and I felt him there. He was back in his prison, but there seemed to be a proud strut to his movements. He could sense my consciousness and sent me images of his deeds.

My stomach churned and I dry-heaved.

"I… killed the guard, didn't I?" I asked when my stomach settled. I wiped the corners of my mouth with my sleeve and rested my back against Nate's desk. The splatters of blood on book spines, the floor, and Nate's towering boxes told the tale of the demon's deeds.

"It was like something took over and…" Nix's voice fell away.

He didn't need to say more. Tears came to my eyes. I had killed. The demon had been freed, and in those few moments he'd completely consumed me and taken the life of the guards. I had no memory of what he'd done, but his images filled in the gaps. He had released the sabers tattooed on my back and sliced the guards' throats.

I squeezed my eyes shut but couldn't block the graphic details, or his roar of triumph.

A sob burst out of me. I covered my mouth and held still as a few tears escaped down my cheeks. I wasn't certain I wanted or deserved any comfort from my dragons or Nix. There was no way I'd ever let myself be controlled again. How had I let it take over? I had to remain in control. It was the only way.

"We have to go to Nate," I said.

Nix offered a hand and I didn't push him away. Everything in me wanted to, but an odd weakness clouded my usually rational mind.

I wobbled on my feet as Nix placed a hand on my back and held my arm. I didn't snatch my hand away. His presence was comforting.

I saw the boot of a fallen guard and started to turn my head.

"Don't look at it," Nix said, shielding my view of the body.

How could he be so nice after what he'd seen me do?

As we walked out into the hall, the demon sent a steady

stream of graphic images my way. Images of his killing blows. Chim sent up a block so I couldn't see them. I wiped away my tears, then looked down and saw the bloody state of my clothes.

"Nate can't see me like this."

"Do you want to change?" Nix asked.

"Yeah, wait here. My room isn't far."

I stumbled away with the dragons in tow, using the walls to keep me upright. I then pulled the dragons back into myself, reducing the strain of our long separation. Their focused power worked to contain the demon and heal my disturbed soul.

Once in the privacy of my room, I couldn't hold back the onslaught of tears. I stripped off my soiled garments and used a wet washcloth to remove the tarnish of blood from my skin. I couldn't look at myself in the mirror as I rubbed away the red. I was so afraid I'd see the demon instead of me.

After I finished, I did risk a peek—to ensure I'd taken care of every visible stain. My own face stared back at me. It was the same as always, but my eyes looked empty and vulnerable, some of my hardened edge having gone missing. On my chest, the demon tattoo mocked me, and a wave of dizziness overpowered me. I steadied myself against the sink, wanting to scream.

In the corner next to the sink, the shower beckoned me. I turned the water on and it poured out over a lip about an arm's reach above me. The water was drawn through the roots from a hot spring. I had no idea how the magic worked but could sense the magic in the tree drawing forth the water. It poured over me like a cleansing waterfall and helped wash away some of the disgust I felt. The water splashed off and pooled around my feet then down another spout and was either absorbed by the tree or dispersed back into the ground through the roots. I had no idea how tree homes worked or how a tree was transformed into something livable. My magic helped me sense this process though.

The demon had calmed down to a satisfied smirk by the time I was toweling myself off. The dragons had reinforced their shielding around his prison, preventing him from taking over again. For the first time, I noticed the individual layers of the dragons' protection, seeing how each dragon worked in tandem with the others. Tupac created a cage, Chim shielded the demon to create separation, and Pat inundated it with calm and sedation.

Thanks, guys. I said, feeling the dragons' pleasure through a warm burst of energy that brought heat to my cheeks.

As I grabbed fresh clothes out of my dresser, I thought of how the demon was able to overpower me and break through the protections my dragons had in place because I had tired myself out and had been so emotional. I decided that I mostly believed Nate when he'd said that forgiving my parents would release me from the demon's impact. I wasn't sure how but my weakness was the demon's strength—an open door for him to take over. Not facing my past and not forgiving my parents left that door open a crack which the demon had been happy to take advantage of in my weakness. But what of my dragons or other tattoos? They were like my arms and leg or a vital organ. I could never part with them.

I quickly dressed, smoothed my hair, and rejoined Nix in the hallway.

"Feel better?" Nix asked with a small sympathetic smile.

"Yeah," I said. But I couldn't make eye contact with him.

He'd seen what my tattoos could do—what the worst one did. It was too much for any elf to handle.

"Can we talk about what happened back there?" Nix asked.

I winced. "No."

"No?"

"No."

As we rounded the corner into the library, Cocoa rushed up to meet us.

"It's Nate," she said. "He's lost consciousness."

* * *

My neck and shoulders ached as I paced around Nate's spacious bedroom. The movement helped work out my stiff muscles and the murkiness in my mind. I had gotten a few hours of sleep, and now Tupac and Chim thrummed silently inside me. Pat was curled up on the bed next to Nate, still sending healing waves into him.

"You're awake," Cocoa said as she entered the room. I jumped and Pat let out a little squawk. "Sorry, did I scare you, Zoe?"

The brownie carried a large tray covered with a rounded lid. The creamy scent of coffee called to me and I sat in a chair next to the bedside table.

"Not really," I said. "I was just thinking of everything that's happened."

Cocoa placed the tray on the bedside table and removed the lid covering the food. My mouth watered at the sight of savory sausages and buttery toast. My stomach let out a growl of anticipation.

I covered my midsection. "Excuse me."

Cocoa giggled. "I guessed you'd be hungry."

As I ate, Cocoa puttered around Nate, adjusting his bedding, pressing her fingers to his throat then over his heart. The brownies' maternal nature never ceased to amaze me. It'd never help in a fight, but their care had certainly helped me heal emotionally from the trauma of my past.

"How's he doing?" I asked.

"He's better. Pat's doing a fine job of restoring him and I think he'll be awake soon."

Cocoa ran her small hand over the back of Pat's head, and the small dragon preened with pleasure. The dragons seldom received this kind of attention from anyone, since I mostly kept them hidden and close to me. Tupac and Chim stirred and I called them forth. Cocoa clapped her hands and gave each dragon their own strokes of affection.

The little creatures deserved it; they were heroes. Last night, they'd worked hard to move debris and free Nate.

"Where's Nix?" I asked, tackling the scrambled eggs, spiced to perfection.

"He's in Nate's study."

"Oh." I focused on my plate, feeling guilty for having slept. I focused on the crumbs of my toast as an attempt to keep the images of the dead bodies out of my mind. Nix must be cleaning up the mess. My mess.

"He said he's looking for something that belonged to his parents."

"Is he an orphan?" I asked.

I thought of all the kids I had known over the years, all the ones who had passed through Nate's home. I couldn't remember a younger version of Nix ever having been there, though, and he didn't seem to be much older than I was. But it was sometimes hard to tell age with elves.

Cocoa tilted her head to the side and nodded. I got the feeling she was puzzled, too, but wasn't saying anything.

I shoveled the last of the eggs into my mouth and sipped from the steaming cup of coffee. Rich. Creamy. Sweet. Caffeinated. Oh, that first sip was heaven.

Cocoa gave each dragon a final stroke of affection and gathered up my tray. "I should get back to the kitchen. Nate will need to eat, too."

I chuckled, watching my dragons as they danced in the air above the brownie's head. "You've made friends for life."

She reached up a free hand and allowed the dragons to nuzzle it. "They're sweet." She turned her attention to me. "Do you need anything further?"

"No. But thank you for the meal. It was perfect." I paused, feeling a bit embarrassed. "Did Nix eat?"

"Of course. He was in the kitchen earlier this morning."

I nearly choked on my coffee. "You let him into the kitchen?"

Cocoa shrugged like it was nothing, then strolled from the room.

Pat resumed her perch next to Nate, Chim lounged on my knee, and Tupac sat on the edge of the bed. They were all looking at me expectantly. I sensed their worry. Since yesterday, they'd been staying extra close and vigilant about their protections around the demon tattoo.

I'm fine, but don't go far, I told them. *I can't stretch myself like I did yesterday.*

They nodded their understanding.

The guards and the release of the demon last night still plagued my thoughts, and I doubted the incidents would leave me anytime soon. I had allowed the unthinkable to happen and now two elves were dead. I shuddered at the memory.

The bedsheets rustled, pulling me from my musings as Nate rolled to his side. He was watching me.

"You're awake," I said, a bit surprised. The tension I'd been holding in my shoulders drained away.

Nate looked tired, but his coloring was a little better. "Pat's done a fine job of helping restore this old elf. My leg barely hurts." He shifted beneath the covers to prove it.

"That's good to hear," I said. "Cocoa just left to get you something to eat. Are you hungry?"

I put my coffee down on the bedside table and leaned forward to grab his hand. This elf was so very much a father to me.

"I'll take whatever Cocoa brings," he said, studying my face. There was concern in his eyes and I lowered my head under his scrutiny. "What happened?"

I lay my head on his bed as he placed his hand on my cheek. I closed my eyes, thankful Chim blocked the images being sent by the demon.

Nate's voice was soft was he spoke. "The demon got out."

I winced. How had he guessed?

"I was weak, Nate. I should never have let myself get that weak, but the dragons had gone to help after the tree was attacked. It was late, and they were using their energies…"

I poured out the tale of the night before, the whole thing, telling Nix about the dragons, the build-up to the demon breaking through, the damage it had done, the lives it had taken. That was the hardest bit, but I forced the words out of my soul.

I had to tell Nate everything. He understood me. He'd know what to do.

As I finished my tale, I became very aware of the silence in the room and the gentle stoke of Nate's hand on my head.

I turned to face him, not sure how I felt inside. But it had helped to talk about what had happened.

I wanted him to speak, to say something, to tell me everything would be okay. I so desperately wanted my life to return to normal, but I doubted I'd ever feel that way again. My parents—and the demon—had stolen so much from me.

As my fists tightened with anger, the demon laughed. The sound echoed in my head, mocking me.

"I'm sorry this happened," Nate finally said. "Do you remember the plant I gave you?"

"Yes. You said something about thorns and weeds growing together."

I once again considered the lesson. He hadn't made his point clear.

"Right. Zoe, the weeds and thorns grow in good soil. It doesn't make a difference. However, the thorns are a part of the plant while the weeds come from other sources."

I nodded, still not understanding.

"Your anger, where does it come from?"

"My parents and what they did to me."

My magic had never felt right after I'd received the demon tattoo. I hadn't been the same since then.

I thought back to the painting of the dove Vaim Na'quab in Nate's office, the one with golden-tipped feathers. The image sparked in me a longing to find peace and relief from the demon tattoo. Was it even possible to be completely free of that tattoo like Nate has suggested? And experience the peace of Vaim Na'quab?

"What they did was terrible," Nate told me. "No child should

151

ever have to go through that. But you did and it can't be undone."

My anger flared at the memories, which were still fresh after so many years.

"So what are you going to do about it?" Nate asked.

I opened my mouth to speak but no words came out. I moved my lips and finally said, "I… don't know. I can't do anything."

"You can. Those are the thorns." Nate rolled onto his back. "Help an old elf sit up. I think Cocoa will be here soon with my breakfast."

I pushed my confused thoughts aside and adjusted the pillows as Nate directed me. He winced when he shifted his leg. Pat chittered and squawked, sending me images of the healing still needed in Nate's leg.

"It isn't quite healed yet," I cautioned. "Pat says that the bone is set, but the tissues will need time to repair."

"That's good. On the mend. Can you put a pillow behind me?"

I bent forward and placed the soft, thick pillow behind Nate's back.

He leaned against it. "Ah, that feels good."

Now that he was in a seated position, my tongue burned to ask for more clarity. "Nate, what are you trying to tell me about the weeds and thorns?"

"You'll have to understand this lesson on your own," he said. I grimaced in response, playing with the hem of my shirt. "You struggle with this because it is tied to your fears. The horrors you went through have made you want to control things. Those are the thorns, the problems you need to deal with. And your demon tattoo will remain as long as you refuse to deal with the thorns."

The dragons perked up their heads and shot out of the room, pulling my attention from Nate. Cocoa's delighted giggle wafted back into the room and through our shared magic, I sensed the dragons swarming her.

"Go talk to Nix," Nate said as Cocoa entered with a fresh platter. "You two need each other, and he has his own story to share."

I left Pat behind to continue her healing work but called Chim and Tupac to join me again. I felt their reluctance to leave Cocoa as they merged back into my skin.

Feeling their energy pulse through me, I went in search of Nix.

Twilight's Curse

Chapter Fourteen

Nix

My fingers caressed the spines of the books on Nate's shelves. I'd been in here all morning, knowing that Nate had stored my father's signet ring, crown, and seal somewhere. So far my search had come up empty, except for one locked drawer in Nate's desk. I would have to wait until he woke up to sift through its contents.

Or I could just ask where he kept the royal symbols.

I rubbed my tired eyes. I'd managed a few hours of sleep, but I was restless. I couldn't shake this urgency over finding the royal symbols. The night my parents had been murdered, Nate had brought me to this room and said he'd keep the symbols safe until I was ready to be king.

Was I just being paranoid about Nate's home having been broken into? I sighed and settled into Nate's desk chair, resting my eyes.

"Tired?"

My eyes popped open at the sound of Zoe's voice. "You're up."

It was a weak greeting, but I didn't know what else to say. Her long hair cascaded around her face, her eyes captivating me. For a moment, the woman who visited my dream blended with Zoe before me, reminding me that her dream-self had promised to help me.

As she approached and sat down, I noticed that there was something different about her. Her edginess was gone and she seemed almost vulnerable.

"How's Nate?" I asked.

Zoe shrugged. "Better. He's awake and eating. Pat says the break in his leg is healed but will need time to fully repair."

She fiddled with her shirt and then it hit me: she was nervous, not as strictly composed as she usually was.

"And you?"

Zoe didn't answer right away. She let her eyes wander around Nate's office. I followed her gaze, wondering what she was looking at.

"Okay," she finally said.

She didn't seem forthcoming about what had happened last night, even though it had to be bothering her.

I grabbed a stylus off the desktop and began twirling it across my knuckles in an attempt to distract myself. I thought of last night and the change that had come over her. It had been like a beast coming alive... she hadn't been herself in that moment. After she'd slaughtered the guards, she had smiled triumphantly, then the dragons had landed on her, causing her to pass out.

And when she'd come to, she was Zoe again. I studied her, fascinated by the enigma she represented.

Chapter Fourteen

Nate had told me to be honest with her. Was this the right time to tell her who I really was? I had been about to do it yesterday, but Cocoa had interrupted. I opened my mouth to speak—

"My parents," Zoe said, cutting me off before I could begin. "Well, I told you they experimented on me."

Her voice was barely above a whisper and she rubbed her chest, her gaze focused on her lap. Her free hand trembled as her thumb ran over the dagger tattoo etched on the opposite forearm.

Zoe seemed so open in this moment. So innocent. When her brow furrowed, there was a slight shake to the way she took a breath. I was humbled by the struggle I saw in her. Here I was, the rightful king of the Twilight Realm, yet afraid to fight for my right to the throne or even admit who I really was.

I looked away, unable to hold her gaze. Her courage shamed me.

"With each new pattern my mother traced on my skin, the ink burned," she continued. "She had such hopes for my magic. They both did. They wanted to manipulate my magic and use it to solidify their control of the Twilight Realm. And they… killed the former king and queen."

My heart stumbled in my chest. It ripped me to shreds to be reminded of what had happened to my parents, but I forced myself to listen. She needed to tell her story, and as her king—no, as her friend—I had to listen.

"Something about my magic resisted my parents' wishes. My magic never bent to their will, and in retrospect I think it's because I was in control. The first time they inked a dragon on me, it was Pat. It took three days and the pain…" Zoe shuddered. "They didn't stop, so I begged for the pain to go away. That's when Pat became a healing dragon. The tattoos didn't hurt as badly after that. Nate thinks my living magic responds to my wishes and needs."

Zoe shook her head. Her eyes seemed so empty and lost as she spoke of the little girl being tortured by her parents.

"Do you believe that?" I asked, not wanting to break the moment or her willingness to tell her story.

"I don't know. If I choose to let go of what my parents did to me, isn't that like accepting that it was okay?" Zoe shuddered. "Somehow I can't quite imagine sitting down to dinner with them like none of this had ever happened… no, dinner will *never* happen."

How often had I wondered the same thing? If my parents had been powerful, why hadn't they done something? And if I let myself believe that there was wisdom in their actions—wisdom I'd never understand—then wasn't that like accepting their weakness? How could they have let themselves be so mercilessly executed?

"My parents, seeing that they couldn't control my magic and noticing how well I handled the pain, decided to try something new," Zoe went on. "They resorted to dark magic and etched a new tattoo into my skin."

Her hand went to her chest and she paused a long time. Her face contorted from the struggle of telling this part of the story.

"Does this have something to do with what happened earlier? With the guards?" I asked keeping my voice soft and words free of accusation.

"It's a demon. They etched a demon into me, a demon controlled by dark magic. My dragons help keep him caged, but yesterday I became too weak to resist and the demon broke free."

I closed my eyes, remembering the moment when her whole face and body had changed, remembering the fierceness in her attack, the vicious way she had struck the guards. It hadn't been her. Zoe could be cold at times, strong and abrasive, but this was something different.

I didn't know how to comfort her.

What I did know was that she wasn't cruel. In fact, she was tremendously compassionate. I saw it in the way she had tried to protect me at the Misty Inn, the way she had spoken of the children, and in how she treated Nate, Cocoa, and her dragons.

"Have you ever considered that your abilities are not a curse?"

I could tell by the way she swayed that my words had an impact on her.

She closed her eyes as tension released from her posture. "Why do you think I consider my abilities to be a curse?"

"You love your dragons and have clearly learned to use your abilities to your advantage," I said, "but you also cover them up and don't want anyone to know about them."

"Nate has always believed in me, and sometimes I've considered him a fool."

I inhaled slowly, carefully considering my response. I didn't think she truly grasped how unique and special she was. "Zoe, I think your gifts are amazing."

She took a long, slow breath. "I'm not sure I'm brave enough to accept that. Nate says all my tattoos are good, save for the demon tattoo. Maybe he's right. They're like tools that help me in my everyday life, to survive and help others. But—"

I saw so much of myself in her. So much of what I wasn't. She had every reason to deny who she was, but I didn't. Who was I protecting by staying hidden? Why didn't I try to take back my kingdom? Why did I let my citizens remain under the tyranny of Lord Leski and Lady Sirina? Why did I allow them to continue their cruelty to children?

My sister. What had they done to her in all these years? That thought punched me in the gut.

Talking to Zoe, learning her story, was exposing my own layers, ripping away the carefully constructed wall of safety I had built up. I felt disgusted with myself and wondered if this was why Nate had wanted Zoe and me to work together.

"Zoe, I can't even begin to understand what you've been through, but I'm glad you told me."

She was quiet for a long time. "Thanks."

I once again thought of the locked drawer in Nate's desk. It was time for me to come clean with Zoe, but first I needed to find the signet ring, crown, and seal.

"Do you know where Nate keeps the key to the bottom drawer of his desk?"

"Why?"

My heart raced in anticipation of my coming confession. "Uh… it's time to tell you the truth about me. But first I need something that I think might be in that drawer. Something that belonged to my parents."

Zoe rose from her chair without a sound and rounded the desk. She bent low and placed her left forefinger against the keyhole. I saw the pin-shaped tattoo on her finger move and assumed it slid into the lock as I heard a distinct click.

"There you go," Zoe said, stepping back.

I stared at her with fresh awe. The smile she gave me lit up the room and I momentarily forgot about my search.

Pulling out the drawer, I looked inside and found a locked box with the royal seal on it. My hands trembled. This was it. I recognized the box and could feel its royal magic in my blood.

"That's the royal seal," Zoe said, leaning across the desk.

"Yes, I'm the crown prince. Phoenix."

Zoe's green eyes grew a few sizes and all the color drained from her face. "Nix... Phoenix." She gasped and stumbled back into her chair. "I'm so sorry. My parents... your parents..."

"It's okay, Zoe. You aren't responsible. I saw Lord Leski kill my parents. I was hiding in the woods near the Royal Tree at the time. Nate rescued me when Leski attacked my home, and he hid me for years."

"Is Nate a member of your family?"

I chuckled at the thought. "Not by blood. He was my father's royal advisor."

"So why haven't you claimed your title?" Her voice held genuine curiosity, but the inquiry stabbed at me.

"I'm a coward. That's why." I spat the words out, pounding my fist on the desk.

"I'm sorry, I was only curious," she said. "I didn't realize it'd upset you."

Zoe lowered her face to avoid making eye contact. At least that was how I interpreted her behavior.

But then Chim wiggled out from the collar of her shirt and leaped toward me, nuzzling my hand. I placed my palm over the small creature and it curled up. A zing of magical energy raced up my arm and dispersed throughout me.

Shocked, I glanced at Zoe. "Is this its magic?"

"*His* magic. Or ours, since he comes from me."

My emotions calmed almost instantly and an easy smile came to my lips. I scooped up the dragon and sat back, my hand brushing the box with the royal items inside. I couldn't believe how good the dragon made me feel.

But as soon as this occurred to me, I regretted it. I held Chim out to Zoe. "I'm sorry. I don't want to exhaust you."

Zoe waved me off and gave me a relaxed smile. "This won't drain me. It energizes me when the dragons use their gifts in this way. Yesterday I was tired and the dragons were scattered around the tree, using a lot of energy. It's the multitasking and extended distance that drained me. But when they're healing or offering comfort, it's like I get the overflow of it."

I shrugged and settled back, letting the small dragon cuddle against my chest like a kitten. I thought of what I'd shared with Zoe so far. For us to work together, Nate had said I needed to be honest. I sighed, feeling the weight of my title and past.

"I was only thirteen when I saw my parents die. And although Nate has done his best to raise me to my station as king, I feel inadequate. He says we—you and I—are to work together, and I had this dream about you."

Zoe's head shot up. "What?"

"It's weird, I know, and I don't want that to sound overly presumptuous." I sighed and rubbed my face. "Sometimes I have nightmares. I see my parents' death, but the last time I had this dream was a few days ago and you appeared and told me you'd help me." I shook my head. "And when I saw you at the fortress…"

"That's why you tried to keep me hidden?"

"Sort of. At the time I didn't know how well you could fight or what you were doing there. I have a protective instinct. I don't like to see anyone hurt."

"That makes sense. Seeing your parents killed left a scar on your soul," she said. "But if you were the crown prince and are now king of the Twilight Realm, you'll have to let your citizens die for you. Unfortunately, this goes with the station."

Her words had a more profound effect on me than I let her see. It felt like she'd dumped a bucket of ice water on me. Refreshing. Awakening. Jolting.

Chim thrummed and more of his comforting energy pulsed into me. I stroked the dragon.

Zoe was right. For a good cause, the citizens of our realm would need to die for their king. But I didn't want even one more child to grow up without a parent… and I didn't want to be the cause of it.

I sighed. "It does go with the station. My parents died for me." I hated being so vulnerable, especially in front of Zoe. I should be strong and kingly—yet here I was, no better than a child. "But you don't understand. I saw my parents die. They died for me."

Zoe was quiet. I wanted her to say something, to respond, and at the same time I hoped she'd say nothing so this moment could pass us by and we could forget about it.

Zoe cleared her throat. "Your parents died for you and for the crown. My parents tortured me and killed your parents for their own purposes. I take it there was some reason you wanted to get into the fortress, or you wouldn't have been skulking around it."

"Skulking?" I raised an eyebrow.

"Calling it like I see it."

A chuckle bubbled out of me. "Thank you."

I placed the box with the royal seal on Nate's desk. Meanwhile, Chim moved to my lap and stared at the small case. He let out a squawk, then sniffed it.

"Do you think you can use your fancy key to open this up?" I asked.

Zoe raised the finger with her pin tattoo and wiggled it at me. "Sure."

She placed her finger in front of the lock and pointed. Fascinated, I watched the same process play out. The lid of the box emitted a quiet pop. I grabbed her free hand, wanting her full attention.

"You know, you're so much more than your tattoos," I murmured. "Own them. You're so gifted and talented. You could do just about anything." I was rewarded with a confused smile. "You're a fighter, a healer, a counselor, a protector... You could just as easily be a thief or an assassin, but there is so much good in you. I know you'd never turn to that."

Her cheeks reddened and she turned away until the heat died down, then she slipped her hand from mine. I didn't feel bad for causing her some embarrassment. I had a feeling no one, or at least very few, had ever told her she had value. She needed to hear it.

Focusing on the box, I lifted the lid. My breath caught in my throat as I pulled out the signet ring and slid it onto my finger. The last time I'd worn it, it had hung loosely and I'd spun it around my finger, but today it fit. I flexed my fingers and admired the ring and accompanying royal seal.

The next item in the box was the crown, crafted from gold.

"The crown, a very simple circle that rests on the head of the reigning monarch," I said, picking it up. It weighed very little. "This has been passed down in my family since the start of time by the first royal elf, Paz Mier and his consort, Nazira, when they established the five realms through their children. My father always told me that the crown is more than the physical object." I held up the circlet. "This is a symbol of the monarch's responsibility. The crown is the elf who leads the people."

"I bet that responsibility feels pretty heavy right about now."

I sighed and placed the crown back in the box.

"Aren't you going to put it on?" Zoe asked.

"A king doesn't crown himself. That's the job of the royal advisor. When Nate places this on my head in a coronation ceremony, I will officially become king. The royal power that was my father's will transfer to me."

"What'll you do until then?"

I put the signet ring back in the box. My hand felt suddenly bare without it.

When I closed the lid, I heard the lock click. I'd have to ask Nate for the key.

"I meant with the box," Zoe said, prompting me for answer.

"The box is mine. As is this." I pointed to *Ascension*, which was lying atop Nate's desk. "He's kept these items all this time, waiting for me to be ready. But I think they need to stay with me now."

I stood, causing Chim to flutter from my lap and settle on Zoe's shoulder. I picked up the box and the book.

"Let's check on Nate," I said.

Chapter Fifteen

Zoe

When Nix and I entered Nate's room, he was sleeping and there weren't any brownies around.

Pat, how is Nate doing? I asked.

The healing dragon, who had been napping on Nate's chest, immediately responded with images of a set bone and tissues, veins, and vessels that were restored but still bruised and tender. The other dragons, feeling restless, joined Pat on the bed. Tupac and Chim curled up on either side of the royal advisor.

Royal advisor. He was someone very important. The thought gave me the shivers. I'd always thought of him as a kind old elf who was a bit of a hermit. I chuckled internally. The old elf had his secrets as well.

My thoughts returned to Nix and his identity. There was no way an elf would make up a story like that. But it was so weird to think of him as the crown prince of the Twilight Realm. As he'd held the signet ring and crown, I had been able to sense his royal bearing, perhaps even the hint of royal magic—a desire to follow. It was unique to the bloodline and drew the citizens to follow their leaders. My parents had mentioned it numerous times while I was growing up and I'd always had a feeling they were trying to recreate something similar.

A thought turned my blood cold. My magic interacted with plants and made them responsive to me. My parents had known that much. They just never realized that my magic had given life to my tattoos; that I'd kept a secret. But what if my parents were really searching for a way to use my magic to control the citizens. They controlled their regent guards. I slid into a chair next to Nate's bed as my knees grew weak. My parents already had control of the Twilight Realm and their guards. Why did they want control of the citizens? My thoughts began to swirl and my heartbeat sped up. Pat sent a calming wave toward me and I decided to save these thoughts for another time.

I glanced at Nix as he sat in a chair Cocoa had used earlier. He was the crown prince.

And I was the daughter of his family's usurpers.

No! I'd long ago stopped seeing myself as Leski and Sirina's daughter. But whenever I thought of it, my stomach rolled.

"What's the verdict?" Nix asked bringing me out of my chilling thoughts.

"Pat says Nate is resting well and should be fully restored within the hour."

"Right. Then we should discuss strategies. You mentioned that a friend told you we need to go to the fortress today."

I thought of Maximon and found that the change in subject a good distraction. "Yes. It has something to do with my parents. They've found a way to subdue the populace."

Nix took a sharp intake of breath.

"Maximon said we could stop them," I added. "But that's all I know. He asked me to bring friends, but my real concern is the kids."

Nix was quiet for a few moments, his fingers steepled in front of him. "You don't trust Maximon, do you?"

"We were friends in the loosest sense of the word. We played together as children, but I don't know what my parents did to him. I never fully trusted him in the fortress. And I don't know how much I trust him now. But he is a way inside."

Had it been stupid to talk with Maximon? Would Nix and I be walking into a trap? Had my parents somehow turned him? I closed my eyes at the onslaught of questions.

"Well, he's a guard now," Nix mused. "Leski and Sirina use dark magic to maintain their hold over their guards."

I didn't like what he said. I didn't trust Maximon, but to think of what my parents did to elves... I didn't wish that for anyone and couldn't think of Maximon becoming one of their minions. Though this did give credit to my earlier thoughts about my parents working toward controlling the elven populace. But why?

Nix leaned forward in his chair. "I'm sorry. I know Maximon is important to you."

"No, it's okay. I don't want to think of him being controlled by my parents, but you're right to question his motives. My parents would stop at nothing to get me back."

"We can get into the fortress, of course, but I have a feeling that won't be the hard part," Nix said. He was fiddling with the book on his lap, running his hands over the cover.

Little did he know how hard stepping into the fortress

would be for me. For years I had tried to re-enter that place to rescue others, but I'd never been able to. The fear always took me.

My dragons, ever sensitive to my emotions, raised their heads to look at me. Courage emanated from Tupac, dissipating my fears.

"What do you think the hardest part is then?" I asked.

"Once inside, we'll be incredibly vulnerable. The hard part will be rescuing the children, stopping your parents, and getting out again."

"True."

Nix fidgeted in his seat, and it seemed clear to me that he wanted to say something else.

"There's more, isn't there?"

Nix nodded. "My sister, Zyanna, is inside."

I closed my eyes, thinking back to all my years at the fortress. I had never seen or heard my parents speak of the princess.

"Are you sure? Although my parents treated me like a lab rat, I was still their daughter and had the relative freedom to wander the fortress. Maximon and I explored every inch of it. If your sister was there, I never saw her. Maybe they recently found her and brought her to the fortress."

Nix's face looked like it lost a bit of color. "How or when doesn't matter to me. If she is there, I have to save her. The regents have announced that she's going to marry Dimas."

"My brother? My parents wouldn't dare." I straightened in my seat. "What could they possibly gain by doing this?"

"Me. They've been trying to draw me out since that night long ago. They called out to me, telling me I could prevent the slaughter of my parents."

I shut my eyes, imagining what that must have been like for

thirteen-year-old Nix.

My chest tightened. "I'm so sorry. That must have been horrible for you."

"My parents gave themselves for me. It's why I've stayed hidden for so long. I didn't want to spoil their sacrifice, but I fear it's turned me into a coward."

"You are not a coward," I insisted. "But you also can't do this alone. It took a lot of courage to tell me what you did today. Even *thinking* about going against my parents takes courage."

I hesitated, afraid to say the next part. He had referred to members of my family by their names, refraining from associating them with me. This emboldened me a little.

"Nix, you are the bravest elf I know," I finally said. "As your subject, I will follow you into battle—to free the children, stop my parents, and save your sister, if she truly is held by Leski and Sirina."

It felt good for me to refer to them by their names as well. It created some distance. They had never behaved like real parents anyway, and my brother hadn't been a brother. Dimas used his mimicry to manipulate and deceive and had been easily controlled by my parents. He was too weak mentally. And I knew he had suffered abuse due to my father's efforts to toughen him up. Was there anything left of Dimas?

"Thank you," Nix said.

I bowed my head. It wasn't meant to be a respectful gesture, I just couldn't hold his gaze any longer. How could I so easily give allegiance to Nix? Was this part of the royal magic?

"What you two need is an army," a voice from the bed said.

I looked and saw that Nate had sat up a bit.

"How're you feeling?" Nix asked.

I leaned forward to squeeze his hand. "It's good that you're awake. Pat says you're almost healed."

"I'm feeling good and ready to serve my king as I was meant to," Nate said. Nix started to protest, but Nate waved him into silence. "What you don't know is that many in the realm are still loyal to the throne. They've been waiting for the crown prince to step forward."

As Nate sat up fully, I helped rearrange his pillows. Once he had shifted into a more comfortable position, he began stroking Pat's back.

"What loyalists are you talking about?" Nix asked.

"The former royal soldiers. The centaurs, dwarves, and other such creatures."

"Centaurs and dwarves. But I thought they'd fled the realm when the Dions took over." Nix's eyes bulged. I knew how he felt and had believed the creatures had been part of myth and legend like Paz Mier, Nazira, and Vaim Na'quab.

"They are crafty and skilled in their magic. And they've been able to find me when needed."

"And do they… swear allegiance to the crown?" I asked, curious since they'd never been mentioned in my sheltered upbringing.

Nate raised a hand and twirled it. "It is a peaceful alliance or co-existence. They do live in our realm, in all the realms, and have their own forms of government, but they've never been subject to the elves."

Nix snapped his fingers like he was suddenly remembering something. "Right. My father always said that, that no one owns land. We live in harmony with it and co-exist with all creation peacefully. It's why elves live in trees, or should live in trees."

Nate nodded. "I'm glad you've remembered. I was beginning to think I'd have to re-teach you interspecies politics. But that's not what you should be focusing on, my prince."

Nix's brow furrowed. "It's not?"

"No. The real question is, are you ready to become king?"

I watched as Nix digested that statement as though he'd swallowed an apple whole.

"I… I don't know that I'm ready." Nix glanced at me and I nodded at him in encouragement. "But it is my station and I've been avoiding the responsibility for years. Many have suffered." When he straightened, I once again perceived that royal bearing in him. "I am not ready. I don't think I ever will be, but I'm no longer comfortable with the way I've been living in relative safety while others suffer… others who I should be protecting."

"Well spoken, my prince," Nate said.

"Yes, Prince Phoenix, your subjects stand with you," I said, feeling truly inspired by his words.

Nix sighed. "Oh please. To you, Zoe, I will always be Nix. I need friends to keep me grounded."

I dipped my head—again, not out of reverence but to keep him from seeing how his words affected me.

Was it possible we were friends? Yes. I wasn't sure when it had happened. Maybe at the Misty Inn when I'd sat with him to protect him from the guards. Or when I'd seen him at the doorway in Nate's office. Or was it when he tried to protect me at the fortress? *My first true and real friend!* Warmth flushed through me. Nate, Dasha, Cocoa and the brownies, and the children were family, but Nix, he was my friend.

My mind shifted to the even greater questions that Nate kept bringing forward with the thorns and weeds. Was it possible to forgive my parents? And would it affect my magic?

I thought back to the night I'd woken up after receiving the demon tattoo and how a part of me had always felt separated, fractured from the rest of me. Would letting go really take away the demon tattoo… and would it take away my other tattoos as well? I would hate to lose my dragons. I'd have to ask Nate more about this.

Nate clapped his hand jolting me out of my thoughts. "Perfect. Now, if you two will excuse me, I need to get dressed and begin summoning your loyal subjects."

"Is there anything we should do?" I asked.

"You will remain with the prince and take him to the Royal Tree. In the meantime, I'll have the brownies return there to prepare it for the prince's coronation."

"Wait. My… what?" Nix's jaw dropped, and in that moment he looked anything but a king.

"Your subjects need their king, and once crowned it'll be much easier for you to overpower the usurpers," Nate said. "Being king and accessing the magic that comes with the privilege will give you the strength and protection you need."

Nix wrapped his hands around the book, *Ascension*, and the box on his lap. "But—"

"I see you've found the royal symbols." Nate nodded. "I did some digging into old manuscripts, and I believe they should open the book."

Nix was silent for a moment as he digested this information. "I suppose I just… I thought there'd be more time. I thought——"

"You thought the perfect time would be a time of peace and safety so no one would get hurt?" I said.

Nix's eyes shot in my direction and Nate beamed.

"You've grown wise," Nate told me, patting my hand. "You

two will work well together."

"I don't want anyone to die for me," Nix added.

"As the monarch, you will have to accept this." Nate turned to me. "Zoe, have you figured out the meaning of what I told you... about the weeds and thorns?"

I scowled. "No, not really."

Nate sighed. "A shame. It's a simple lesson. Well, no worry, you'll figure it out soon enough."

The royal advisor turned and stared straight ahead. I followed his gaze to the wall, but there was nothing there.

"What lesson are you talking about?" Nix asked.

"Nate gave me a plant and told me that weeds and thorns grow together," I explained, trying not to roll my eyes. "Apparently you can't do anything about the thorns, but you can about the weeds."

Nate chuckled. "I said more than that."

I narrowed my gaze. "Barely."

Nix looked as confused as I did. That at least gave me some comfort.

"Well, you'll figure it out," Nate said for the second time. "Now, out of my room, the two of you. There's no time to waste." He threw the covers aside, forcing my dragons to crawl off the bed and return to me.

Nix and I took our cue and left.

Once we were on the other side of the door, Nix ran a hand through his hair, leaving it completely disheveled. He blew out a stream of air and gave a relaxed smile.

He'd entered Nate's room as Nix and left it as the crown prince who would be king in a few hours. It was a lot to take in.

"That was... unexpected," he said.

I chuckled and Nix joined me.

"I'll bet. You just went from being an average citizen to… well, it's safe to say your whole life's about to change."

Nix turned toward me and folded his arms across his chest.

"I feel good, actually, and kind of excited. I've been avoiding thinking about being crowned king, running from thoughts of it, resisting it since I saw my parents killed. But now… when Nate asked if I was ready to be king… you summed it up perfectly. I've been waiting for a right time, a perfect time to take my station as king. And now that the decision has been made, it feels surreal but right, like a burden has lifted."

"I'm happy for you." And I meant it, but a part of me felt just a little bit irritated due to my own puzzle to solve, or perhaps resolve was more accurate. "Do you think if I really forgave my parents, my demon tattoo would be taken care of?"

"I don't know. If Nate believes it, I'm sure it's true."

"But what of my other tattoos? I would hate to lose them."

"That's a tough one and I don't have an answer. I don't think anyone could answer with any certainty. There's never been another elf like you."

I turned from him, not particularly satisfied with what he'd said. But at least it was honest.

As we walked down the hall, I thought again of Nate's lesson about weeds and thorns. What did it mean?

Chapter Sixteen

Nix

Zoe and I left Nate's tree and walked through the forest. As we went, I wondered what Nate meant about rounding up loyal citizens. How would he do it? It seemed an impossible task, but Nate had his ways.

"So where's the Royal Tree?" Zoe asked.

"You've never been there?" Her comment struck me as a bit odd since it was one of the oldest inhabited trees in the Twilight Realm. The Royal Tree's location was common knowledge.

Zoe shrugged. "My parents brought me to the Twilight Realm when I was four. Raised in a fortress for eight years and then I've always stayed close to Nate's. I didn't want to run into any of my parents' guards."

My heart warmed at her admission. Not at what she experienced but that she told me this part of her life willingly and because I'd get to show her the Royal Tree. "Then it'll be my pleasure to show you."

I relaxed. It felt good to have her with me. I didn't know what the day would hold, especially if the coronation happened quickly, but I had hope when we were together. I didn't know what it was about her. Perhaps it had something to do with her life-giving magic. I liked having her with me and whether it had something to do with her magic or just her, it didn't really matter.

I stopped myself from reaching out and squeezing her hand. Would she accept the gesture or threaten to cut off my arm? I hid my smile at that image. I hoped one day she'd let me hold her hand. This thought seemed so natural and perhaps I should have been surprised as I'd never considered this with another elf, but instead I only found myself looking forward to the moment it would happen.

"I want to stop by my tree," I said, adjusting the satchel thrown over my shoulder. It held *Ascension* as well as the royal symbols. "There's something I need to pick up."

"May I ask what it is?"

"It's a pendant."

She didn't respond, just gave a quick nod.

When we got to my tree, we went inside and stopped in the middle of the living room.

"You can wait here," I said. "It'll just take me a moment."

Zoe crossed her arms and began a slow circle around the room.

I ran up the stairs to my bedroom and grabbed the pendant from my bedpost. I looped it over my head, ran my thumb over the tree engraved on the surface, and then tucked it under my shirt. The pendant itself wouldn't help me gain access to the Royal Tree, but wearing it felt right.

When I got back to the living room, Zoe was standing next to my desk with a book in her hand. It was one of the books that Nate had given me.

I shook my head. Had it only been yesterday that I'd met Zoe? It felt like at least a week.

Zoe's head jerked up as I entered and she snapped the book shut. "This is about your family line."

"Yes."

Her gaze ran over me as if looking for the pendant.

"This book says the royal family has a kind of magic that helps them govern," she said.

I shrugged. "The magic gives us favor and because of it, the kingdom had enjoyed relative peace for thousands of years. This is common knowledge among elfkind."

"Need I remind you again of my upbringing?" Her tone was soft and calm.

"Nope. Did your parents not teach you about this or at least send you to school?"

A huff of air left her. "No. I was never allowed to leave the fortress and the education I did receive... well I can read and write and do math, oh and of course science since that's my mother's specialty, but the history of the royals? My parents had no interest in expanding my knowledge on that subject. They did talk about the royal magic, but not like this." She waved the book at me. "They made it sound like the royal family controlled elves with their magic."

"Then it's a good thing we're friends. We can clear up any of your misunderstandings."

I rested my hand on the book, acting as though I was going to take it from her, and chanced letting my fingers brush against hers. It was an innocent gesture, but it would let me know if she would allow it. She looked down and frowned but didn't yank her hand away. Maybe there was potential for more—one day.

"Are you aware that this magic will transfer to you once you're coronated?" she continued.

"Where'd you read that?" I think I'd read something about magic being involved in the coronation. Royal magic, like all eleven magic, was innate, but maybe there was more to it.

Zoe hefted the book, flipping through the pages to a spot about a third of the way in. "I was scanning through while I waited for you. Here."

She passed the book over and I read the section she'd pointed out. I became very aware of how close she was. I had to step away to help me focus.

"It describes the coronation ceremony and the royal advisor's role," I murmured while reading the passage. "It says that when the crown is placed on a new monarch's head, a transference of power comes upon said monarch and expands over the whole kingdom."

I swallowed against a lump in my throat, again reminded of how little I knew about what was expected of me. I'd probably read this a dozen times over the years; skimmed was probably more accurate. I had always taken the royal magic for granted. But this wasn't a game; it was my *life*… and the lives of all the citizens of the Twilight Realm.

"Thanks for showing me this," I said, closing the book and placing it back on the desk. The new information, while adding to the weight I was already feeling about my coronation, also gave me added determination to take up my rightful position.

"Thought you should know." Zoe hesitated. "Did you get

what you needed?"

My hand went to my chest and felt the pendant beneath my shirt. "Yes. We should get going."

Judging by the rays of the sun, it was already mid-morning. That would hopefully give us time to figure out how to enter the Royal Tree. I patted the satchel over my shoulder, certain the royal symbols and *Ascension* would help me.

I led Zoe to an older part of the forest where a stream flowed next to the path we had taken. It was the same stream that had comforted and given me strength on the night my parents had been killed. I stopped, listening to the water.

Zoe tilted her head. "It sounds almost happy. Is that normal?"

"Yeah. It's called the Rivers of Laughter, and the myth is that if you follow it, it'll lead you straight to the Day Realm elves. The water sounds happy because it reflects the joyful heart of the Day Realm elves." I shrugged when Zoe raised a skeptical eyebrow. "It's what my parents told me."

"Riiiight." She elongated the word. "Did you say *rivers*? I only see one."

"According to the history I was told, Paz Mier and Nazira established the five realms with their children as rulers. There's a river in each realm that leads to the Day Realm. Each river has the same name, so *Rivers of Laughter*."

"So is the Day Realm supposed to be the center of power?" Zoe raised her hand. "And before you ask, no, my parents told me nothing about Paz Mier and Nazira either, so no I don't know a lot about them. I've learned a bit from listening in on the odd lessons from the classes the kids take at Nate's tree though the lessons are pretty simplistic and don't go into a lot of detail. Nate's taught me some as well, but I never bothered learning about our founding leaders or the royal family."

"Can I ask why?" I found this odd. Nate would have more than enough information in his library alone to educate anyone on the history of elfkind.

Zoe didn't answer right away. "I suppose learning about Paz Mier and Nazira as well as the royal families made me think about my parents and what they'd done. I couldn't focus as I'd always end up feeling angry at my parents and reshelve the book like it was diseased."

"Well, perhaps you'll have reason to learn now." I winked at her and I was rewarded with a scowl as she turned away.

"We're almost there," I said as we continued walking. "The Day Realm isn't the center of power. Paz Mier and Nazira wanted their children and their descendants to always remember that they were family. The Day Realm is where Paz Mier and Nazira ruled from, and they always wanted their children and descendants to think of it as home."

"Thanks for telling me." Zoe walked steadily beside me. "I've never been to this part of the forest. The trees are so huge here. And dense."

Tendrils of her hair got caught in the twigs of passing branches and she had to pick them free. Despite the canopy of trees towering above us, the sun filtered through and offered a warm glow.

"The Royal Tree is at the center of the Twilight Realm and the oldest part of the forest," I explained. "Just past here."

My steps quickened over the crunch of the leaves as I entered a small clearing. My heart thrummed with anticipation and lightness at arriving at my childhood home. Happy memories came to mind, along with the laughter of my sister Zyanna.

I stopped in front of the Royal Tree. Its trunk was huge and the branches grew long and heavy with fresh growth drooping toward the ground and brushing the earth with their tips. New growth. Perhaps the tree sensed my return and was preparing for its new king. The thought warmed me. I patted the smooth bark. It felt ancient and pulsed strongly with familiar magical energy. I'd sensed this magic in my nightmares whenever I dreamed of the night my parents were killed. Only here, it was more alive, more potent and I felt it reach out to me in recognition gently tugging me closer.

"It's a wonder my parents never tried to take over the Royal Tree," Zoe said, standing next to me.

"It'd be impossible. The royal magic protects it."

"Then how did Leski manage to infiltrate it and kill your parents?"

"That's a mystery we've yet to figure out. Nate has suspicions he's yet to share with me. But only the royal family and the brownies who serve the royal family have access."

Zoe nodded, and I sensed that my comment had stirred some dark thoughts for her.

"Something bothers you."

I touched the sleeve of her shirt. She glanced at my hand but didn't pull away.

"I just thought of Maximon and his eagerness to take down my parents," she said. "Is he my parents' weakest link? Or ours? I confess the idea troubles me. I'm worried that we might be walking into a trap, that I might be leading you into one."

I pulled in a long breath of air. "This is my choice as much as it is yours."

"And if it is a trap?"

I studied Zoe and raised my hand to brush my thumb across her cheek. "We have to try."

Zoe frowned, but she didn't flinch away. She did, however, grip my hand in hers and pull it from her face. "You take too many liberties."

"My apologies." I clasped my hands behind my back and gave her a slight bow.

She scrutinized me for a moment, then turned and released her dragons. As they fluttered about her, I noticed a small upturn of her lips. I exhaled, thankful that she didn't seem too offended by my actions, but I would have to be careful if I wanted to build trust.

She was younger than me, and although I didn't know how young, she had to at least be a child-adult. I sighed. While some child-adult elves married before they reached their one hundredth birthday, it wasn't common. Perhaps when all this was over and the Twilight Realm was re-established under my rule, I could find out where Zoe stood on the subject of relationships, dating and marriage. Marriage seemed like a quick leap since I'd only met her... yesterday, but being with her felt right.

I walked up to the Royal Tree and pressed my hand against it. The magical energy within hummed.

"Is that the doorway?" Zoe asked.

"It should be, but it's not opening. As the crown prince, it should sense me and open automatically. I guess it's been sealed since the attack."

"You mean you haven't been here since?"

"Nate brought me a few times, but we never tried to go inside. It was safer to leave it sealed until it was time for me to become king."

I shifted my stance and felt the satchel bump against my thigh. It was time to dig out the royal symbols. I squatted as I laid the box and book on the ground.

"I'll need your key again," I said.

Zoe sighed. "What would you do without me?"

She knelt to let her pin-key do its work, and a moment later the lid popped open. I pulled out the signet ring, slid it onto my index finger, then returned the other items to the satchel.

Zoe crouched near the entranceway, running her fingers over an etching at the base of the tree. Her hand flinched.

"What's that?" I asked.

"It's like someone carved into the tree."

I peered over Zoe's shoulder as she rested her hand over the marking. "The magic's old and weak."

"Do you think it has anything to do with opening the door?"

"I don't think so. The magic is different from the tree. It feels cool and slippery."

Zoe reached out again to touch the marking. "You said a guard let my parents into the tree?"

"That's the rumor, though it's weak since aside from the brownies who serve in the tree, no guards had the ability to freely enter. Though guards always watched over the tree day and night, so no one inside could have given the Dions entrance. Is the carving suspicious to you?"

"The magic feels familiar. I'll come back later and study it."

"Let me know what you find out. Now to figure out how to get into the tree…"

I placed my hand over the door and felt it shimmer. The tree's magic reached out to me and entwined around my arm like lace. I closed my eyes, concentrating on the flow. It was warm and inviting and I could feel the tree reading me, searching me, embracing me because it recognized my lineage.

Then it welcomed me. With a soft hiss, the door peeled open. The tree had been waiting for me to wear the royal seal; that was what had broken the protective seal.

"You did it!" Zoe said, following me as I entered a large foyer. She looked around with wide-eyed astonishment.

The foyer was massive. In front of us was a sweeping staircase that flowed from the center of the room and branched to the left and right. Other corridors led away from the foyer, and just behind the stairs was a huge set of open doors.

None of this was quite what I remembered. My younger self had never appreciated the beauty of this place. It had just been my home.

It was *still* home, but its meaning was much deeper now.

"Is it familiar?" Zoe whispered.

"Yes, though it seemed bigger in my memories."

"Seriously?"

"I was thirteen when I was last here. Perspective, okay?"

"Good point."

A soft padding of feet sounded from a corridor on the left. "Your Majesty, welcome home."

I spun at the familiar voice. Cocoa stepped forward to greet us.

"Thank you, Cocoa," I said. Seeing her here completed this moment. The brownies were the last to leave the Royal Tree the night my parents were killed and probably had something to do with the seal that had been placed on the tree. They had also been responsible for the upkeep of the tree. Plus Nate had said something about the brownies making the tree ready. It should come as no surprise that Cocoa and her family were already here. Brownies could pop in and out of anywhere they wished. "It's good to be home. Is everything being prepared?"

"Everything should be ready within the hour for your coronation. Would you like to change in your room?" Cocoa asked.

"Yes." I glanced at Zoe, who looked a little uncertain. "Please take care of Zoe. And you can send up the royal advisor, Ignatius Elek, when he arrives."

"Of course, Your Majesty. The Lady Zoe will be well cared for."

Zoe tried to hide her cool discomfort. I wanted to offer her some assurances but held back, remembering her words to me about taking liberties.

"Will you be okay?" I asked instead.

"You've gone from sounding casual and average to suddenly so… formal."

"I'm still Nix to you, and I always will be. But I do need do a few things. Cocoa will stay with you and help you. The Royal Tree is yours to discover."

I swept my arms wide around me, wiggling my eyebrows at her. She rewarded me with a slight wrinkle of her nose.

"Thank you…" Zoe paused, uncertain.

"Nix. With you, it's just Nix."

"Nix." Zoe relaxed and breathed a little easier.

I bounded up the stairs, eager to see my room again. From the top of the stairs, I glanced back to catch Zoe and Cocoa in discussion. Smiling, I patted my satchel and continued on.

There was an odd mixture of joy and discomfort as I gazed at my old room. It had been organized and the bed was made. I appreciated how the brownies had taken care of the Royal Tree in my absence.

Feeling suddenly weighted down, I closed the door behind

me and fell into a chair. Soon I'd be crowned king. It'd be official.

I grabbed *Ascension* from my satchel and rested my hand on the cover. The book began to glow and I felt its magic read me just as the tree had—and when the glow faded, I found that I was able to open the cover. I had a very short amount of time before the coming ceremony. If my father had been alive, he would have trained me for this, but he wasn't and I couldn't dwell on that.

I started to read about the coronation. The text went into great detail about the magical abilities gifted to my lineage. Apparently peace would fill the Twilight Realm when I was installed as the rightful monarch, and my power would lend me favor and persuasion over my subjects. In turn it would be my responsibility to lead with wisdom.

Much of the information was familiar to me, and so I skimmed some passages, deciding to study them later. However, I couldn't answer one piercing question: had my parents and previous monarchs become a bit complacent in the peace of the realm?

A memory came back to me of the days before my parents' murders. Lord Leski, having been exiled to the Night Realm, had asked to return to the kingdom, and my father had chosen to welcome him back. I'd been in the throne room on the day of his return, observing my father in his duties—something he'd required me to do at least once a week. When Leski entered, my father hadn't even brought in any guards.

I also remembered that Leski had smiled—not a pleasant smile, but one of victory. Had Leski been planning his takeover during his time in the Night Realm? Had he known something about the royal magic, something we didn't?

I flipped to another page but was interrupted by a knock at the door. Nate strode in, clapping his hands and smiling.

"The elves are coming," he said. "It's time to prepare, my prince."

I sighed and left the book on a side table. Was I ready for this? No. But it was what I had to do, the reason I had been born. Today I would become king.

Twilight's Curse

Chapter Seventeen

Zoe

I watched Nix happily run up the foyer steps, wondering if it was the excitement about being in the Royal Tree or if there was something else I didn't know about. He seemed to be looking forward to taking up his station. Well... maybe not happy, but he was more at peace with it. A few hours ago, he had struggled with admitting his identity to me. And now? The quick turnaround seemed odd, but perhaps the mere act of telling me had helped him accept what he'd been born into and stripped away the fear that he'd been carrying. Maybe being in his childhood home helped him forget some of the horrors from his past as well. I was sure the emotions would catch up with him again, though, and perhaps under the happy veneer, there were other deeper emotions he was processing.

I shrugged off my wandering thoughts, accepting this logic. My own soul churned with turmoil at the prospect of entering the fortress again after all these years and facing my parents. Would forgiveness release me from my constant battle with the demon tattoo? It was hard to believe this war inside me could really end after having lived with it for so long. Could letting go bring release? Was forgiveness that powerful?

Cocoa cleared her throat. "Excuse me, Lady Zoe..."

I jumped in surprise, and she rested a small hand on my forearm.

"I'm sorry, I didn't mean to disturb you," she said.

"It's all right." I took a deep breath to relax my tense muscles. "And Cocoa, it's just me. There's no need for you to call me *Lady*."

"You are His Majesty's lady. It is indeed proper."

A bark of laughter burst out of me. "I'm not his lady. I think we're just friends."

Are we friends? I wondered. *Maybe. I don't know.* It felt odd, but I'd decided we were. Sometime last night we'd become friends. A warmth crawled up from my belly. I just wasn't used to having friends. That was all.

Cocoa gazed at me with a serene look, and I scrunched my nose in irritation. I'd get nowhere with her. She'd call me Lady Zoe no matter what I said. It was the brownie way.

"Would you like a tour?" Cocoa swept her arms wide.

Having helped Nix enter the Royal Tree, I had nothing else to do until the coronation other than strategize and figure out how to rescue the children. I nodded. A tour would be a pleasant distraction.

Before we could get going, Nate strode into the foyer from a corridor off to the left. "Ah, good. You're here, Zoe. Is the prince upstairs?"

"Yes," Cocoa said. "He's in his rooms preparing."

"Good."

"Nate, how did you get in?" I asked, remembering what Nix had told me about the Royal Tree's protections. No one but the royal family could enter. And the brownies.

"One of the brownies let me in through the kitchen," Nate explained.

"If they could let you in, why didn't they let Nix in?"

Cocoa bounced on her toes. "The tree was sealed, so to unseal it, someone of the royal line needed to do so."

"I get that, but why? Would the brownies not have been able to let him in?"

Cocoa twisted her lips. "It is a bonding process between the tree and Nix." She clamped her mouth shut.

That sort of made sense, but by the way she averted her gaze, I doubted she'd tell me anything further.

Nate cleared his throat. "Now, before I head up to the prince, there's something you need to know, Zoe. A group of elves, former soldiers and guards of King Alistair and Queen Calla, are on their way here. The leader, Commander Adothlin, will speak with you about entering the fortress. Make sure you meet with him after the coronation."

My throat tightened. I didn't often speak with anyone I didn't know. My dragons sent a surge of peace through me, settling my nerves.

"You found them?" I asked.

"Yes, those loyal to the crown have been biding their time, training for this day."

I raised an eyebrow. "And where? How have they gone unnoticed?"

"Where will remain a secret for now. It will be up to Commander Adothlin to reveal that knowledge. But how…

a touch of magic." Nate winked at me. "Now if you'll excuse me, I need to attend to the prince and you can find a suitable meeting location with the commander."

I didn't really like his answer but accepted it. Those loyal to the monarchy had to stay unnoticed from my parents. "Of course. Cocoa was just about to give me a tour."

"Good then." Nate patted my shoulder, then ran upstairs, taking the steps two at a time.

I turned to Cocoa. "It seems we'll need a meeting space to talk with this Commander Adothlin."

"Perhaps the library would suit your needs?" Cocoa said.

I nodded. "That should work."

"Right this way."

The spacious library housed floor-to-ceiling shelves filled with books. The first floor had a seating area with clusters of plush furniture. The walls stretched up for what might be two additional levels, though there was no ceiling separating the various levels. There were just stairs winding up along the walls and walkways that circled the circumference of the room to access the books on the higher levels.

"Will this meet your needs?" Cocoa asked.

"Yes, but is there a table we could bring in?"

I imagined pulling the chairs in a circle or lining them around a large table. It seemed the meeting would likely include Nix, Nate, Commander Adothlin, and myself, although there could be other officers as well.

"I will have the brownies bring in a table," Cocoa assured me.

"Thanks."

A bit of noise pulled my attention back to the foyer. I peeked out the library door to find the foyer already crowding with elves.

Cocoa came up beside me. "Many have already come."

"How are they getting in?"

"There are a few brownies standing out front. When they sense the guests, they permit them entrance."

I squinted at Cocoa hoping for more of an answer.

"The elves can't see them, but the brownies activate the door for them."

"And do the guests have access to the whole tree?"

"No. When they enter, they only see a path leading them to the throne room where they'll remain for the prince's coronation."

I tilted my head trying to imagine this. "You mean the brownies are blocking them from access to the rest of the tree."

Cocoa wobbled her head from side to side in her yes-no-maybe gesture. "Sort of. It's a mixture of brownie magic and the magic of the Royal Tree. The Royal Tree will not permit entrance to anyone but the royal family."

"And brownies and friends like me and Nate."

Cocoa planted her fists on her hips and pursed her lips.

"Magical trees are connected to the elf who resides in them and who they allow entrance. The guests for the coronation are only permitted access to certain areas like the main foyer and the hallway to the throne room."

"And brownies?"

"We've added some illusions so the guests only see what we want them to see. The guests won't see the staircase leading to the private quarters or the hallway to the kitchens. They will only see an open foyer with a corridor leading to the throne room. The walls will be like regular walls in any tree."

"Cocoa, is there a reason for all this security?"

"The royal guard has yet to be established and there wasn't time to put them in place for the coronation. Nate thought this would be best for today."

"I see."

I focused on the growing crowd then gasped as I noticed a tall, lithe elf walk through the others, his eyes darting from side to side. He reminded me of the guards who served my parents, though far less muscular. My palms grew slick with sweat.

"That's Commander Adothlin," Cocoa said. "I should introduce you."

I trailed behind her, taking in slow breaths to calm my pounding heart. Adothlin may have been smaller than my parents' guards, but he still elicited the same visceral response. My protective instincts fought to take over and my dragons needed to send me calming waves. Meeting the commander, talking to someone military… it unsettled me.

Cocoa brought me through the perceived wall that she'd told me about and I imagined if any guests were looking in our way, they'd see us as suddenly appearing. I felt a slight buzz of magic pull at me as we passed through the wall, but no one on the other side responded to our sudden arrival. I wondered if this was common in elven homes. Aside from my parents' fortress, Nate's and Nix's trees, I'd never been in another elf home, so my knowledge was limited.

"Commander Adothlin, this is Lady Zoe," Cocoa said. "Royal Advisor Ignatius Elek asked me to introduce the two of you. You will be strategizing together."

The elf straightened and with fluid grace offered a slight bow. His long, silvery-blond hair fell forward, but he brushed it back over his shoulder. He seemed young. He was a full adult or he wouldn't be a commander, but I doubted he was more than two hundred years. Perhaps my parents had killed the senior guards.

"It is a pleasure to meet you," Commander Adothlin said, crossing his arm over his chest in a salute.

I copied his gesture and licked my dry lips. "It is a pleasure to meet you as well. Nate… uh, Royal Advisor Ignatius Elek said we are to strategize on how to breach my parents' fortress."

The elf blinked and narrowed his eyes. "Your parents?"

I glanced at Cocoa, but she had already disappeared. "Yes. I assumed you had been informed. I escaped from them when I was still a child. I was raised by Royal Advisor Ignatius Elek."

"I see. Advisor Elek is sufficient."

"Pardon me?"

"Royal Advisor Ignatius Elek is a mouthful. Advisor Elek is sufficient. And you can refer to me as Adothlin as you are not part of my guard." His voice was cool but not rude, as it would have been had it come from one of my parents' guards. He also came across as formal, but in a friendly sort of way.

"Okay. Thank you. So… we'll be meeting in the library. Is that suitable for you?"

"Yes, I look forward to it once the ceremony is over and the Twilight Realm once again has a king." Adothlin bowed again.

As he walked away, my legs nearly turned to jelly. That hadn't been as bad as I had imagined, but I was relieved it was over. Although a bit serious, he held no malice.

The foyer began to fill up with various elves. Nate's call to the crown prince's supporters had traveled fast. But I didn't know anyone here.

The room was stuffy and I needed some air, so I ducked

outside as the next group of excited attendees arrived. I shook my head trying to shake off how overwhelmed I felt at being around so many people. It was worse than being in Haven. I understood how these elves felt though; the return of the king created the anticipation of freedom, but it also portended a future battle. Nix's coronation would mark the beginning of... what? A war with my parents? Or would their demise be quick? It was hard to say, but change was coming.

I sighed and took another meandering walk around the circumference of the Royal Tree, not wandering too far so I could slip back in before the coronation. I wouldn't miss Nix's moment even if the ceremony itself held no interest for me.

The dragons zoomed around me in an odd game of tag. I couldn't figure out the rules, but it entertained them and that's all that mattered. They wanted to be visible for Nix's crowning, but I worried about the questions this would raise.

I sensed the dragons' emotions shift toward excitement and turned to find Cocoa approaching.

"Oh, hello there," Cocoa said, giggling as the dragons flew up to her. "They are magnificent creatures. And so loving, like you."

Her delicate voice grated on my nerves. It wasn't her. It was what she said. I didn't see myself as loving. I turned away to hide my discomfort. My eyes caught the marking at the base of the Royal Tree, the one I'd seen earlier. I crouched to get a better look at it, and as I traced its lines with my finger, I recognized my mother's artistry. The marking formed an uneven circle with scattered lines running through it.

Chim, come here, I called. He was immediately beside me.

Within moments, Cocoa and the other two dragons drew

up behind me. Chim flew to the ground and sniffed at the marking. He nuzzled my arm, letting me know that the pattern held no magical properties.

I cupped my hand over the symbol to read it with my own magic. And remembered the odd but slightly familiar cool magic I'd felt earlier. The faint trace of my mother still resided in it, and it dawned on me that the image wasn't meant to depict a circle at all, but a stone. But I still couldn't figure out its purpose.

"What is it?" Cocoa asked, crouching next to me.

"It's a stone, and my mother made it. I'm sure of that much."

My mind continued to work, and through my magic I sensed that the drawing had been done before my tattoos. Had my mother perhaps put this here as a way of propping open the door? Maybe it could explain how my parents had gotten into the Royal Tree that night.

As a scientist, my mother had dabbled in the dark magic of Nosh Dem, deity of the Night Realm. I wouldn't put it past her to have done something like this.

"Cocoa, did you serve King Alistair and Queen Calla?" I asked.

"Yes, my lady."

I rested on my haunches, wrapping my arms around my knees as the other dragons continued to inspect the artwork. "Do you know what happened the night the Royal Tree was invaded?"

"It is a fuzzy memory, Lady Zoe. The whole household was asleep, and it's always been assumed that a traitor let them in."

"Is that what you think happened?"

Cocoa shook her head. "No. The entry was too clean, and those who serve the royal family cannot betray them."

"Why?"

"Those of us who serve the monarch do so willingly, not for the glory of attaining a high position in the realm."

My lips twitched. I was unsure of how to respond to that. It didn't really make sense to me. "Are brownies the only ones who serve the royal family?"

"We are the only beings, other than the royal family, who resided in the Royal Tree."

My mind spun. "But what about guards? Certainly the royal family needed protection, and Nix said that Nate was there to help him escape that night."

Cocoa puffed up her cheeks indignantly. "You underestimate the fierceness of nurture." She blew out a stream of air. "When the Royal Tree was breached, I went to Nate and brought him to the tree."

I digested this, chewing on my bottom lip. I didn't know what to make of it all, so I filed it away and called for Chim.

I want to deactivate the mark, I told him.

As Chim lent me his energy, I inhaled deeply and closed my eyes. I focused on the mark before me, needing to figure out how to break this spell of my mother's.

My hands grew warm but my magic was slow and sluggish as usual. It made its way throughout my body at a steady pace—this was more than my regular magic, which gave my tattoos life. It was magic from my core that I seldom touched since my magic had fractured.

Another wave of strange yet familiar magic pulsed through me and I felt the demon in my chest weaken. The dragons in turn buzzed around me, darting around the Royal Tree with renewed energy. When they flew far from me, I didn't feel the usual drain on my power. What was happening?

I focused more intently on the marking, wanting to rid the tree of it completely. Suddenly, a third surge of magical energy flooded over me. It encompassed me in a cocoon of warm sunlight and a calm peaceful joy. Was it the tree? Royal Magic? Or something else, something strong like Vaim Na'quab? All my focus centered on the marking, and with a burst it completely disintegrated.

I smiled and the dragons chittered with excitement.

"You are one powerful elf, my lady," Cocoa said as she wiped her brow.

"I don't think that was me," I replied, pondering what had just happened. I replayed the sensation of this new magic and its effects on my tattoos. I stored it in my mind and determined to explore it later.

I stood a little shakily and brushed off my clothes. "Come, Nix's ceremony should be starting soon."

The dragons melded back into me, giving off mild protests. They wouldn't miss anything, though; they'd be able to observe the proceedings through my eyes.

But something about them felt different. That surge of energy they'd received had affected them. They were still mine, undeniably, but they also felt like independent entities.

That unsettled me.

We entered the tree and made our way to a throne room, which was buzzing with energy, packed with elves and brownies.

I peeked over the heads of the crowd and saw the dais, empty save for a brilliantly white throne. The royal chair must have been carved from a great tree, its legs stretching to the floor like roots; interwoven vines crawled up its sides to create armrests. Atop the throne, branches sprouted to create a canopy of leaves. It reflected elfkind in its exquisite beauty.

Nate strode from a door off the side of the dais and walked to the center of the platform. As he clapped his hands, the excited murmur in the room died down and every head turned toward the front.

"Friends of the royal family, it is an exciting day," he began. "For today we bring forth the crown price, who has come of age and is ready to be crowned king."

A cheer arose from each being in the room, followed by a reverent hush. Everyone turned as one to face the doorway I'd entered a few moments ago, and there, framed in the entrance, stood Nix—or rather, Crown Prince Phoenix. My eyes unexpectedly welled up with tears at the sight of my friend in his royal attire. It wasn't much different than casual wear in style. The fabric was softer and had detailed embroidery. From his shoulders flowed a long cape that trailed behind him on the floor. He stood taller, more stiffly, as he nodded while passing his subjects. I doubted he saw me with the masses between us, but a desire rose within me to bow. Cocoa had been overcome by the same desire, for she had kneeled. I followed her lead, for it felt uncomfortable, even disrespectful, not to honor the monarchy.

The crown prince stepped onto the dais and knelt before Nate. Then a brownie appeared at Nate's side holding a plush purple pillow with the circlet resting upon it. The royal advisor took the circlet between his fingers and held it above Nix's head.

"In the name of our first ruler, Paz Mier, who established the line of the elven monarchy, I crown thee, Phoenix, as the king of the Twilight Realm."

Nate lowered the circlet onto Nix's head. As he pulled his

hands away, a pulse of energy flashed through the room and a soft murmur of surprised voices filled the silence.

"The blessing and seal of the royal line is confirmed," Nate said. "Rise, King Phoenix."

As Nix rose and turned to face his subjects, my knees once again gave out and I bowed out of respect for my friend. Afterward I felt his eyes on me and even perceived the flicker of his smile. I smiled in return, hoping he'd sense my support.

He looked like my friend, but in this overwhelming moment his movements seemed stiff, his previous casual comfort having disappeared. My heart swelled for him as I tried to imagine his emotions. He'd confided in me his deepest fears about becoming king and others dying for him. How was he feeling now?

Twilight's Curse

Chapter Eighteen

Nix

It took every bit of my self-control not to show how nervous I felt. The crown, *my* crown, sat for the first time on my head. It wasn't heavy, but the weight of what it represented was keenly felt. And I knew in my heart what my father had told me years ago: *"The crown is merely a symbol of the elf wearing the crown."*

I scanned the elves and noticed a number of brownies interspersed among those gathered in the throne room. The crowd was standing, waiting for me to speak. I was amazed at how many had remained loyal through the years. Hope inspired me as I considered the task ahead: soon, we would take down the usurpers who had killed my parents and plagued the Twilight Realm for too long.

But as I searched the crowd, there was only one face I wanted to see. When my eyes landed on Zoe at the back of the room, I felt grounded once again. She knew me as Nix, not King Phoenix. But seeing her and having Nate with me on the dais, I inhaled deeply as new courage rose in me.

I cleared my throat, ready to address my subjects for the first time.

"Citizens," I began. My voice came out softer than I intended, so I squared my shoulders and projected so the sound would carry all the way to where Zoe stood. "Inhabitants of the Twilight Realm, welcome! And thank you for coming to the coronation of your king. It is my humble duty to serve you and our lands. There are many who could not be here today, as the time was short. I offer now my sincerest apologies. It was not the intention of the Royal Tree to offend any or deny the opportunity to attend this joyous occasion, but as you all know, there is an evil among us that has existed for too long. It is because of this evil and under the wisdom of the Royal Advisor Ignatius Elek that I have been kept from this position for a period of time until I had grown in physical stature and mental fortitude. I am merely a child-adult without the council and guidance that my father would have bestowed on me, but I am your king and I humbly take this position to serve and restore the Twilight Realm to the peace it has known for millennia. I am sorry for all we have suffered under the usurpers, Leski and Sirina Dion. As the crowned king and rightful heir, I ask you to partner with me in purging the evil from our land. Those who murdered my parents." I paused. "Those guilty will be brought to justice."

The crowd applauded and cheered as Nate guided me to the side of the dais. We entered a private chamber as Commander Adothlin took his place on the dais behind us. Nate had informed me that the commander would be choosing subjects to fill the military and guard roles in the kingdom, positions fitting their skills.

My subjects. The words felt strange. Just this morning, I had still been a common elf with no one subject to me at all. But that wasn't completely true. If anyone had known my true identity, and if they were loyal the crown, I would have had an immediate ally. The reality of that thought sent warm tingles dancing over my skin and I shivered with mild excitement and cool dread. The idea of not being so alone—more than me, Nate, and Zoe—felt nice, but imagining any one of those elves dying for me made me sick.

A flash of memory assaulted me. It was my father dying. I squeezed my eyes shut. Since that moment, I had vowed that no one would die for me… and now that I was king it was very likely that one of those loyal subjects just might. I shook off the unsettled feelings and flopped into a chair in a very unkingly fashion.

"I'm glad that's over," I said.

Nate raised an eyebrow. "I know you've enjoyed your private life, but in order to face the Dions, you need to be king."

"Are you finally going to tell me why?"

Nate sat across from me, his elbows perched on his knees and his fingers tapped his chin. "You know the surge of magic you felt when you were crowned?"

I nodded. The energy had rushed into me and then pulsed outward. I could still feel its encompassing magic, not just within me but surrounding me as well.

"This is the magic entrusted to your line," Nate explained.

I remembered what *Ascension* had said about a kind of magic that gave the monarchy favor and persuasion over the masses.

"But why the rush for a coronation?" I asked. "Certainly we

could have waited until after Zoe and I went to the fortress—"

"Zoe and you." Nate's lips lifted into a small smile. "I'm afraid, my king, that you cannot do this alone, just the two of you. You must stand alongside those faithful to the crown."

I squirmed in my seat trying to avoid this very subject. "I don't want anyone to die for me or the crown."

Nate squeezed the bridge of his nose with his two index fingers. "That's not your choice. Being crowned king ensures the Dions can take no further action against you or the Twilight Realm."

"I refuse to let anyone die for me. Not one child will grow up without a parent."

"I'm afraid that is beyond your control."

"But I won't let it happen. I won't willingly allow it to take place."

"My king, I understand where this comes from. Perhaps time will help you understand. It is the way of things. It is the burden of being a monarch."

"A burden I'd gladly do without." I sighed. A part of me knew Nate was right and I'd have to accept that elves would give their lives for me, but... not today.

Nate cleared his throat. "Let's go back to the royal magic and the reason for your coronation. The Dions influenced their guards with dark magic. It's similar to the royal magic you carry in your veins, but where theirs is manipulative and controlling, yours is not."

"So the citizens of the Twilight Realm have the freedom to choose whether to serve the monarchy?"

"Yes, they do."

Back at the Misty Inn, the guards had been large—unnaturally so. And all these guards had an unswerving loyalty to the Dions.

However, as I reflected on Nate's words, I realized they were true. The guards who had served my parents had always been free to voice their opinions and serve at their own discretion. The thought of my parents' contented laziness reared its ugly head again. I didn't like this thought—it felt treacherous—but Nate had served closely with my father. He might be able to assuage my concerns.

"Nate, did my parents grow too complacent in their royal magic?"

The royal advisor tilted his head to the side. "Are you asking if your parents were lax in their duties?"

"No. I'm asking if they took their position and favor for granted. They didn't anticipate the threat of a coup because they trusted too much in the royal magic, choosing not to ensure the loyalty of their subjects."

"Perhaps," Nate said. "But your father fell on the sword Leski Dion held to his throat. He didn't allow himself to be killed."

"You're saying that he sacrificed himself for the kingdom."

"Yes. By sacrificing himself, he broke the power of the Dions. If they had killed him, the Royal Tree would have lost its power and the Dions would have been able to rule. They would have taken the crown."

All this time, I had seen the Dions as murderers who had killed my mother with every intent of killing my father. But my father had died for me and his kingdom. He had acted as a hero. When this was over, I'd ensure that was how he was remembered.

"My father's sacrifice prevented that..." I mused, digesting this new information. "And if I'm killed now?"

"You won't be, my king. The magic you received at your coronation will strengthen you against the Dions while weakening their guards and causing confusion among them."

That seemed to raise an important question: "Why didn't this work for my parents?"

"I don't know how the Dions were able to enter the Royal Tree," Nate admitted. "My guess is that it had something to do with Sirina's dark magic. It wasn't until after your parents died that the Dions had any sway over the inhabitants of the Twilight Realm. Those who were initially loyal to them all came from the Night Realm." Nate sighed. "I don't know if King Alistair took the royal magic for granted. But it's good for you to ask these questions. It will make you a good king. A better king."

For the moment, I needed to focus on the future—and I suddenly realized that I needed Zoe. I wanted her here and a part of this moment.

"Nate, can you get Zoe?"

My advisor nodded. "She is on her way. Cocoa is with her."

"Good." I smiled at my mentor. "I'm glad you're here and that the ceremony is over with."

"I fear, Your Highness, that this is only the beginning. There will be many other ceremonies."

I sighed. Gone were the days of my freedom. But at least I was doing this for the elves in my life—for my sister Zyanna, for Zoe, and for the children being held captive in the fortress.

A knock sounded at the door and Cocoa popped her head in. When the door opened wider, Zoe followed the brownie inside.

"Zoe," I said, feeling relaxed at seeing her.

She bowed low. "Your Majesty."

My teeth ground. "Oh, please, save that for ceremony. In private, I'm Nix."

"Right, Nix," Zoe said, though her voice sounded a bit forced.

I wondered if she was okay with me being king—not that either of us had a choice in the matter. Well, after we dealt with the fortress, I'd make sure Zoe and I had time to talk about this change. For now, we had to focus on the task at hand.

Nate rubbed his hands together. "Right, now to talk strategy. Zoe, I believe the library is being prepared for us?"

Zoe nodded. "Yes, the brownies have taken care of it."

"Excellent." Nate nudged my shoulder. "Are you ready, my king?"

I raised an eyebrow. "Lead the way."

* * *

I studied the crude map Zoe was sketching of the corridors in the fortress. We were sitting at the table in the library, joined by Nate and Commander Adothlin.

"Your memory is amazing," I said.

"The dragons are helping. Tupac remembers the fortress best."

A lock of her unique hair settled over her shoulder, partially obscuring her face. My fingers itched to move it out of the way. Would she remind me that I was taking liberties? I held back but I leaned closer and she didn't shift away from me.

I glanced at Nate and Adothlin, who were chatting softly.

"You and I will enter together," I spoke in a whisper.

Zoe nodded. "And the brownies. We'll need them for the

children, but don't you want to enter with the royal soldiers?"

"If we enter as a large group and the Dions do have my sister, there's no telling what they'll do to her if fighting breaks out between the royal soldiers and regent guards."

"And you don't want to risk anyone dying."

I gave a slight nod. Zoe knew my story.

"I understand but I'm not sure it's wise." Zoe turned back to her drawing.

"Where would be the best place to separate?"

"You want to go through the corridors alone?" Zoe's eyebrows lifted to her hair line.

"I want to find my sister."

Zoe bit her bottom lip and pointed at the map. "In the foyer. The children should be near there and the magic imbued in the corridors lessens after that. At least it did when I lived there. Are you sure?"

"That I want to search for my sister?"

"That you want to go alone."

"She's my sister."

"Are you almost finished?" Adothlin asked. His abrupt voice cutting into our secret planning.

"Almost," Zoe said. "Though I'm not sure how good these diagrams will be."

"Do you not remember its layout? You *did* live there. The Dions *are* your parents."

A part of me wanted to tell the commander to back off.

"Biologically, yes," Zoe replied without emotion. "My mother was skilled at creating illusions. Before my escape, I spent many days running through the corridors, pretending to play, but really searching for a way out."

Adothlin turned down his lips. "Your memory is all we

have."

Zoe nodded. "I think our best bet is for me to enter the fortress—alone."

"Can we trust her, Advisor Elek?" Adothlin asked, turning toward Nate, who was seated comfortably in a cushioned chair across from us.

"Zoe has no love for her parents," Nate said. "Her reasons are her own."

Adothlin gestured toward Zoe. "I will not risk the life of our king on her."

"Nonetheless, I will go with her." I stood and rested a hand on Zoe's shoulder. She didn't shift away, but I felt her muscles tense under my touch.

Adothlin spun toward me. "You will not."

"I will. Zoe is risking her life for the kingdom, and she is our best hope at defeating the Dions."

Adothlin huffed. "What say you, Advisor Elek?"

"It is the king's choice in the matter." Nate winked at me as his eyes landed on my hand on Zoe's shoulder. "I agree that they, together, represent our best hope against the Dions. However, I do not support them heading into the fortress alone."

"This is ludicrous," the commander said.

I breathed deeply, collecting my thoughts and letting the royal magic inside me intensify a notch. Despite the objections of Nate and the commander, I couldn't risk anyone dying. I knew I was being stubborn, but I felt Zoe and I could enter with greater stealth than a company of soldiers. "My father gave his life for this kingdom. His sacrifice makes it necessary that I enter the fortress alone with Zoe." I glanced at Nate silently attempting to remind him of our brief conversation after the coronation and my feelings about no one dying.

"And if you're killed?" Adothlin's eyes drilled into me.

"I won't be."

"No?"

"No. And while we're inside, we'll rescue the kidnapped children and look for my sister."

"All on your own? Without your royal soldiers? Your Majesty, you insult us." Adothlin folded his arms. "Are we to wait outside until you come out?"

Zoe stood up. "No, you won't merely wait. Before the coronation, before Nix—"

"King Phoenix," Adothlin corrected.

Zoe cleared her throat. "Yes, my apologies. Before King Phoenix and I entered the Royal Tree, I noticed an etching at the base of the tree near the entrance. Upon inspection, I detected my mother's signature upon it. My dragons and I were able to disable it."

"Disable it how?"

Zoe licked her lips. "I think my mother used the mark to gain entrance into the Royal Tree on the night King Alistair and Queen Calla were killed. It was shaped like a stone, and I believe it was used to keep the door from fully closing. In undoing that etching, I've come to understand the magic that was used to make it. I can assure you that my mother will have found ways to improve this practice, and these markings will now be all over the fortress. Their purpose, I believe, is to create confusion. The markings create illusions, transforming the normally orderly rooms and corridors into a maze."

Nate nodded at her. The advisor steepled his fingers in front of his face, making it impossible for me to read his expression. Was he pleased?

"The king and I, along with the brownies, will enter the fortress first, but you may follow soon after," Zoe said to Adothlin. "My job will be to disable these markings, which will make it much easier for your troops to enter and navigate the fortress."

Zoe clenched her fists and licked her lips. "A childhood friend will be waiting to let us in. He asked me to come with friends. King Phoenix coming as my friend Nix and the brownies will seem less forceful and less obvious than a troop of royal soldiers."

"And is your friend loyal to your parents?"

Zoe paused. "I don't know. But right now, he's our only way in."

"I don't trust this girl. And brownies! We are about to lose our new king," Adothlin muttered, eyeing Zoe. "What does she know of her mother's magic? She was nothing but a child when she left."

Zoe huffed and stepped away from the table, rolling up the sleeves of her blouse and allowing her daggers to drop into her hands. Meanwhile, the dragons slipped out between the slits of her clothing and fluttered into the air around her.

Adothlin's eyes widened at the sight, but he didn't stand.

"Are you challenging me to a fight?" Zoe raised one of her daggers. "I was my parents' first experiment, so I know my mother's magic better than anyone. Never question me or my loyalty."

Zoe held her stance until Adothlin turned away. Her daggers slid back into place on her forearms, although the dragons remained free.

"I do not know the abilities of the brownies, but Cocoa has repeatedly reminded me to never underestimate them. So neither should you. If the markings inside the fortress are anything like the one I found on the Royal Tree, you should be joining us within a few minutes."

I beamed at Zoe and wanted to hug her, but I was certain she'd call that *taking liberties*.

"Right then," I said. "I will be joining Zoe as she enters the fortress. Commander Adothlin, you and your soldiers will wait until Zoe disables Sirina's markings and then storm the fortress!"

"Sounds like a plan," Nate said from his seat.

With my advisor's hands still in front of his face, I remained uncertain about whether he supported my decision—but I had been called to rule, and this *was* the right decision. No one would die for me and I'd put no one in danger before myself.

Except Zoe, of course. She had a right to face her parents.

Chapter Nineteen

Zoe

I crouched next to a bush, peering out at the wall of my parents' fortress. My heart pounded and I could barely breathe. I closed my eyes, willing my racing pulse to slow down. I had to stay calm and in control or the demon tattoo would break out again; I could already feel him pacing his cage, rattling the bars. The dragons did what they could to reinforce the cell, but I knew it was just a matter of time before he broke free again.

"When you're ready," Nix said, his breath tickling my ear.

I didn't like him so close, but our need for stealth required close quarters. The brownies were invisible but otherwise close by and would follow us in.

"How are you doing?" Nate asked from his hiding place behind us.

"We have to do this," I whispered back.

"That's not what I asked."

"I know."

Nate reached out and I felt his hand on my shoulder. "Are you up for the task?"

"Yes. We have to do this, and I want to." The words came out flat, but I could sense the truth in them as they fell from my lips. This was the last place I had ever wanted to go—back into my childhood house of torture—but I gained courage from knowing that others stood with me. To ignite my resolve, I thought of the children we were here to rescue. I squared my shoulders. We *could* do this.

"Have you given any more thought to the thorns and weeds?" Nate asked.

Seriously? He was bringing this up now, of all times? This hardly seemed like the time for an object lesson.

"I've been a little busy..."

"Thorns grow with you," Nate said. "Weeds grow around you."

I shook my head, shifting my focus back to the fortress in time to see its back door edge open. A lone figured stepped out.

"Is that Maximon?" Nix asked.

My heartrate sped up as I recognized my childhood friend.

"Zoe?" Maximon spoke in a loud whisper.

I rose from my hiding place and made my way toward him. "Maximon, how'd you know we were here?"

He shrugged. "I guessed."

"That's it? You're not going to tell me?"

He smirked and nodded toward the door.

I didn't like not knowing but right now he was our ticket in. And if he gave us trouble, I was certain we could handle him between Nix, myself, and the brownies.

"Did you bring friends?" Maximon asked.

"They're here," I said quietly. Just then, the brownies emerged from the foliage as if suddenly materializing with Cocoa leading them. They huddled around me.

Maximon's eyebrow raised. "These are your friends?"

"They've come to help rescue the children."

Maximon's eyes lifted past my shoulder and I guessed he had probably seen Nix drawing up behind me. We had decided to keep Nix's identity a secret. I didn't know where Maximon's loyalties lay and I didn't know what he was capable of. On top of that, I didn't know what my parents had been up to these last six years since I fled the fortress.

Maximon turned back to the door. "Follow me."

My body froze, and suddenly I was unable to move forward. The demon in my chest gleefully roared. Fear flooded through me, fear of the years I had spent at the mercy of my parents.

Nix came up beside me and cupped my hand in his. I didn't mind this gesture of support this time. I turned my head to meet his gaze.

"You've got this," Nix whispered.

A small hand slipped into my empty one and Cocoa squeezed. I felt a strong pulse of her magic flow with mine, giving me courage.

I inhaled sharply and took my first step toward the doorway. Before I crossed the threshold, one of my mother's markings on the external wall beside the door caught my attention. I only gave it a passing glance as I headed into the torchlit tunnel. From that brief look, it seemed to me that the etching had been shaped like an eye.

In a rush, I remembered the night I'd escaped and the eye, very similar to this one, I'd seen outside my bedroom door.

I'd wondered about it then and I had a pretty good guess to its purpose now.

I should deactivate it and summon Commander Adothlin and his soldiers. But Maximon was inside and watching me. A cool shiver trickled down my spine.

My mind flickered back to what Maximon had said outside of Nate's. He said he'd know when we arrived. Did that mean he, the regent guards, or even my parents knew we were already here? Not for the first time, I wondered if we were walking into a trap.

I squeezed Nix's and Cocoa's hands reminding me they were with me and there were at least twenty more brownies filing past us into the fortress. We stepped through the doorway and the door slammed with a thud. It was too late to turn back now.

We followed Maximon down a narrow corridor, which then ended and made an abrupt turn. As a child, my brother and I had raced through these twists and turns. Something niggled at my mind about that, and I toyed with the thought but was unable to make sense of it.

I knew my parents had placed magical properties in the fortress causing the passageways to shift, making it impossible for an elf to navigate them. I had tried to find a way out for years. Yet somehow, I'd been able to escape. It was like that one night the magic had been down and the path unblocked.

The tunnels grew more familiar the longer we walked, and soon I began to sense the proximity of the children. We were coming up on the foyer—near where I had found Dasha's room years ago—and the children were there, or in a room close to the foyer. For some reason, I was feeling more relaxed. This struck me as odd, but it occurred to me that this place didn't have the same hold on me anymore. Perhaps that was because I knew I would be leaving.

Maximon was walking in the front with the brownies noiselessly filling the gap as Nix and I made up the rear of our small procession. I squeezed Nix's hand and felt it slip from mine. My hand felt suddenly cold, and the first true friend I'd ever had was walking away to rescue his sister. The difference between my friendships with Nix and Maximon was that I trusted Nix and I'd felt safe enough with him to tell him my story. After all these years, Maximon was still an enigma.

Nix had the crude map I'd drawn of the fortress in the library earlier. It showed where I thought his sister was being held—if in fact she was in the fortress. I watched him head down the hallway alone; he paused and glanced back at me and gave a nod. I nodded in return, swallowing against the tightness in my throat. I didn't like him going off on his own.

Within about ten more steps, we entered a large open foyer.

"Here we are." Maximon paused just outside a large metal door and inserted a key into the lock. The sound of the key clicking was magnified in the silent foyer.

The door creaked open. Stale, musty air rushed out at me. I wrinkled my nose.

"Where are the guards?" I asked.

"They're occupied elsewhere with Lord Leski and Lady Sirina."

When Maximon smiled, it sent another wave of chills down my spine and all my instincts told me to run. Something about his tone of voice didn't sit right with me. This was too easy. Had we walked into a trap?

Just get the kids and get out, I thought. *That's what we're here for.*

I placed my hand on the doorway and peered into the room. The brownies crowded around me and gazed in at a network of cages, each holding a child. Some of them were crying. Others sat and stared. Still others screamed.

"There's so many," I whispered. I recognized the small handful from Nate's home, but there were at least twenty or thirty more than our original fifteen. My heart sank for each child here.

"We'll get them all, my lady," Cocoa said.

That caught Maximon's attention and an eyebrow peaked. "My lady?" he asked.

I turned and nearly crushed my nose into his chest. How had he gotten so close? I stepped away from him. "How do we get them out?"

Maximon held up a ring of keys, jingled them, and then handed them to Cocoa. With that, she and the other brownies slipped inside the dark room.

"I see your friend has left you." Maximon gestured behind me, then shoved his hands casually in his pockets as he relaxed against the doorframe.

"He had a different errand," I replied. I couldn't tell him any more than that.

"Oh, really? And is he more than a friend? He seemed a little protective of you when you first entered."

The way Maximon said that made my muscles tighten. His manner reminded me a lot of my brother, Dimas, who had been sweet and innocent until my father's cruelty finally began to wear off on him. After that he'd become another tormentor.

"We're just friends," I said, folding my arms across my chest.

"Right." Maximon shifted closer and leaned in. "And have you been hanging around with him ever since you left your parents? They've missed you and the work you helped them with."

Maximon's voice trailed off. I didn't like the direction his thoughts were going. Almost like he saw their torture as a good thing and was persuading me to return.

"It's their work and I never asked to be a part of it." My voice was flat.

"Don't you think you should help them?"

I studied his eyes, searching for any indication that this was a trap. I looked away—and in the process my eye caught another one of my mother's designs embedded in the wall.

My heart pounded in my chest and I felt ill. I needed to release those symbols so Nate, the commander, and his troops could enter. I'd already wasted too much time. It was supposed to have been the first thing I did. The others should be with us. I mentally kicked myself for not acting earlier.

Maximon shifted his weight.

"I understand that they misused you as a child, but now, you could be in control. You could work with them. I'm sure they'd respect you."

A harsh laugh belched out of me. How could he even suggest that? I shook my head. He and I had been friends in this horrid place. And he'd been stuck here all these years while I'd been free of it. Maybe he wanted me back. Or maybe he'd missed me and felt trapped.

Perhaps it was my turn to help him. Maybe... somehow I could break the hold my parents had on him and rescue him as well.

"Think about what you want." I grabbed his hand and held it up between my own. "You can come with me. You don't have to stay here. You can escape with me tonight."

Maximon pulled his hand away and placed it on my cheek. It wasn't an affectionate gesture, though. I felt the calluses on his fingers scratch my skin and the coolness of his touch felt like my mother's magic.

"Don't tempt me to go against the Lord and Lady," he said.

"But why? I left. So can you."

Maximon stepped back from me and crossed his arms. "Things have changed."

That was all he said, and the meaning was lost on me. What had changed? He himself? My parents? Our friendship? Or lack of real friendship. I hoped Maximon hadn't been corrupted by my parents.

Get the kids and get out. The mantra marched through my mind, helping me to focus on the room and turn from my childhood playmate.

The smell was musty and I coughed, feeling my chest tighten. The low lighting gave the chamber a dismal feel.

The brownies worked quickly, and within a few minutes most of the children were huddled together near the door. Many of the children I didn't know wore vacant expressions. We had to get them out of here.

My fingers shook as I ran them through my hair. I searched the faces of the children, I couldn't find Dasha…

"We're done, my lady," Cocoa said, coming up next to me.

"What about Dasha?" I asked, trailing my gaze over the kids again. My heart sped. Where was she?

I turned to Cocoa. Her eyes were round, filled with the same concern I felt. *My mother.* The thought took the very breath from me.

The children would be safe with the brownies and whatever nurture magic they had. They'd be able to get the children

224

out of the fortress. I didn't know how, but I knew enough of the creatures' ways to know they were capable of this.

"Take the kids and get them out of here," I said as anger rose up in me. "I'll find Dasha."

My demon tattoo rattled against the confines of his cage, but I felt the power of my dragons working against him.

It was time to finish this.

"But what about you?" Cocoa asked.

"I'll be fine."

Cocoa looked at the huddled mass of children. There were two to three children for every brownie. "There's more than enough brownies to escort the children out. Some could help you as well."

"And what could a brownie do to protect me?" I gripped my blades, feeling the impatience in me. Every second lost was another Dasha would suffer at the hands of my mother.

"You underestimate the power of nurture," Cocoa said. "Let me come."

Her eyes were so sincerely fierce that I doubted she'd accept a second refusal.

"No, go with the children," I decided. "When they're safe, if you want to risk your welfare for me, then you can return." Cocoa looked like she was going to argue, but I cut her off. "The children first." I leaned down and whispered in her ear. "Get Commander Adothlin. I don't trust Maximon and things aren't going to plan. We need the royal soldiers."

Cocoa nodded curtly and the brownies filed past me with the children. A few children who recognized me greeted me as they shuffled by, but otherwise the group remained silent.

Maximon drew up next to me. "You're not going with them?"

"There's one missing," I said without turning.

"Go with them. I'll find the remaining one."

I turned to face him. "She's my responsibility. Besides, I have a good idea where she is."

"The laboratory?" Maximon asked.

I nodded. "My mother will be experimenting on her, eager to use her."

When the last of the children had left the room, I began walking back toward the corridor Nix had taken earlier.

"Coming?" I called over my shoulder to Maximon. I heard him follow, his feet scraping against the smooth floor. I didn't want him with me, but I didn't want him with the brownies either. I felt better knowing where he was.

I knew my way through the maze of hallways now. Perhaps it was just the corridors closest to the exits that were governed by my mother's illusions.

Once again, I thought of my brother and I running through these corridors, playing for countless hours.

Dimas. I hadn't thought of my brother often. Perhaps I should have, or at least pitied him. After getting my first tattoo, Dimas had held me and let me cry into his shoulder. As time went on, though, he changed. By the time half of my body had been covered in tattoos, he had delighted in adding to my pain.

He'd even attempted adding his own tattoo once, thinking it was fun and laughing at my screams. The small of my back prickled at the memory of burnt skin. He hadn't pushed the ink far enough into my skin and the result had been a burn mark. Pat had healed the injury, but the scar remained. My parents never left me alone with Dimas again.

If Nix's sister really was here and was to marry Dimas, then

I pitied her.

When Maximon and I turned a corner in the hallway, my throat suddenly constricted. I heard screams filling the air. Ghosts of memories past flooded over me. I couldn't move.

Maximon tugged my sleeve. "Zoe?"

I closed my eyes and breathed deeply. Those weren't just anyone's screams… they were Dasha's, her terror mingling with my own recollections.

I had to save her. I had to help her.

Nate's confusing lesson about the thorn and weeds once again squirmed into my thoughts, but I thrust them aside. This wasn't the time.

All the same, I felt a mental nudge to let go and forgive my parents. I couldn't do it… I couldn't risk losing my dragons…

I squared my shoulders and felt the dragons' calming effects. I had to focus. I had to do this. Now.

"Let's go," I said to Maximon as I pointed at the door with my daggers.

With each step, my heartbeat thudded loudly in my ears. Within moments I had reached the doorway to my mother's laboratory. I steeled myself, then turned the knob and swung open the door.

Twilight's Curse

Chapter Twenty

Zoe

The room was brightly lit, with white walls. It was a stark contrast to the rest of the fortress. It hadn't changed from my childhood, with my mother's desk in the back and an operating bed to the left with medical beds on the right. The rest of the room had shelves of beakers and test tubes. Some were filled with colorful liquid while others sat empty.

To the right, my mother hovered over a crying Dasha strapped to a medical bed. My breathing came in shallow gasps. It was like walking into a memory of me six years ago.

My mother twirled and beamed at me. "Zoe, darling, the runaway daughter has returned. And just in time. Thank you, Dimas. Now be a dear and go tell your father that your sister has returned home."

I fought with everything in me not to show my surprise. The demon within me raged against its cage and I turned to regard Maximon. Before my eyes, my friend's face slipped…

and instead of Maximon, my brother was standing in the doorway, smiling back at me.

"Hello, sister," Dimas said.

"Where's Maximon?" I raised my dagger and held it against my brother's throat. I knew of my brother's magical ability to mimic others. So where was my friend? Anger pulsed through me and the demon roared with glee.

Maximon and I had been the ones to explore the fortress. But now that I thought about it, the three of us had never played *together*. It had always been me and Maximon, or me and Dimas… My stomach lurched and bile rose in my throat. I swallowed it back.

"He never was," my mother said in a soft voice, so sincere and conversational.

"What?"

"It was Dimas all along."

Before me, Dimas suddenly shrank in appearance, transforming into a young boy. The last child who had come to Nate's home about a week ago.

"And Anansi," I whispered, my blood running cold as the boy transformed back into my brother. Why hadn't I listened to Cocoa when she'd said there was something odd about him?

"Now run along, Dimas," my mother said. "You've done well."

Dimas beamed. "It's great to have you home, sis."

He reached out a hand and pinched my shoulder. The pain ran down my arm and I knew there'd be a bruise if it wasn't for Pat.

"We'll be picking up right where we left off." Dimas strode back toward the door, but then turned before going through.

"We knew you'd come for the girl. I've been waiting all day."

"Is that why you changed the time?" Thinking back to the forest near Nate's and him changing his request from two days to one day.

"You got it, sis. Just wanted the family back together." His chilling laughter remained like the stench from a rotten egg.

My heart plummeted. My one friend in this fortress, Maximon, had never really existed… and now I was trapped. Tricked! Again. Delivered right into the hand of my mother.

I thought of Nix. Where was he? I hoped he had found his sister and gotten out, but a part of me felt more certain than ever that Zyanna had never been here. I suspected my parents had been trying to lure him inside. *Why?*

My one hope was that Cocoa, the brownies, and children had made it out and Commander Adothlin and his soldiers would be storming the fortress soon.

Dasha's whimpers reached my ears.

No, I couldn't let myself drown in self-pity. I had to fight. I had to fight for her. I had to fight for every child and elf my family had ever hurt or killed. I had to fight for Nix, my friend and my king!

I pivoted slowly, raising my dagger.

Lady Sirina laughed. "Put those silly daggers away, darling, and come greet your mother."

She held out her arms as if expecting me to run to her—and when I didn't, she shrugged as though it didn't matter and turned her attention back to the weeping Dasha. The child's face was stained with tears and her breathing was ragged. Her arm was red with a fresh tattoo. Though barely started, I saw enough of the original template to turn my stomach. It was a demon tattoo like my own.

It took every ounce of self-control not to surrender to the terror and anger I felt inside. The demon roared in pleasure at my emotions, and it took the combined efforts of my dragons to keep him in line.

"Let her go," I commanded, keeping my eyes focused on my mother.

"Nonsense. I've perfected my technique. Having learned from you, I've discovered how to eliminate any interference by the personality of the host."

My skin felt hot and flushed with anger as I took a step closer to Dasha. But I didn't want to take my eyes off my mother.

"Zoe," Dasha called out.

"It's all right," I said. "I'm here and I'm getting you out."

My mother burst into a round of giggles. The sound scraped at my ears. She was mocking me, attempting to control me with her indifference. It usually worked—I'd seen elves fall under her charms time and again—but I knew her too well.

"Don't even try it, Mother. I came for Dasha and I'm leaving with her."

Trying to show the same indifference, I took the last few steps toward the child. With a racing heart, I scrambled to untie the knots binding her wrists. My fingers slipped and I needed to use my dagger to slice through the material. I should have done that in the first place, but I hadn't wanted to accidentally nick the child.

Once free, Dasha slid off the table. She gripped the back of my shirt in her fists and cowered behind me.

"And just where do you think you're going?" Given her cheerful expression, my mother seemed delighted with my efforts.

"I told you. We're leaving."

Dasha drew up next to me. The few lines of fresh ink on her arm were angry and raw. I'd have Pat look at her the moment we were safely away from here.

I inched toward the door, not daring to turn my back on my mother. She had never been a strong elf, but she always seemed to be a step ahead of me.

"No, I'm sorry, but that just won't do," Lady Sirina said. "You see, I have need of you, darling daughter. As you now know, I used your brother's ability to mimic the appearance of others to lure you here."

Maximon... Anansi... I wanted to kick myself for falling for the trick.

My mother had her ways and had probably sensed me, Nix, and the brownies the moment we crossed the fortress's threshold. Perhaps she'd used those markings to do it. How had I been so stupid? She had prepared this place against any intruder.

I moved closer to the door, but a beefy hand clamped down on my shoulder. My muscles tightened as I fought against the previously unseen guard's hold. Chim should have helped me sense him, but I'd been distracted and my dragons were working hard to keep the demon in line.

"Stay close," I said to Dasha, pointing where she could seek shelter in a corner. "Right there."

As the girl scooted toward relative safety, I rolled my shoulders, preparing to fight.

I whirled on the guard with my daggers flashing at my sides. I felt my dragons flutter, straining for me to release them, but I was afraid. If I let them out, I might lose control of the demon.

I ducked and rolled as the guard brought down his fist, aiming for the side of my head. I dodged out of the way as he lunged; he was big and reminded me of the guards I had fought at the Misty Inn. Frustrated, he roared and it occurred to me that he seemed more animal than elf. The guard tore at me and scooped me over his shoulder, then slammed me against the wall. The air in my lungs vomited out and I gasped. He grabbed my waist, but I twisted free and landed on my feet.

There was no way I could take out this guard alone, so I summoned the dragons. The beasts fluttered out of the folds of my clothing and immediately launched an attacked on the guard, giving me a brief reprieve to come up with a plan.

My mother clapped her hands in delight, but I did my best to ignore her. A quick glance behind me assured me that Dasha was still folded into the corner.

The guard threw off my dragons and Pat landed on the ground and skidded into a tray. All the instruments clattered to the floor as Chim and Tupac tore at the guard, attempting to gouge out his eyes. The guard flung his hand up and brushed the dragons aside, but they quickly pivoted and re-engaged.

The guard turned his back to me. Seeing an opening, I ran at him with my daggers ready to strike. I raised the weapons in a swift movement and landed on his back, wrapping my arms around his chest and shoving the blades deep into his chest. I wasn't sure I could kill him. His chest was too muscular and thick for my blades to sink deep enough for any serious damage to his heart, but if I could incapacitate him, puncture his lung… anything would help. He stumbled backward and I jumped aside, expecting him to fall.

Instead he looked at the blades and yanked them out. They

dropped them to the floor.

He smiled... and my blood stopped flowing, my knees buckling. I forced myself to remain upright as the demon within me lurched at his confines. It took every bit of determination and will power I had to hold him back. I could feel his taste for blood.

I summed my daggers back to me. They flew into my waiting hands.

The guard beat his chest as the flow of blood stopped. My attack hadn't even hurt him.

I sensed my dragons' confusion. It mingled with my own. What had my mom done to this elf? Was he even an elf anymore or had she somehow perverted him into something more dangerous?

The guard flew at me with such speed that I didn't see him move. His fist cracked against the side of my skull and I sank to my knees...

A flash of bright white light exploded behind me. Stars danced across my vision and I slammed shut my eyes, everything glowing a vibrant red behind my eyelids.

When I thought it was safe, I squinted my eyes open and discovered the guard and my mother both prone on the floor. The guard looked like he'd been thrown back about five feet and my mom had smashed into the wall before crumpling to the ground. Both were out cold.

What had happened?

I staggered to my feet and spun to check on Dasha. Cocoa was there, helping her out of the corner.

"Was that you?" I asked the brownie, my jaw hanging slack in relief and surprise.

Cocoa glanced up at me and smiled. "Never underestimate

the power of nurture. It's like a mother bear robbed of her cubs."

I nodded, feeling dumbstruck. "I will never underestimate any magical creature again. How'd you find us?"

"I followed you and waited until you needed my help."

"And the children and brownies?"

"Safe. Brownies delegate; I gave the task of escorting the children out to another. And the commander should have entered the fortress by now."

I held my tongue, uncertain whether I should feel relieved that help was on the way or irritated that she hadn't obeyed me… or that she'd waited so long to step in and rescue me from my fight with the guard.

"We've got to get out of here," I said as Dasha darted for me and threw her arms around me.

Cocoa waved her hand toward the door. "This way."

Once we'd put a few hallways between us, I noticed another of my mother's markings on the wall. I stopped and inspected it. The carving was shaped like an eye, with lashes fanning above it and an inner circle representing the pupil.

I would have to deal with this. If I had done my duty when we'd first entered, the royal soldiers would have been with us. It was foolish. The commander and the royal soldiers could have held Maximon, or Dimas, while I'd deactivated the mark. I shook my head not sure if the royal soldiers would now be of help. Although as brave as Commander Adothlin and his troops were, I doubted they were any match for my mom's guards.

I called for Cocoa to slow down, and the brownie skidded to a stop. Trotting back to where I was crouched next the carving, she let out a hiss.

"It's just like the one on the Royal Tree," she said. "But much more potent."

I cupped my hand over the mark and let my sluggish magic flow into it. "There's dark magic here. Cocoa, help me deactivate it or my mother will be on us in no time."

As I concentrated on breaking the spell, the dragons pushed their own magic, blending it with my own. Cocoa joined forces with me, and soon even Dasha contributed her young magic.

Sweat poured down the sides of my face. Despite our concentrated efforts, this was too strong for us. But if we didn't break it soon, we never would. My mother would certainly find us and bring more guards.

I felt the steady flow of magic weaken. A bit more of the demon's rage was leaking through his cage, despite every effort to hold him back.

"Thorns and weeds..."

I nearly screamed in frustration as Nate's voice floated through my mind. How could any of this philosophical mumbo-jumbo help me now?

You'll never be able to access the full strength of your magic until you deal with your thorns. It wasn't exactly what Nate had said, but close enough to irritate me.

Panting, I pulled back from the mark as if expelled.

"It's too strong," I said, catching my breath.

"Do you want to try again?" Cocoa asked.

I shook my head. My mind was too distracted with thorns and weeds to concentrate. "It's not worth risking our lives. Let's get out of here."

We scrambled back to our feet and took off. Before long we'd reached the foyer.

I glanced around, hoping to spot Nix. If he wasn't here, then maybe he'd made it out. But I knew that probably wasn't the case.

"Cocoa, take Dasha and go," I said, pushing Dasha into the brownie's arms. She clung to my wrist and cried. "Dasha, you have to go."

"No!" the girl cried.

I hugged her, but then stepped away. "Take her, Cocoa. Keep her safe."

Cocoa held the squirming child in her embrace. "And you, my lady?"

"I have to…"

I let my voice trail off as I thought of Nix. Cocoa nodded sharply and turned, pulling a sobbing Dasha behind her.

Tears filled my own eyes at the thought that I might not see her again. But at least she would survive.

Turning back, I called on Chim's stealth, praying that it would hide me from my mother's spying eyes. I headed deeper into the fortress, hoping my instincts would lead me to Nix.

Chapter Twenty-One

Nix

I followed Zoe's map, but despite my best efforts I determined that I was hopelessly lost. I shifted the map in my hand, certain that I had followed it precisely, but the layout of the fortress must have been under some influence of Sirina and Leski, as Zoe had suspected.

As I stepped down a hallway, a cluster of voices in the distance grew closer. So far I had been lucky enough to avoid guards and servants, but I knew I now had to hide.

At the first room I came to, I ducked inside. Like the rest of the fortress, the room was dimly lit. It had a desk to the left and a bookcase decorating the wall beside it. There was a seating area in front of me with a couch and two chairs.

The voices were louder and stopped just outside of the room I had entered. When the doorknob rattled and turned, I dove behind the couch.

"She's here," an older elf said when he entered the room.

I couldn't see anything from my hiding place but those two words were enough for me to recognize its owner: Leski Dion, the traitor.

"Yes, Father, she's with Mother now."

Dimas. I shifted my position, hoping to get a view of the father and son as they spoke, but I couldn't move without giving away my hiding place. I settled for listening in.

"Good," Leski said. "Now we just need to get a hold of that elusive crown prince and our plan will be complete."

"But the ruse of my engagement to the Princess Zyanna hasn't worked," Dimas said.

"I thought it might draw out the prince. I even sent him a letter, nudging him to the Misty Inn, but he never showed. Rather our guards received a walloping by that talented but misguided daughter of mine. Oh well. That will all soon be taken care of."

I winced, thankful that Zyanna hadn't been condemned to a life with Dimas, but the way Leski spoke of Zoe troubled me.

"That the prince hasn't responded to the letter makes me wonder," Leski said. "Though I'm certain he's here…"

Sweat dripped down the side of my face. *Does he know I'm in the room?* I wondered.

"So what's the next move? We've already captured a pawn."

Leski laughed. "Don't refer to your sister that way. She's useful." He sighed. "She never should have run away all those years ago. Your mother and I had relaxed our defenses that night, thinking she would be recuperating… well, no bother. She's home now, and your mother has refined her technique. We merely need the prince to step forward. We'll draw his blood, which is infused with a unique magic that subdues this realm's subjects. Combined with your sister's ability, the royal magic will finally allow us to control the Twilight Realm. She will serve as a proper regent."

"*She'll* control the Twilight Realm?"

"That's right, son. It's a shame that she hasn't fallen in line like you did."

"But I thought…"

Leski chuckled. "Thought what? That we'd really leave the ruling to you?"

Dimas cleared his throat. "But if the monarchy has this special ability, why didn't King Alistair and Queen Calla use it to save themselves?"

"They were weak, my dear boy, and distracted with petty issues. They trusted too much in their magic and became lax. Why, the takeover went smoothly, their deaths came quick. The only chink in the plan was that the prince got away. But I believe my patience has finally been rewarded. Isn't that right, Prince Phoenix?"

How had he known I was there? In confusion, I lunged from my hiding place and pulled my sword from its scabbard in a smooth motion.

Leski stood near the door and smiled as if I were nothing more than a child jumping out from behind curtains to surprise him. To my right, I heard the cool brush of steel as it was released from its scabbard; I glanced at Dimas and noted the blade in his hand.

"Well, well, well, delivered to my doorstep. Thank you for coming." Leski looked me up and down. "Welcome, Prince Phoenix."

"It's King Phoenix." I wasn't sure why I gave him this information, but from the slight waver of Leski's smile I guessed he hadn't expected it.

"You can put those away," Leski said, pointing first at my sword and then Dimas's. I strode closer as Dimas put his away, but I just tightened my grip. "I guarantee, there's no escape. My dear wife has eyes all over this place and I've been watching you make your way through the fortress. Why, I even had our guards clear the way. Were you not curious as to why the fortress was so barren, or how I knew you were hiding behind the couch? Now come, I've waited a long time for this moment. If you had only obeyed all those years ago when I called to you, your parents would most likely still be alive. But you, foolish boy, cared nothing of them. You are responsible for their deaths."

Had Leski truly been after me alone? I doubted it. Their attack on the Royal Tree had been too well planned, too calculated. I recalled what Nate had told me about the power. If Leski had succeeded in his plans all those years ago, he would have killed my parents regardless.

Still, the weight of his words rested heavy on my shoulders. I had always blamed myself for their deaths.

Leski stepped aside and motioned to the seat beside him on the couch.

My eyes narrowed, realizing that I should have stayed with Zoe and not ventured off on my own. My throat constricted at the thought of her being alone in this place. Despite what I'd just overheard, I hoped it was a lie and she was safe and out of the fortress with the brownies and the children.

"What exactly did you want with my blood?" I asked hoping he'd share a little more of their scheme. I got the impression that Leski was quite full of himself and would enjoy sharing their plan. Plus, it'd give me time to think of how to escape and perhaps lull them into a sense of comfort before I attacked or ran.

Leski stretched his arm over the back of the couch. Dimas lowered himself slowly to his chair, keeping a watchful eye on me.

"Its magical properties are unparalleled, of course," Leski explained. "You heard our conversation. Don't play dumb, King Phoenix. It doesn't become you."

"You said you wanted it to control the realm's subjects. What does that mean?"

A smirk lit up Leski's eyes. "You really don't know?" The elf sighed. "I supposed you were quite young when I killed your parents. A shame, really, that they had to die but nothing can be done about that now."

Irritation rose in me and I leveled my sword against his throat. "Enough with the delaying tactics!"

Leski studied the sword, then me, and his expression cooled. "All right. If you insist, I'll school you. The monarchy has a unique magical ability. You probably sensed it at your coronation."

I lowered my sword but didn't sheath it. I remembered the burst of power that had flooded over me in the throne room earlier in the day. It was like I had suddenly connected to each of my subjects.

Leski continued, "Well, most monarchs have taken it for granted. Your parents, for example. I mean, what monarch would dare believe his subjects would betray him when they were under such a compulsion?"

Had my parents really been as passive as I suspected? As much as I hated to admit it, Leski did have a point. If the royal magic worked the way he said, it was possible that my parents had fallen victim to overconfidence.

"It's impossible to take another's magic," I pointed out. "Magic can only be willingly blended with another's." I thought of Zoe and what she'd told me earlier about receiving her tattoos and the pain she endured. Forced magic always hurt, but shared magic was as comforting as slipping into a tub of warm water.

"My dear king, this is where you are wrong. My brilliant wife was trained in dark magic by the followers of Nosh Dem." Leski stroked his mustache. "She learned how to blend and manipulate the magic of another. We tried for years with Zoe and the poor girl suffered until dear Sirina came up with some way around it. Too bad Zoe's not interested in joining our cause. She would be a true leader if she'd only embrace her potential."

I thought of Pat, Zoe's healing dragon. *Are her parents so clueless about how her magic brought the tattoos to life?* Out of the corner of my eye, I saw Dimas wince. Perhaps he had wanted to be the leader and Zoe had stood in his way.

I cleared my throat, not interested in hearing Leski wax eloquent about his aspirations for Zoe.

No wonder Zoe's tattoos had hurt so much when they were burned into her skin; it had been the process of foreign magic mixing with her own. Although I had only seen her arms, she'd told me the extent of her tattoos. I couldn't imagine what that must have been like, to endure the repeated process for as long as she had. What parent would subject their child to such torture?

"Once Zoe has been marked by my wife with the mixture of royal and dark magic," Leski said, "we will finally be able to control her. She will be made regent over the Twilight Realm, and subsequently we'll finally be able to mark the rest of the elves, too, and enjoy true dominion. Why, I'd even be willing to let you be king, with my daughter at your side, if you would join us. What say you, *King* Phoenix? My daughter is quite beautiful and unique."

The way Leski bartered with his daughter's life, as though she were nothing more than an item to sell at market, made my stomach roll. Zoe was beautiful, true, but no way would I consider what her father was suggesting. Zoe deserved her freedom and the right to choose her own spouse. I wouldn't allow such things in my kingdom. The elves of the Twilight Realm had suffered enough at the hands of the Dions.

My hand tightened around the hilt of my sword. I was learning nothing new from this fool.

"We decline your offer," I announced. I raised my arm and moved to strike the older elf. I'd knock him out and deal with him and his wife later.

Dimas's sword clanged against mine and I twisted my blade and pushed. Dimas stumbled back a few steps and I knew this would be an easy fight. He was a poor swordsman. He retreated until he was backed against the bookcase. I then swung and bashed the side of his head with my hilt. Dimas fell to the floor, knocking a few rows of books from the shelf in the process.

I turned to face Leski. "For your crimes against the crown, I place you, your wife, and your son under arrest to be tried in a court of justice."

Leski laughed—a deep and hearty belly laugh. I lifted my arm to strike his head, having had enough of him, but he held up his hand to stop me.

"Dear king, please. Let us speak civilly and come to an arrangement. After all, what about your sister? I know where she is."

Zyanna. "What have you done with her?"

"Nothing, and that's the truth." He shrugged. "Don't believe me? Her nurse took her to the Night Realm where she remains to this day."

Anger flared within me as I wondered whether he spoke truth. All these years, was she even alive?

"Relax, she's safe," Leski added. "If you spare me, I'll take you to her."

I saw the same glint of triumph he'd shown to my father when the king had offered him leniency.

My arm swung and the hilt dug into the side of Leski's head. He crumpled onto the couch, then slid to the floor. Defeating him had been easy, too easy, but then perhaps he never intended to let me escape. I thought of the markings on the walls and what Leski had said about leading me to this room.

I leaned over his prone body and confirmed that he was out cold, like Dimas. But the two of them would come to before long.

I didn't have much time. I had to find Zoe and get us out. Then we'd come back and deal with the Dions.

Catching sight of a magical symbol on the wall, I guessed that Sirina was paying attention. Chances were she'd already sent guards to intercept me.

I ran from the room, trying to guess my way through the maze of dimly lit corridors by instinct. Before long, I realized that I was lost again.

The sound of approaching steps alerted me to guards, so I checked to see if any of the nearby doors were unlocked. They weren't. Out of options, I hefted my sword and prepared for the fight of my life.

The guards were on me in moments, and I swung my sword without much guidance. I blocked a blow to the head, then elbowed my attacker in the temple. He staggered away, soon replaced by another guard, who I stabbed in the gut. I paused my movements out of shock. While Nate had trained me in sword fighting, I had never struck a blow that could mortally wound another. I recovered after a moment of hesitation. As the guard grunted and fell, I swept my sword out around me to catch the next attacker—

Only there weren't any.

I looked down at one of the fallen guards, gasping for breath, and I guessed he didn't have long left. Blood spurted from his wound and our eyes locked; there was recognition there, and a flicker of his magic reach out to me. I winced but it felt like what I'd experienced at my coronation. I knelt. My magic merged with his and I sensed his loyalty, his devotion to the crown.

"My king," he gasped. "I'm sorry."

I rested a hand on his forehead. How had Leski and Sirina managed to enchant him? Leski and Zoe had both mentioned Sirina's ability to manipulate magic to control others. I thought back to what Zoe had told me of her demon tattoo and what I'd witnessed when it had taken over. How had Sirina done it? Questions for later. The how wasn't as important to me as undoing what the Dions had done. I wanted my kingdom freed.

Now that this elf was near death, all he had were the memories of his enchantment. I shook my head both in pity for the elf and at the evil thrust on him by Leski and Sirina.

"You did well," I assured him. I didn't know what else to say.

Peace rested on his face as a slow exhale rattled from his chest. I bowed my head and closed his vacant eyes. He was gone.

The other guard stirred, and I turned to him, knowing that he too had been under the spell of the Dions. Perhaps he still was. Not wanting to take a chance, I got up and sprinted down the hallway.

I continued in my worthless navigation through the confusing corridors, kicking myself that I had gone off on my own. Nate and Commander Adothlin hadn't wanted me coming in here alone, but I hadn't listened, and now I seemed to be running in circles.

Heading down another dimly lit corridor, I slowed to a walk to conserve energy. When I heard footsteps up ahead, I held my sword at the ready and turned slowly in a tight circle.

Nothing in front of me. Nothing behind me. Nothing beside me.

Suddenly, a solid mass slammed into my back and I spun to greet my newest attacker.

Chapter Twenty-Two

Zoe

I wasn't sure how long I wandered through the darkened corridors of the fortress, but Chim's shielding held strong and I didn't run into any of my mother's guards. I hadn't found Nix yet, and that had me worried. I rubbed my sweaty hands over my pants, and then I found myself staring at another of my mother's markings. I ran my hand over it, sensing its magic. Its power didn't feel as strong as the one I had tried to work on earlier with Cocoa. Maybe I would have a chance at deactivating it.

I called forth my dragons to stand guard as I summoned my magic, but it flowed slow and at its fractured pace through me. Why had it been so strong at the Royal Tree but not here in the fortress?

A flare of frustration toward my parents rose up in me. Why were they doing this? Not just with these markings, but with everything they'd done to the Twilight Realm in killing the royal family, experimenting on children, and attempting to rule by force. I shook my head. I would never understand it.

I knelt next to the mark and took a deep calming breath, hoping to expel some of the tension I felt. I closed my eyes and cupped my hand over the mark. It buzzed with energy and dark magic.

Pat and Tupac perched on my shoulder, providing a magical boost while Chim kept watch and kept me shielded. As our combined magic flowed into the mark, it seemed to me that the mark fed on it and pulsed with renewed power.

I pulled back. We hadn't only failed to deactivate the mark but had succeeded in making its magic stronger and giving away our location.

Let's go, I ordered the dragons as we hurtled down the corridor. We didn't have long before my mother or her guards would be upon us.

Distracted by my thoughts, I crashed into something and bounced back. My daggers landed solidly in my hands and I took up a fighting stance.

Then I realized who I'd bounced into.

"Nix?" I said as the daggers melded back into my skin. Seeing my friend made me want to give him a hug, even though it was unlike me. I held back this surge of affection.

"Zoe, what are you doing here?" Nix asked, his eyes round with surprise.

He grabbed me in an embrace and I patted his back, allowing myself to enjoy it for a moment before pulling away.

"We've got to keep moving," I said. "I think my mother's not far behind."

Grabbing his hand, we entered the next corridor. While jogging, Nix filled me in on his conversation with my father.

I couldn't suppress the anger I felt at the revelation that they planned to use me to control the citizens of the Twilight Realm. Though it shouldn't have surprised me.

As my irritation grew, I felt the demon inside me strengthen. I had to stay focused and in control of my emotions, and not let it overpower me. Pat sent a calming wave through me and Tupac reinforced the barriers holding the demon in.

Panting, I stopped and gripped my knees. I needed to catch my breath.

"We're lost!" I said. "We should have reached the main chamber by now."

Nix's gaze swept the corridor. "Rest for a moment."

Spotting another one of my mother's marks, I grimaced. "I have to find a way to deactivate these."

I ran my hand over the engraved stone. My parents had gone to great lengths to etch tattoos into my skin... there had to be something I could use. I began taking mental inventory of the tattoos covering my body...

I leaned against the wall and inhaled sharply. "Come, stand next to me."

He hesitated. He'd given me space since I'd told him he'd been taking liberties at the Royal Tree. He'd been respecting my request and that sent a little flutter through my stomach.

"Chim's shielding me from my mother's spying eyes. I want you to be covered, too."

Nix stepped beside me. "Smart. It's not too big of a power drain?"

I shook my head.

Nix took my hand and I was about to protest when I felt a warm surge of energy pour into me. It was like a burst of sunlight on a hot summer's day and it cascaded into me in a golden stream. This was Nix's magic! I sensed his personality mixed with the warmth.

I started to pull my hand away. "Thanks for the boost, but I don't want you to weaken yourself."

Nix nodded slightly in acknowledgment but didn't let go. The reprieve was welcome and his boost really did help me to focus.

I continued the process of mentally ticking off my tattoos. There were other weapons, including two swords on my back that ran alongside Chim's body, not to mention a knife along my calves. Most of my tattoos were weapons. Then there was that pin tattoo on my finger, and a flower tattoo on my palm...

"What are you thinking about?" Nix asked.

I glanced up at him and realized he'd been studying me. My cheeks warmed with a rush of embarrassment.

"I'm trying to figure out which of my tattoos might help deactivate my mother's markings."

"Come up with anything?"

"No," I said sullenly. "When I use my magic, it bestows life and power, which makes deactivating these extra challenging..."

The silence of the corridor and fortress gave me time to rest and think. My mind flipped through the options my tattoos offered, but nothing seemed useful.

"You're not like the Dions, you know," Nix said.

I stared in futility at the mark. "I'm their daughter."

"Being their daughter and being like them are two very different things."

I didn't have a response, but his words sank into my thoughts and mixed with the maelstrom of emotions I was wrestling with. They were my parents, but I wasn't like them.

"Weed and thorns..."

Nate's voice interrupted my thoughts and reminded me of the object lesson in his greenhouse. Weeds and thorns grew in the same soil. Thorns were a part of the plant, but weeds grew around the plant. Hadn't Nate said something about the thorns being my responsibility and the weeds being things that had happened to me? Was it possible that the anger, fear, and shame my parents stirred in me were my responsibility—but what they'd done to me was their responsibility? The two felt so intertwined that it was hard to determine where one began and the other ended. But if I separated the tattoos from the emotions I felt about the tattoos…

I slumped, feeling the weight of everything press down on my shoulders. I equally hated and feared my parents. Waves of memories hit me. Me as a little girl, begging them not to ink the next tattoo. Clinging to my mom as she laughed and placed me in her lab chair. A slap across the cheek that sent my head spinning when I tried to fight back. The aloneness of being dumped back in my room when they were done with me. I'd cry in the dark, my hands covering the spot where the newest tattoo had been inked. My skin burning with the foreign magic, unwelcomed, inside me, feeding my own magic into the wound, giving it life and believing it was something better than what my parents had intended.

In my abandonment, out of my crippling pain, I realized what I'd done. I had desperately needed relief, so I'd released my magic into the tattoos… remaking them, changing their very *nature.* I had craved friends, needed the pain to stop…

And so my dragons had been born.

As my dragons now fluttered around me, I caught Nix

watching me. I knew that I was on the verge of fully understanding Nate's lesson.

Instead of pulling back, Nix wrapped an arm around my shoulder. Despite my reservations, I leaned into him and let myself relax.

My mind walked through my life after leaving the fortress. I'd left physically, but not mentally or emotionally. I'd been holding onto everything that had happened to me as a child. I felt Pat butt her head against my chin.

I finally understood that part of the magic I'd wielded as a child had been blocked off by the demon tattoo. I had never allowed my magic to merge with it like I had my other tattoos. I had woken up with a sense of loss. Something inside me had fractured.

There was no way for me to take down my parents with only a portion of my magic. In truth, since the night the demon tattoo had taken up residence on my chest, I hadn't been able to access all of my magic. It was sluggish. I needed to use *all of my magic*. My mind snapped as Nate's lessons and my memories connected. *All of my magic. Weeds and thorns.* And in my desperation as a child, when I merged my magic with the tattoos, my magic had changed them and given them life.

There is only one way to free yourself of that particular tattoo. You have to forgive and let your magic merge with it. Nate's words from yesterday echoed in my mind. I knew it was time to forgive and let go.

I stroked Pat's skin, thinking of all the things my parents had done to me and all the emotions I had attached to them. The onslaught overpowered me. Forgiveness might mean I'd lose all my tattoos, but something told me I wouldn't, and that I was doing worse damage to myself in my current state.

I remembered the image of Vaim Na'quab, the dove, hanging in Nate's office and the longing for peace it symbolized... a deep internal peace. I wanted that more than anything, but I didn't know if it was possible to achieve. I was determined to try. Anything was better than this torment, this war with myself.

I let all these emotions and memories surface, and I pictured them as a ball wound tight and ready to explode.

I choose to forgive, I thought, covering the sphere with my magic. *I choose to let go.*

The sphere in my mind pulsed with magic, shaking, and then bursting into millions of strands. As each snapped, they dispersed into nothingness, taking from me all the tension that had been attached to my memories and emotions.

I felt like I was falling as the rush of this release overwhelmed me. New strength infused me and I felt my demon tattoo shrivel. He weakened and weakened until he was utterly gone.

A giggle bubbled up in me, and I covered my mouth. He was gone... he was really gone! And so was all the anger and hurt I'd carried for years. I was free of it—of everything.

My eyes shot open and I slid my arms around Nix. His arms slowly encompassed me probably because he wasn't sure what to make of my sudden display of affection.

He stepped back and his hands gently held my arms. "Zoe, you glowed."

"Excuse?"

"Yeah, a soft white light. It came from within you and increased until this corridor shone with the light of day. I could barely stand to look at it. It burned my eyes, but you looked so content. And your face was peaceful. What happened?"

I explained to him what I had just experienced. Excitedly, I turned to my chittering dragons to confirm that they were, indeed, still there. I hugged each one in turn and felt their strengthened energy, which when combined flooded through us and made us feel full. This was the fullness of my magic. How it used to feel before the demon tattoo. How it was supposed to feel.

After I'd danced around with the dragons in jubilation, I checked what tattoos I could. They were all still there, including my daggers, the pin, and the flower. I was confident that all the tattoos were intact, save one; my hand rested over my heart and felt only warm energy radiating from it. I was free. The curse of my demon tattoo, of my negative emotions—or the thorns, as Nate had called them—had been destroyed.

Nix stared at me with a goofy grin. "Congratulations."

"Thanks, but we've still got to get out of here. I'm sure my mother and her guards will be on us in no time."

It felt weird to hear myself say that, since I no longer felt any of the usual pangs of fear and anger.

I squatted down and placed my hand over the mark on the wall, feeling the dark power emanating from it like before—but this time, there was no interference from my demon tattoo.

As my dragons settled on my head and shoulders, I heard a loud scuffing sound behind us. I whirled, daggers in hand, as my mother's guards descended on us.

Chapter Twenty-Three

Nix

I raised my sword and swung at the first guard. He fell. I bashed the next in the head as well, but the third engaged his scimitars, one in each hand, and repelled me. I regained my footing and struck, but the elf kept up his defense. I had no time to check on Zoe, but from the clang of weapons I knew she was still fighting. We needed to end this and get out.

Using a trick Nate had taught me, I twisted my blade, catching the guard unaware. His arms folded in an unnatural manner, causing his blades to fall from his hands. He stumbled into a wall and I easily knocked him out.

I caught my breath and watched as Zoe delivered a crushing blow to the back of one of the other guards' head. He crumpled.

"That's the last of them," I said, making a quick survey of our crowded hallway.

"For now." Zoe wiped her daggers with the shirt of a fallen

guard before letting them meld back to her forearms.

I wasn't sure what it was about her, but there was a new confidence in her stance and a calm on her usually tense face.

I cleaned my sword but kept it ready for the next wave of attackers.

"Let's go," I said.

We took off down the corridor, leaving the fallen in our wake. At the next turn, a group of three guards fought us, but once again we were able to drive them back and continue through the confusing building.

Eventually we came to an intersection of three corridors.

"Which way?" Zoe asked, holding her side and breathing heavily.

"You're the expert." I smiled so as not to show my frustration.

Zoe shrugged. "At this point, your guess is as good as mine. I'm lost."

I turned in a circle, gauging which might be the best direction. A flutter of black darted past my periphery. It was one of Zoe's dragons. Her other two dragons took off, one in each of the corridors before us.

"I'm sending them out to scout the best route," Zoe said.

"Won't it weaken you to let them range so far?" I asked.

"I don't think so, not anymore." A grin split Zoe's face.

Suddenly, a new thought occurred to me. "Wait. With everything that's changed, is it possible now to use your magic to deactivate your mother's marks?"

She tapped her finger to her lips and studied a mark on a nearby wall. "Maybe..."

I glanced around our surroundings and saw at least five markings. "You should try. If any guards come, I'll hold them off."

Zoe knelt next to the closest pattern and cupped her hand over it. I hoped she would be successful. We needed to disable Sirina's ability to track us, otherwise I feared we'd just keep running in circles.

She squared her shoulders, rested her hand over the mark, and closed her eyes. A moment later, the dragons zoomed back down their corridors. I guessed from their sudden focused attention on Zoe that they were helping her.

I gazed back along the path we'd come from, then shifted to peer down the other three. When the guards came—and I knew they would—which direction would they come from?

I didn't have long to wait. The attack came from every direction at once as four elves, each bellowing in rage, streamed out of the dark. I gripped my sword tight in preparation for the onslaught. I kept my back to Zoe, guarding her with my life. Keeping her safe was all that mattered.

The first guard was on me in moments. His sword flashed and I struggled to keep up. I did manage to send him sprawling, but only for a moment before the next guard faced me, launching a dual attack, joined by a third man. I swung at their swords, dancing and defending myself on all sides. It took all my concentration to hold them off; it was the royal magic working through me, but in truth I knew I shouldn't have been here alone from the start. Nate and Commander Adothlin had been right. And I hoped I'd survive to tell them.

My arms were growing tired, but I couldn't let my blade fall or it'd be over in a moment. I took another swing and tried lunging at one of my attackers, but he quickly regained his footing and pressed forward on me again.

In the blur, I thought of my parents and their folly, thought of my forces standing ready outside the fortress with Nate. I had been foolish not to let even a small detachment join me.

I swung an arc around me and the guards stepped back, giving me room to move, but only for an instant. Sweat poured down my face and stung my eyes. I wiped at it, but I couldn't clear away the fog that had been clouding my judgment. I'd let my own cowardice and pride get in the way of good leadership, just like my parents had taken for granted the power of the royal magic to protect them, failing to remain vigilant against their enemies.

I had acted like a total and complete fool. What kind of king would I be if I survived?

As another strike rained upon me, I stumbled and my arms dropped. A guard sliced at my arm and a howl escaped my lips.

This is not the end, I thought as my knees buckled. *This cannot be the end.*

I couldn't be the last ruler of the Twilight Realm. We had existed for thousands of years. I raised myself up, decided to fight one-handed if need be.

Preparing for the next strike, I gripped my sword, closed my eyes, and focused on the royal magic within me. With grim determination, I realized that I needed help.

A sudden flood of magic came at me from all directions. I could sense all my allies—Nate and Zoe, and Adothlin, and even elves as far away as the small city of Haven, including Yoli, Toli, and Nyla. Magic surged into me from elves and creatures I'd never met, from the royal brownies to the children we'd rescued, each of them lending me a small piece of themselves.

Nearly as soon as it entered me, all this magic pulsed out of me in a shockwave.

The building shook and the guards wore awed expressions. Pat then landed on my wounded arm and her healing power rushed into it.

"Thanks, Pat," I said, raising my sword again.

The guards leered at me and charged.

Twilight's Curse

Chapter Twenty-Four

Zoe

The clash of swords rang out and I felt the brush of battle behind me. The coppery smell of blood drifted to my nose and the grunt of the guards pulled at my instincts to join the fight. With great effort, I closed my mind to these distractions and gave all my attention and energy to the wall before me. I didn't want to pour any magic into the markings until I felt certain I could deactivate them. I had figured out that my mother had taken dark magic and mixed it with her own, and I would need to separate the two—but I wasn't sure how.

My mind raced through my arsenal of tattoos. Aside from my usual tools, there were a few along my left shin that I rarely thought about; these had been among my mother's earliest experiments and had no obvious purpose or life to them. There was an elaborate oval, which perhaps my mother had meant for a shield, but nothing had ever come of the design.

Maybe these tattoos don't do anything because I got them before I started using my magic to give my tattoos a purpose, the idea springing up with giddy excitement. Testing this theory, I fed some of my magic into the oval-shaped tattoo. This time my magic flowed smooth and fast. My magic was whole once again! I had to concentrating on controlling the flow and giving the tattoo a purpose. What I needed was something to absorb the dark magic from the wall markings.

I felt a sword swipe near enough to my head to ruffle my hair. Adrenaline raced through me as the dragons chittered and swayed. I didn't know how many attackers Nix was holding off, but experience told me he couldn't keep it up much longer.

As I concentrated on the oval tattoo, it suddenly released from my skin and dropped onto the toe of my boot, taking the form of a beautifully embroidered cloth. Surprised, I held it up and pressed it against the mark on the wall. Would it work?

I fed my magic into the cloth, activating its purpose, and felt the dark magic immediately begin to respond. Success! A smile wove its way across my lips as the cloth absorb the dark magic. No, not absorb it; it disintegrated it.

Not wanting to rush but feeling impatient, I muttered at the cloth, willing it to hurry. The last thing we needed was a sloppy or incomplete removal, but Nix had to be tiring. I refocused my efforts, trying to strengthen the magical flow. If Nix fell, we were done for.

When the last of the dark magic had seeped into the cloth, I quickly moved to apply the same technique to the next mark. When I placed the cloth against the wall, however, nothing happened. I moved to the next one, and each mark within reach, and realized I had inadvertently cleaned them all; only my mother's magic remained.

I let the cloth meld back into my skin and set to work on the last step: deactivating my mother's magic. This was easy enough. I'd done it at the Royal Tree earlier today.

As I let my magic flow, I enjoyed the sense of rushing fresh water, its cleaning stream hitting the wall marking and spreading through the entire fortress. In response, I felt the fortress shake around us.

It had worked. The markings no longer had any magical properties. I couldn't help the giggle at my triumph.

But there was no time to celebrate. Nix grunted behind me and Pat sent a picture into my mind of his wound, which she was trying to heal.

Releasing the sabers on my back, I jumped into the fray, giving Nix a reprieve for Pat to finish her healing work. Chim shielded me against the guards' blows and Tupac lent my strikes greater accuracy.

Within moments, the guards had all fallen unconscious.

"Are you okay?" I asked, rushing to Nix's side and studying the healing tissues on his arm.

"I'll be fine." He nodded toward the wall. "The marks?"

"Done."

"Great. Let's find the next ones—"

"No, they're all down."

Nix got to his feet and ran his hand over the closest markings. "How?" he asked amazed.

The steady flow of steps alerted me to more guards headed our way. I gripped Nix's hand, pulling him along.

"Later," I said. "We're about to have company."

Commands made their way through the tunnels:

"Spread out and search."

"Right. We'll find them."

Nix and I looked at each other, then at the direction of the voices. That wasn't my mother's guards; those were the voices of our allies!

"That's Nate," I said.

"And Commander Adothlin."

We both turned and shouted as Nate, Adothlin, and the host of the royal soldiers surrounded us. It was a relief to see them. I glanced at Nix, noting the bloody smears across his face and arms. I took in my own apparel and realized that I didn't look much better.

I ran into Nate's arms and gave him a tight hug. The royal advisor stiffened, doing a poor job of hiding his surprise from this very uncommon show of affection. In all the years we had known each other, I had never initiated a hug. In response, though, he wrapped his arms around me in the warmest embrace.

As he pulled back, I saw a grin on his face.

"I think we'll have a few things to discuss," he said.

I waggled my eyebrows at him. "Weeds and thorns."

Nate laughed as he moved to embrace Nix while the rest of the royal soldiers began to bind up the arms of our enemies and line them up along the wall.

"Your orders, sire?" Commander Adothlin asked.

Nix turned to me. "Zoe, your parents did something to their guards that makes them obedient. Do you think you could free them? Remove the evil like you did with the marks?"

I glanced at the enemy guards, wondering if such a thing were possible. It wasn't anything I had ever considered before.

"I'll try." I knelt next to the closest guard. Startled, I realized it was Derek, my fighting tutor whom I hadn't seen since

I'd left the fortress over six years ago. I brushed his hair back from his face and remembered his training. He was never mean. And as I considered our hours spent training together, I remembered catching almost wistful moments in his expressions. Had my parents changed him? Probably. I rested my palm on the side of his face.

New resolve welled up in me. Who would Derek be if I set him free of whatever my parents had done to him? I hesitated before taking the step of flooding him with my magic and potentially burning him. With Chim's help, I allowed my magic to pour into the guard, searching for evidence of what my parents had done.

My magic flowed through the elf, touching his own. It was like the guard's magic was eager to encounter mine and even lead it to where it needed to go. At his core, I felt the confluence of my mother's magic, his own stifled magic… and now mine. Mentally, I reached for my cloth tattoo and wielded it psychically, feeling my mother's magic begin to draw out, absorbing into the cloth.

Finishing, I opened my eyes and moved on to the next guard.

"Did it work?" Nate asked.

I had been so focused on my task that I hadn't even felt him crouch next to me. "I think so," I said.

There would be no way to know for sure until the guard woke up.

As I performed the same procedure on the other guards, I found each of their magics eager for my help, eager to be free of my mother's hold on them.

By the time I finished, Derek was coming around. Nix was kneeling next to him.

"What happened?" Derek's words slurred. He shook his

head as if trying to throw off a deep slumber and looked around like he didn't know where he was.

"Are you all right?" Nix asked.

The elf's eyes settled on him and nearly popped out of his head. "Your Majesty! I beg your pardon…" Derek bowed his head and tried to stand.

Nix stopped him. "Can you tell me how you feel?"

I came up behind Nix and peered at Derek. Through my magic, I could tell there was no remaining trace in him of my mother's influence.

"He's clean," I said. "And given the hold my mother had on these guards, they might not even know what happened to them."

"Forgive me, but you look familiar." Derek squinted his eyes.

I knelt next to him and smiled. "Welcome back."

He tilted his head to the side then gasped. "Zoe? How? It can't be! Did you do this?"

I smiled. "It's good to see you, old friend."

"You know him?" Nix asked.

"This is Derek. He was my weapons trainer."

"Your parents… What they did to you and at such a young age. It never felt right. Even when I was under—" Derek tilted his head back and inhaled.

I patted his hand. He gripped it in his thickly calloused hold. "It's best to forget it."

Nix turned on his haunches and peered up at one of his own soldiers. "Stay with these elves. We need to find Leski and Sirina."

"You're looking for the Lord and Lady?" Derek asked.

Nix looked back at him. "Yes."

268

Chapter Twenty-Four

"I can take you too them," he said, trying to stand again.

"Are you sure?" Nix asked. He helped Derek to his feet.

Commander Adothlin stepped forward. "Not a wise decision, sire."

But Nix seemed to disagree. "I trust Zoe's work and I'd like to deal with these traitors quickly."

"Yes, sire…" The commander eyed me, then bowed his head.

"Besides, I have the rest of the royal soldiers with me," Nix added.

"As you say." Adothlin then steadied Derek. "Lieutenant Alwythin, help this guard."

An elf separated from the others and bowed. I guessed he was probably close to my age, and I further guessed that he might be related the commander. He looked like a younger version of Adothlin. A brother, maybe?

Adothlin and Alwythin stood on either side of Derek, helping him to walk—and also making sure he wouldn't suddenly turn on Nix. They didn't trust him and were doing their duty to keep the king safe. I knew it wasn't needed; the elf was free and loyal to the crown. But it would take time for the others to see that.

Thankfully, Nix trusted me. A deep sense of pride welled up in me in the work we had accomplished today. My magic was finally being used to help others, the way it should have been all along.

Twilight's Curse

Chapter Twenty-Five

Nix

With the fortress's guard leading us, we made great time through the corridors and I actually started to recognize some of the areas we passed. I had been down this way before.

Zoe walked next to me. I wanted to say something to her, but words failed me. She'd amazed me by how she'd handled her fears and chosen to forgive her parents. Her magic was so unique and special... *she* was special. My heart swelled with pride in knowing her and the changes she had brought out of me. Watching her courage had helped me face my own fears. What should an elf say to such a woman? What should he say to a hero?

I reached for her hand and squeezed. She gave me a questioning gaze.

"Still going strong?" I asked, nodded toward her dragons, who flitted around in the air. Being apart from them so long had tired her before, and it had once again been a while since

271

they'd last returned to her skin.

"It's different now," she said. "It's like they have their own strength, their own life. They don't draw energy from me anymore. It feels a bit odd, but…" Her face transformed into a brilliant grin. "I like it."

"You did great back there, by the way."

"Thanks." Zoe ducked her head and I saw a pink tinge to her cheeks.

"I'm proud of you." The words were out of my mouth before I had time to think, but based on the pleasure emanating from her, the words seemed to be appropriate.

When I let go of her hand, she pulled away a little bit—but we had time. She was younger than me and we were both incredibly young for elves. Plus, we'd only known each other for two or three days. I wasn't sure how much time had passed while in this fortress. But being with her felt right, and once this was all over, I wanted to get to know her.

She was smiling at me. I wanted it to mirror my own desire and say, *Yes, I'd like to get to know you more, too.*

I had noticed that the brownies were already calling her "my lady," but I thought that title was wrong since she wasn't of the royal line. Still, the brownies had a way about them. They knew things, sensed things, the rest of the world didn't.

Ahead of us, the fortress's guard came to a stop in front of a door that I recognized. It was the room where I'd hidden earlier, the one where I'd overheard the conversation between Dimas and Leski.

"Are they in here?" I asked.

"I believe so, Your Majesty," Derek replied.

I nodded my appreciation toward the guard.

"Your orders, Your Majesty?" Commander Adothlin asked.

I glanced at Zoe, trying to gauge her reaction. Though I didn't like to associate the traitors with her, these were her parents we were talking about.

"What do you think, Zoe?"

"Offer them mercy first," she said in an even voice.

I had to guess this was hard on her both emotionally and mentally. Nate came up beside her and draped a fatherly arm over her shoulders.

Turning back to the commander, I said, "We will confront the usurpers and offer them mercy. Imprisonment instead of death."

"And when they refuse?" Adothlin asked. "It is a strong possibility."

"If they refuse, mercy will not be given."

It wasn't easy for me to give that command, since I never wanted to take a life. Life was precious. But for these crimes, there could be no other option. They had killed my parents, caused my sister to be raised in the Night Realm, tormented children, and brainwashed and controlled their guards. Their crimes were too numerous. For them, death would be the smallest punishment I could give them and keep my morality. I did not want vengeance, but justice.

I nodded to Derek and he swung the door open.

Leski and Dimas were seated in the same places they had been before, and Sirina was standing next to her husband, her face shot with surprise at our entrance.

"Traitors to the crown," Adothlin said, stepping aside to let me enter with my soldiers.

I held the royal posture my father had taught me as a child. Even Zoe straightened and held her head high.

Sirina gasped. "Impossible! How did you get in here?"

So she hadn't been able to sense when Zoe broke her enchantments.

I ignored her question. "By order of the crown, we are here to offer mercy. Please accept this offer, as it will only be given once. You will be stripped of your title as regents and sentenced to serve the remainder of your lives in the royal prisons. For your crimes against the Twilight Realm, its citizenry, and the royal family, you will be spared an unnatural death. This is mercy."

Sirina laughed. It sounded like a delicate bell, soft and subtle. "We will accept no such offer."

Leski shook himself as if in a stupor. "No, the offer is unacceptable."

I turned to their son, who stared at the coffee table before him.

"Dimas?" I prompted.

Dimas looked up and glanced at Zoe. Everything in me wanted to shield her from that stare, but she held her posture and did not return her brother's gaze. Her jaw muscles twitched.

Dimas stood up in a fluid motion and moved to his mother's side. "I cannot accept your offer."

"So be it," I replied. "You have been offered mercy and the gift has been rejected in the presence of witnesses. You will now be sentenced to an unnatural death."

There was a sharp intake of breath from Zoe as she turned and left the room with Nate at her side. My soldiers stepped forward and bound the Dion family in magic-blocking cuffs around their wrists and ankles. The Dions would be taken to the commander's training grounds to be executed. I'm not sure if an execution had ever taken place before in the history of the Twilight Realm. Certainly it had never been recorded in the histories. This crime, however, could receive no lighter sentence.

"Your Majesty, if you please." Commander Adothlin motioned to the door.

I nodded and left the room, wanting to check on Zoe. I had just sentenced her parents to death. The weight of this settled on me, as did a cold dread.

Will she ever forgive me? I asked myself. *Not King Phoenix, but me, Nix, her friend?*

It didn't take me long to find Zoe. Nate had taken her to a room across the hall, similar to the one we had just been in but with more bookshelves. They were seated beside each other on a couch. The older elf patted her shoulder. Tears slid down the sides of her cheeks as she twisted a handkerchief between her fingers.

"Zoe," I said softly as I entered. Her posture stiffened at my presence and my heart fell. "I'm sorry. It has to be done."

Her glare shot into my chest and I paused halfway toward her.

She raised an eyebrow, then stood and took a step in my direction. "Is that your excuse? You are no better than they are."

Her accusation pierced me and I winced. Nate rose from the couch silently and closed the door behind him, giving me and Zoe privacy.

Zoe closed the distance between us and looked at me. Her cheeks were stained with tears and I wasn't King Phoenix in this moment; I was Nix, and as Nix, her friend, I wanted to comfort her. I reached out and wrapped my arms around her. Thankfully, she didn't pull away. I let her cry into my shoulder until her tears subsided.

"Don't you fear that in killing them you will become just like them?" Zoe asked, sniffing.

"No, the Dions killed for reasons of selfishness and to overtake the kingdom. I do not take their lives lightly and I do not agree with taking a life unless absolutely necessary."

"And this is necessary?"

"I offered them mercy. They did not accept it."

"You could still choose to give it to them."

I pulled back. "Zoe, what would you have me do? They killed the royal family, and because of their actions my sister was raised in the Night Realm. How many countless lives have they taken? Think of the guards you just set free from their magic. Think of the children. And their crimes against you." Zoe's face softened, encouraging me to continue. "I do not take their lives for revenge, nor do I take their lives because I don't value them. I take their lives for justice. They committed great crimes against the crown and those who live in this realm. My father even gave them a second chance after their exile to the Night Realm. It is the only rightful punishment."

I raised my hand to brush a lock of hair away from her wet cheek.

Zoe turned and slowly made her way back to the couch, still holding that handkerchief in her hand. She wouldn't look at me. Everything in me wanted to go to her.

I took a step. Even if she yelled at me, it wouldn't matter; she was in a tremendous amount of pain right now and I had to be here for her. If our friendship meant anything, if our friendship had any possibility of growing into more, I couldn't leave her. Not now. Not when she needed a friend the most.

Chapter Twenty-Five

"Please don't be angry at me," I said.

"I know… I know they deserve death." Zoe hiccupped. "And until a short time ago, I wanted them dead."

I sat beside her on the couch and gripped her hands in mine. "What changed?"

"I finally got rid of my thorns."

"Excuse me?"

Zoe explained the object lesson Nate had given her. "The thorns represent the anger and hatred I've felt, which I rid myself of when I finally accepted what happened to me. No, I don't want my family to go free, but I don't want them to die either."

A soft knock sounded at the door, and reluctantly I went to open it. I cracked open the door and encountered Commander Adothlin waiting in the hall.

"Your Majesty," he said, stepping aside. "We're ready."

I softly called for Nate then, and motioned for him to come toward me. I hated that I had to leave Zoe now of all times and didn't want her to be alone. But as the king, I had to witness the Dions' execution.

"Nate," I said. "Stay with her."

Nate nodded in understanding, then moved to the couch and took up his post.

Before leaving, I returned to the couch and laid my hand gently on her shoulder. She didn't flinch or pull away. "I have to go. I'm sorry, but I'll come back and we will talk more."

She didn't respond. She didn't even turn to look at me.

I walked toward the door and was about to open it when she spoke.

"Please, don't." Her voice was just above a whisper and sliced through my heart.

I wanted to turn back and comfort her. She was in pain and needed time to process all that had happened tonight. I understood a little of what she felt. My parents had been taken from me at a young age and a part of me had always longed for the lessons I could have learned from them.

But the Dions had taken that from me.

I knew Zoe had no love for her parents, but as their child she must hold a spark of hope for their redemption, clinging to the chance they might one day change. I now had to take that chance away from her. This, I felt certain, was why she grieved.

I schooled my expression, squared my heavy shoulders, and left the room. I joined my soldiers as we left the fortress with the Dions in tow.

Chapter Twenty-Six

Nix

I flipped the envelope in my hand and studied the name I'd written on the front: *Zoe.* I missed her and our friendship. Aside from Zoe and Nate, everyone treated me as their king, and in the past five months of officially establishing myself as monarch of the Twilight Realm I hadn't been able to see Zoe. She avoided me and my every attempt of contact.

My heart ached and I massaged my chest with my free hand. I then turned from the desk to stare at my bookshelf, all the while continuing to rotate the envelope between my fingers.

A sharp knock sounded at the door.

"Enter," I called.

Derek, the guard Zoe had freed at the fortress, opened the door and filled the doorway with his bulk.

"Pardon the interruption, Your Majesty, but your royal advisor is here."

"Very well. Send him in, Derek. We have an appointment

and are not to be disturbed."

He nodded and then stepped aside to give Nate room to enter. I stood, though I didn't need to given my royal position. But Nate was a trusted friend and confidant. He'd raised me in my parents' absence. He deserved the respect and honor.

When the door was closed and we were alone, I relaxed my posture and embraced the elf. "Good to see you, Nate," I said, motioning to the couches in front of my desk.

Nate settled on the right, so I took the seat across from him. "You are doing well?" Nate asked.

He always asked about my welfare, and it felt good. Outside of a physician, no one sincerely asked after my welfare.

"Well enough," I said. "You? Your home?" I wanted to ask about Zoe specifically, since I knew she still lived in Nate's tree. How could she not, with all the newly rescued children bursting its trunk?

"We're well, Nix. Zoe is busy with the children and doing an excellent job of keeping everything in some semblance of order. One would think that someone who received such little nurture as a child wouldn't be so good at taking care of children, but she comes by it naturally. Just the other day, one of the more adventurous boys somehow managed to climb to the top of one of the bookshelves in my study—without tipping it over, and without my notice. He wouldn't leave or come down, so Zoe gave him a warning. When the boy refused, she sent Tupac and Chim after him and they gave the boy a chase. My library did suffer some disturbance, but the boy has been much more cooperative since."

A chuckle spilled out of me as I imagined the scene.

After a moment of silence passed between us, I asked the question I knew Nate expected, and which I almost couldn't bring myself to say: "She is happy then?" I couldn't hold back the touch of sadness that coated my words.

"She is well enough. Give her time. She's very young."

Nate's gaze was pointed. It felt like a father telling me to back off.

I nodded. "Of course."

"I do think she misses you, but grief…" Nate shrugged.

I leaned back against the couch and stretched my arm over its top. Before continuing, I decided to turn my attention to the reason Nate had come today. "As you know, Zyanna is still alive."

"The royal princess, yes. You mentioned that the Dions sent her to the Night Realm."

I shook my head. "Actually, her nurse took her there the night my parents gave up their lives."

"Right, forgive me."

I waved it off. "Do you know why she was taken there? Did the nurse have any connections to the Dions?"

"More like the nurse felt it would be a good place to hide the princess. She was from the Night Realm herself and had come here seeking refuge."

I nodded and digested this information. "Have you any way of contacting her?"

"No, I'm sorry. She was dedicated to your family, though."

"I'm glad to hear this. Hopefully she's been able to raise Zyanna well."

"I'm sure your sister is cared for. Your parents wouldn't have trusted the nurse otherwise."

I cleared my throat. "I want to bring my sister back."

Nate shifted in his seat, rested his elbows on his knees, and leaned forward. "Have you tried official channels?"

"Yes, I've sent letters monthly to King Edmund of the Night Realm, but he has not responded. Either my communications haven't gotten through or he's ignoring me."

"Be wary of the king and what you say."

"Meaning?"

"He is manipulative. If he finds your sister, he may use her against you."

I shivered. Blood ran from my upper body and settled at my feet. Had I already put Zyanna's life in jeopardy?

"And have you looked for your sister unofficially?" Nate asked, tilting his head.

"Our spies? They are looking for her, but nothing yet. Either Leski was lying or my sister has grown up in obscurity."

Or worse, I thought, not wanting to voice it. I shook my head and pinched the bridge of my nose.

Not wanting Nate to read in my expression all the worry I held over Zyanna's wellbeing, I shifted to the edge of the couch and leaned forward.

A long sigh trickled from Nate. "What are you considering?"

"Rescuing her… making an official visit… something along those lines."

He tapped his bottom lip with his finger. I'd known him long enough to recognize it as a thinking gesture. He was my advisor and trusted friend and confidant; his opinion on the matter was important to me, so I waited.

"Your Majesty, I understand your concern over your sister. I too would love to see the return of the princess—"

"Go on."

The conflicting emotions were clear on Nate's face. He knew I wouldn't like what he was about to say, or he didn't want to say it. Or both.

Nate looked me directly in the eye with perfect sincerity. "Your Majesty needs to first turn his attention to his own kingdom." He held up his hand to stop me when I opened my mouth to respond. "Please let me finish. Your kingdom is still recovering from more than a decade of harsh rule. If you leave now, those in the Twilight Realm may lose faith in you. They may feel abandoned and consider you unfit to rule due to your young age."

"I'm twenty-seven."

"Our kind live thousands of years. You are a mere child-adult."

My shoulders slumped. Despite his directness, I knew Nate was right. Not for the first time, I felt a pang of longing for my parents and the wisdom I'd missed out on by not having the opportunity to be trained by them. As Nate had said, I wasn't much better than a child to my subjects, a child-king, and I would be until I was at least one hundred years old, if not two hundred.

A wry smile settled on my lips. "Then what do you suggest?"

"I suggest you continue through diplomatic channels and communicating with our informants in the Night Realm. Perhaps she will be found. And in a few years' time, when you have proven yourself as a capable leader and the Twilight Realm is stable, you may decide to go after her yourself."

I hated to hear this, and my guts twisted at the thought of living free while my sister rotted in the Night Realm. She deserved to come home and be with her family.

"And perhaps by that time you and Zoe will have made amends," Nate added.

I glanced up at him with a raised eyebrow. What had made him think of that? And what did it have to do with my sister?

"She's a worthy fighter," he went on, keeping his gaze steady. "She would perhaps best connect with Princess Zyanna."

Understanding clicked. Zoe had abilities no one else had. She also had an amazing sense of empathy. Where I might lack the necessary skills to nurture my sister, Zoe would not.

I ran my fingers through my hair, leaving it a disheveled mess, but I didn't care at the moment. I needed to make things right with Zoe, one way or another. I still needed her in my life. I *wanted* her in my life.

I stood, fetched the envelope from my desk, and handed it to Nate. "It's an invitation to the winter ball."

Nate slid the envelope into his pocket.

"Do you think she'll come?" I asked.

"I'll speak with her and make sure she doesn't throw it out like the other invitations you've sent."

My heart sank and irritation stirred in me. "Does she hate me that much?"

"I don't think she hates you. If anything, it may be the opposite. Zoe doesn't get close to others. She protects herself. I think she's afraid of how much she cares for you. Be consistent and patient. Give her time."

Nate's advice never proved wrong. He had told me that Zoe and I would need to work together to restore the kingdom, and that to work with her I would need to earn her trust. In my thoughts, I pictured her soft green eyes and uniquely beautiful hair.

One way or another, Zoe, we're going to be friends, I decided.

But my heart pulsed an excited rhythm as I digested what Nate had said. Perhaps he was right, and her feelings for me scared her. If that was true, she didn't hate me.

Feeling lighter than I had in weeks, my mind spun with

ideas on what to do next. I circled to the seat at my desk, running through them all. I'd wait and build a friendship...

And then one day, I thought, *maybe more.*

Chapter Twenty-Seven

Zoe

I walked down the hallway of Nate's tree to the giant playroom where all the children studied. A smile stretched across my face as I peeked through the doorway. Pat chittered from her perch on my shoulder.

Quiet, I told her. *You'll disturb the children.*

She stretched her neck and rubbed her head against my jaw, thrumming with delight.

Since I'd forgiven my parents, my dragons had been more independent. Right now, Chim and Tupac were somewhere else in the tree, and if I focused, I could sense their location. Although they were enjoying their newfound freedom, sometimes they did meld back into my skin to rest, such as when the kids got to be too much for them.

All my tattoos were different now. They were stronger, and I'd also discovered new abilities. I could now change the shape of my knives, making them longer or shorter depending on my need. I'd nearly stabbed my new fighting coach, Commander Adothlin, in an accident a while back; his quick reflexes had saved him. The memory of him jumping out of the way made me giggle. As well as the change in his attitude toward me. It seemed that in removing the dark magic my mother used and restoring the former guards of my parents helped the commander think better of me.

The only tattoo that had disappeared completely was the demon on my chest. After the events at the fortress five months ago, the first thing I'd done upon returning to the tree was strip off my clothes, wash away the grime, and study my chest to make sure the demon tattoo was really gone. There was no evidence it had ever been there and I could no longer feel him.

In fact, in its place a new tattoo had emerged. This one was a beautiful depiction of a dove, white with golden accents. It resembled Vaim Na'quab. Seeing it now always made me giddy. I hadn't yet figured out its purpose, but I would.

I left the children behind and turned toward the kitchen. Since we'd picked up so many new residents, Nate had officially made me head of the household. I oversaw everything, one by-product of which was that the brownies finally let me enter the kitchen—their sacred place. Cocoa still lived here; she'd assured me that the Royal Tree had plenty of other brownies to serve the newly crowned king.

When Nix's face floated across my thoughts, I immediately ignored it. I didn't like to think about him.

As I entered the kitchen, I found that it was a hub of activity, like usual. A brownie stood at the glass-topped stove, stirring a pot while three others chopped vegetables beside him. I guessed they were preparing some kind of soup. At another counter, cookie dough was being scooped onto baking sheets, bread dough being rolled out. And at the sinks there was an assembly line of washers, rinsers, and dryers.

"My lady," Cocoa said when she caught sight of me. Her arms were laden with boxes stacked three high.

"Here, let me help you." I took the top two boxes from her.

"Thank you." Cocoa shifted the weight she was carrying. "Is there something you need?"

"No, I just came to check in. Doing my rounds." I nodded to the boxes in my arms. "Where do these go?"

She hoisted her packaged up onto a nearby counter. "We can leave them here. Would you like a cup of coffee?"

I set my boxes down next to hers, smiling. She knew my love of the beverage, but I'd already had two cups this morning and could still feel the effects of it.

"No, thank you," I said. "Has Nate returned from his visit?"

He had told me he was going to the Royal Tree, and I knew it was for a meeting with Nix. I hesitated, unable to bring myself to talk about Nix with anyone. I wondered when this feeling would leave me.

"I believe he just returned," Cocoa said. "I was going to take him his afternoon tea. Would you rather take it?"

"Sure. There are a few issues we need to discuss."

Cocoa darted into the congested part of the kitchen and moments later returned with a tray. She nimbly navigated around brownies. It was like watching a complicated dance.

"Here you are, my lady," Cocoa said, presenting me with the tray.

I winked at her and took the tray. All my best efforts at trying to discourage the use of "my lady" had failed. Cocoa claimed that it was improper to call me anything different.

Once I'd made my way to Nate's cluttered office, I weaved my way through the maze and caught a glimpse of him at his desk. He was twirling a cream-colored envelope between his fingers.

"Zoe, good to see you." Nate smiled, set the envelope down, and rose to take the tray from me.

I settled into the chair opposite him. "Cocoa sent me with your tea. I thought it'd be a good time to have our weekly meeting."

Nate raised an eyebrow but said nothing. He must have thought I purposely chose to have these meetings right after his regular visits with Nix, but it wasn't true. At least, I didn't think that was the reason. It seemed logical to get all his business over with in one day.

"Everything go all right?" I asked. A part of me did wonder about Nix, but talking about him directly would leave me feeling troubled for days, so I avoided it.

Nate settled back into his chair and moved the envelope to the side of his desk.

"Would you like a cup?" Nate asked, holding up the teapot that had been on the tray.

It was then that I noticed Cocoa had included enough tea for two. I shook my head. "I'm good for now. Thanks."

Nate poured a cup and added a spoon of sugar and cream. He then added a cookie to his plate and sat back his chair. He chuckled as the dragons zoomed into the office, circling around the periphery of the room.

"Do you mind?" I asked, taking a few cookies.

"Of course not."

I broke them up into little pieces and left them out for the dragons. They eagerly surrounded the plate and devoured the morsels. Once the plate was empty, they fluttered to perches around the room and set to preening themselves. I shook my head and marveled at the change in them; before unblocking my magic, they had never shown interest in food.

"So what's the news?" Nate asked.

"Well, there's not much to report. The children are settling in well with their new routines. I've also been able to enlist some of the older children to tutor the younger, relieving the brownies. I think that's gone well also."

Nate sipped his tea.

I continued with my report. "I have one idea for the older children. Some will be leaving in a few years, and it would be wise for them to learn a trade, and perhaps gain an apprenticeship so they can become self-sufficient."

Nate bit into his cookie. "That's a good plan. We should be thinking ahead."

My cheeks warmed under his gaze.

"I was wondering if you could approach your contacts about this," I said. "You seem to know just about everyone in the Twilight Realm. Perhaps we could set up a trial run of sorts?"

"Do you have any children in mind?"

"I do." I pulled out a folder sheet of paper from my pocket and passed it over to Nate.

He scanned the list. "I see you've also suggested possible careers for them."

"That's right. I considered their strengths and natural interests."

Nate chuckled and his shoulders shook. "I see you've suggested that Sabastian intern with me."

"Not as royal advisor, of course. I know... I know only the king chooses that candidate. But Sabastian has a great deal of curiosity and charm. I think he'd do well as a professor or historian one day."

"This is great." He put down the paper and pushed it to the side of the desk. "Anything else?"

"No."

Nate reached for the envelope and my stomach clenched. Was this another of Nix's invitations? I hated turning them down, but the thought of seeing him again... my heart sped up. I'd known him as a friend. Then as the prince. Then the king. We'd tramped through the neverending corridors of the fortress together. We'd fought together. He'd seen me at my worst, when the demon tattoo had taken over.

I knew he considered me a friend. But that was part of my problem. What if when I saw him again, he'd act like nothing had ever changed. Like he hadn't sentenced my family to death. In my heart, everything had changed. The emotions swirled in my chest.

He'd promised to talk, to return after the death of my parents, but he never had. Instead, I'd been the recipient of invitations to one royal affair after another. Where was Nix my friend? Not Phoenix the king.

Eventually Nate passed the envelope to me. I saw my name elegantly scrawled across the front and wondered if Nix had written it.

"Are you going to open it?" Nate asked.

"No." I let my hands fall to my lap with the envelope secured between them.

"He misses you. He's trying."

"I know."

"Then what's the problem?" Nate moved the tea tray and leaned forward, resting his elbows on the desk. "You won't talk about him. You avoid any mention of him. Don't you think it's time?"

A long exhale left me. Nate was right. Perhaps avoiding the subject was what had brought me to this emotional impasse.

"What is there to say?" I asked. "He is king and I'm... me. My life is here and his is at the Royal Tree."

"Are those the only reasons?"

My gaze darted at Nate, then back to my lap and the elegant scrawl of my name across the envelope.

When I didn't answer, Nate pressed on and I assumed I was in for one of his cryptic lessons.

"You've been through a great deal in your young life." He stepped around the table and took one of my hands in his. "Zoe, I would hate for you to live out the rest of your life in self-imposed isolation."

Laughter flooded out of me as I thought of Nate's tree bursting with children and brownies. "I'm hardly isolated."

"You have elves and brownies around you, but who are you actually *close* to? Nix was good for you. He was the first friend you ever had."

"I had Maximon. I have you," I said, fighting the tears that were working their way to my eyes.

"Maximon never really existed and I'm like an uncle."

I flinched at his words. He still didn't know that he was like a father to me. Perhaps one day I'd have the courage to tell him.

"Nix was the first elf you ever told your story to other than me," he continued. "You risked vulnerability and received acceptance. That was a big deal to you. Is it possible that perhaps you're afraid of seeing where your friendship might go if you give it a chance?"

I puzzled over this. For the first time in as long as I could remember, he was speaking so plainly!

"Maybe." It came out as barely a whisper. A tear dripped down my cheek and landed on the envelope. I missed Nix. "This is another invitation to a social event, isn't it?"

"Yes, the winter ball."

I looked up at him. "I don't want to go."

Nate sighed and rubbed his face. "I could make you."

Horror washed through me. "No, you can't."

"As royal advisor, I could interpret it as an insult to the crown, you rejecting His Majesty's every offer, and force you to attend."

"You wouldn't dare."

A twinkle sparked in Nate's eyes and I realized he was joking.

Nate patted my hand and then moved back to his chair. "Just think about seeing him again. It doesn't have to be at the ball. I'm sure if you came up with an alternate suggestion, Nix would accommodate you."

My mind flipped through ideas, considering what other scenarios would be appropriate for a meeting with the king… no, with my friend. I stood suddenly, nearly knocking over Pat, who had silently fluttered down onto my seat's armrest.

"I'll give it some thought," I said, gathering up Nate's tray.

"I'm sure you will. Send in Sabastian when he's done with his lesson."

I smiled, pleased that Nate seemed to have decided to put into action my plan to find the children mentors.

Upon leaving the study, my dragons flew at my side, darting back and forth in their game of chase.

As I made my way back to the kitchen with Nate's tray, my

thoughts remained on Nix and the short time I had known him. He was a good elf, but was he worth the risk of knowing more intimately?

My heart pounded in my chest. Nate was right. He understood me better than I understood myself, and there was an odd comfort in that.

A cool sensation crept over me. Being vulnerable was scary, but if there was one elf I would willingly take a risk on, it was Nix.

Feeling lighter than I had in months, I started making plans. Perhaps he and I would have a simple meal. We could have it here, just me, Nix, and maybe Nate. And if His Royal Highness wasn't too busy, it could even happen this weekend.

After depositing the tray in sudsy water in the kitchen, I went to my apartment to write a quick invitation of my own. I left Nate's tree and headed for the Royal Tree. This invitation I'd hand deliver instead of sending with Nate. My heart sped with excitement at seeing Nix and nervousness made me jittery about taking this step forward. Perhaps the way past my jumble of emotions and the way to friendship was in seeing Nix.

Memories of our adventures filled my mind. I saw the softness in his eyes and the ways he reached out to me on numerous times. *Was it possible Nix wanted more than friendship?* My cheeks warmed. I was only eighteen, barely a child-adult, and I wasn't ready to think about romance. Most child-adults didn't pursue dating until they were closer to one hundred years old.

My dragons chittered happily. They sensed where we were headed and were feeding my thoughts with their own memories of Nix.

I reached the Royal Tree. It hadn't changed much since the last time I was here. Though it did look healthier and stronger, like a tree waking up after winter. I reached the front where I'd entered with Nix when Derek approached from the side.

"Miss, can I help you? Oh, Zoe, are you here to see the king?"

Feeling suddenly out of my element, I fingered the small envelope with my invitation. *This was stupid.*

Nix came up behind the guard. His eyes popped when he saw me then softened to the familiar look.

"Leave us," Nix said softly to Derek.

"Yes, Sire." Derek gave a slight bow to the king and nodded toward me as he strode off.

"He leaves you? Aren't royal guards meant to stay with you?"

"He's close by, but with enough distance to give us privacy." Nix took a step toward me. "It's good to see you."

I felt flustered with the mixture of happiness at seeing him, the softness in his eyes that held warmth, and my own uncertainty about how I felt. He'd been my first real friend. I inhaled deeply.

Nix shifted his feet and I got the sense that he was uncertain. "I'm sorry I didn't come back to finish our conversation. I did return to the fortress, but by then you and Nate had left."

My heart pounded. This was Nix but my tongue that usually functioned properly twisted and refused to work. "I'm not interested in balls and royal gatherings." I forced out quickly.

A smile lifted the corners of Nix's mouth and his posture loosened. "Not really your style?"

"No. But maybe, if you're not busy we could take a walk sometime or you could come over for dinner." My voice was growing with confidence, and I was falling into the familiar comfort of being with him.

"I'd like that. How about now?"

"Now?"

"We could take a walk and you could tell me about all the new children. You can listen to how unbelievably boring and tedious my life has become and if you're comfortable, we can talk about the Dions."

Nix extended his hand.

I glanced at it and hesitated to accept the offer. My eyes flicked up to his and I saw that his eyebrow was raised.

"Taking liberties?" he asked.

A giggle spilled out of me. *Was I ready for this? For friendship? For possibly more?* But then I hadn't been ready to take down my parents. I hadn't been ready for a friend. Nix hadn't been ready to be king… I reached out and took his hand. Nix's whole body relaxed like he'd been holding his breath.

We strolled into the trees toward the Rivers of Laughter. We weren't dating. Maybe one day… But in this moment, we were friends. Nix and Zoe. And that was enough. For now.

About the Author

K. M. Wray makes her home in Canada but lived in Pusan, South Korea for seven years. She enjoys working with language learners and immigrants of all ages as an English teacher and has over two decades of experience as an instructor. In her free time, she's learning how to garden, cares for two cats and if she isn't enjoying a good book, she's trying to write one.

Thanks for reading Twilight's Curse, Book 1 in the Twilight Realm Trilogy. I hope you enjoyed the journey of Zoe and Nix. The adventure continues in book 2, where we learn what's happened to Zyanna, Nix's sister, and book 3 (2022), the satisfying conclusion to the darkness threatening the Twilight Realm and Night Realm. Please take a moment to leave a review. Reviews and word of mouth are the best methods of helping authors.

If you'd like to connect, you can visit me at the following or join my newsletter. It'll be great to have you as part of the adventure:

You can connect with me on:

🌐 https://kmwray.ca

f https://www.facebook.com/Wray.K.M

Subscribe to my newsletter:

✉ http://eepurl.com/hFLqBP

Also by K. M. Wray

Hidden

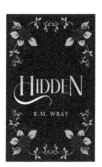

All Tully wants is to find a quiet place in the Midland Meadows. A place free of anxiety triggers, the stares of the Kellans and where she no longer needs to wear the cloak.

She's never questioned anything in her life. Not the story around the barrier that surrounds the Kellan Lowlands. Not the cloak she's forced to wear. Not her disease. Not the savage Arelians. There's never been a reason to.

Until now.

During the annual celebration, a dark creature hovers in the sky and Tully hears a voice in her mind. Her cloak fails in a crowded market and every story every myth unravels. And Tully's left searching for answers.

Everything she's been told about herself, the Kellan-Arelian conflict, and the barrier is a lie.

Now she's forced to flee with enigmatic Ciaran who intrigues her in ways no Kellan man ever has. But can she trust him when everyone and everything tells her she shouldn't?

Hidden is a young adult coming of age clean romantic fantasy for anyone who's ever felt, 'everything about me is wrong'.

Join Tully who learns that everything she thought was bad was designed with purpose and should be celebrated.

Breaking Enchantments

Erin likes her life. It's simple, uncomplicated and comfortable. But all that is about to change with the arrival of her relatives from the Korean side of the family. They speak a language and have customs she doesn't understand and what's the big deal with *Kimchi*? Suddenly it available for every meal including breakfast!

And then there's this mysterious abandoned property she stumbled onto that calls to her. She can't stay away and isn't sure she wants to, particularly when it empowered her with magic that helps her control time. Perhaps, this is exactly what she needs to help her with her relatives and the bullies at school who've taken an interest in her.

Breaking Enchantment is a young adult fantasy book. Join Erin on her journey filled with discovery and enchantments as she battles a far greater threat tied to the ancient magic threatening more than her simple, uncomplicated and comfortable life.

Made in the USA
Las Vegas, NV
20 December 2024

15013387R00184